LITTLE LOOSE ENDS

LITTLE LOOSE ENDS

BONNIE TRAYMORE

Little Loose Ends
Copyright © 2022 Bonnie L. Traymore
All Rights Reserved

This is a work of fiction. Names, places, characters and incidents are either the product of the author's imagination or are used fictitiously, and any resemblance to any actual persons, living or dead, businesses, organizations, events or locales is entirely coincidental.

No part of this book may be reproduced or transmitted in any form or by any means, electronic or mechanical, including photocopying, recording, or by any information storage and retrieval system, without permission in writing from the author.

First Edition

Cover Design - Ivan Zanchetta
Publishing Coordinator – Sharon Kizziah-Holmes

INDIE PUB PRESS

Indie Pub Press
an imprint of Paperback Press, LLC
Springfield, MO

Paperback ISBN - 13: 978-1-956806-77-9
eBook ISNB – 13: 978-1-956806-78-6

For Erica, my little bundle of joy

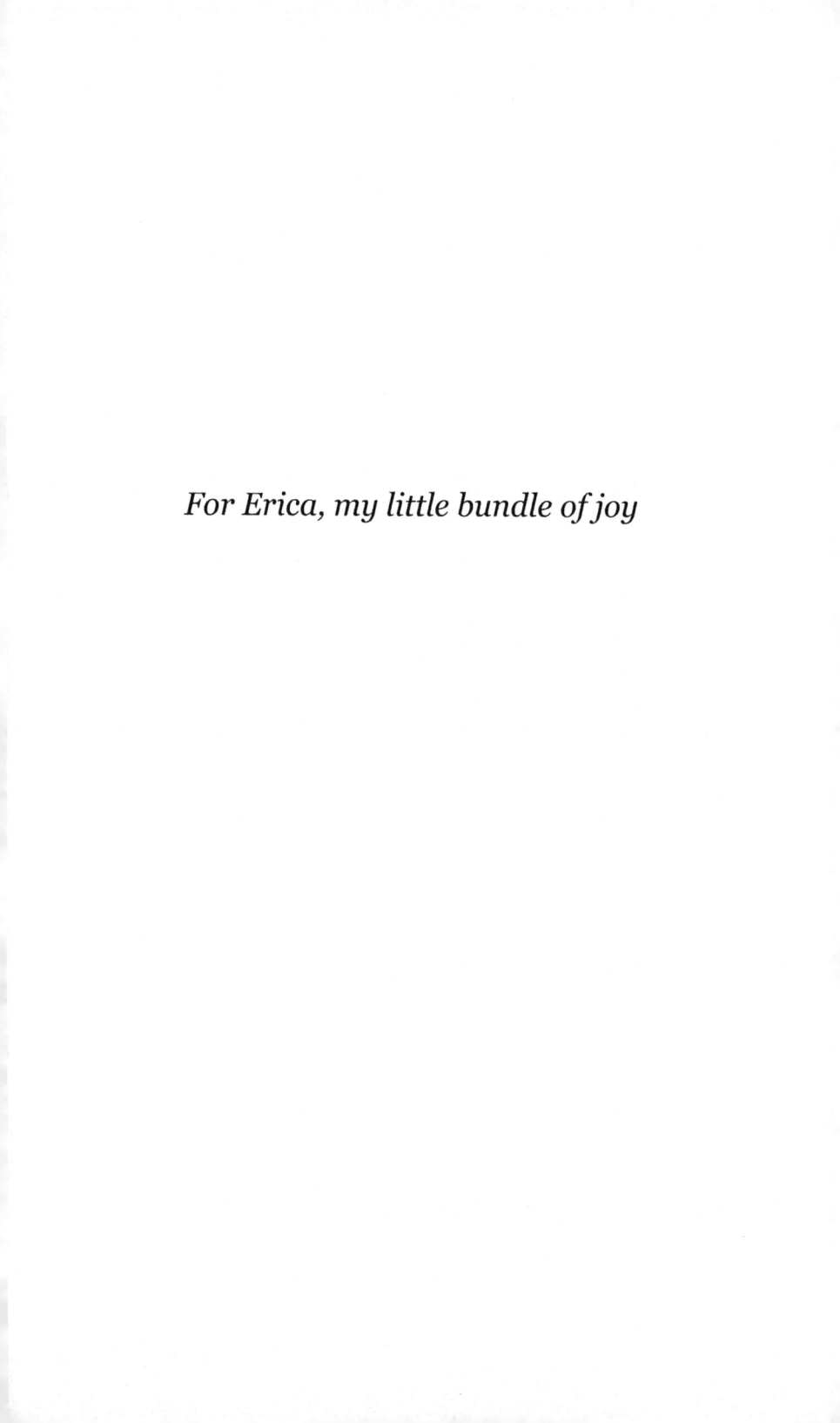

CONTENTS

PART ONE   i
One   1
Two   13
Three   26
Four   33
Five   41
Six   53
Seven   62
Eight   68
Nine   79
Ten   91
Eleven   100
Twelve   112
Thirteen   123
Fourteen   131

PART TWO   139
Fifteen   140
Sixteen   150
Seventeen   159
Eighteen   168
Nineteen   177
Twenty   190
Twenty-One   202
Twenty-Two   209
Twenty-Three   219
Twenty-Four   229
Twenty-Five   237
Twenty-Six   249
Twenty-Seven   258
Epilogue   268
Acknowledgments   272
About the Author   274

PART ONE

"A woman always has her revenge ready."
—MOLIÈRE

ONE

One thing Jenna knew for sure was that he would pay for what he did to her. She wasn't sure where it would happen. She wasn't sure when. But she was sure he would pay.
Getting the police involved seemed futile. What would they even do? It was his word against hers. Plus, the punishment she had in mind was a lot worse than anything they would do through official channels. She'd just lie low for a while. Let him think he'd scared her off. Then she'd make her move.
She pulled up her banking app. Just a few hundred dollars left in her account, but she had one more paycheck coming and a pretty big credit line at her disposal. She'd figure something out. She always did. That was one thing everyone said about her. She always landed on her feet.

Victoria clung to the edges of her dream, longing to linger in its warm, sensual embrace. But as she crossed the threshold into wakefulness, reality flooded back with a vengeance, and she was wide awake.
She reached for her phone in the predawn darkness

to check the time, hoping it was at least close to a reasonable hour to rise. Even though the baby was sleeping through the night these days, she still woke up in anticipation every few hours. Or maybe it wasn't just anticipation. Maybe it wasn't just the baby. Things were strained between her and her husband, and that made her restless. And then, of course, there were the threats. The ones she still hadn't told him about. No more secrets, they'd promised. *Yeah, right.*

She was trying so hard to get past it all. The infidelity. The lies. The hurt. But she'd taken him back. Given them a second chance as a family. The few times they'd made love since his affair, it wasn't awful; it was just bland. Like eating a gourmet meal with a head cold, the distant memory of all the delicious flavors—delicate and bold, spicy and sweet—rendering the muted experience a profound disappointment.

But there was too much at stake to worry about things like her marriage or if she'd ever get some spice back in her life. Lila, their little bundle of joy, was all that mattered, and Victoria would do anything to keep her safe. She looked over at Nick, sleeping soundly next to her. Her husband. The father of her child. *What secrets are you keeping now, Nick?*

Well, she had secrets of her own, like the reason for her upcoming jaunt out of town. She looked again at the latest text she'd received. The final threat that had propelled her to take action.

You're a mother now, Victoria. Be careful. The world's a dangerous place.

It was three forty-three in the morning. Not much chance of falling back to sleep, so she got up and started her day, treasuring the quiet stillness. She brewed some fresh coffee and got to work poring over the data she'd received a few weeks prior from Wade Higgins—computer hacker and self-proclaimed psychic who'd come to be her trusted investigator—trying to decide her next move.

She wanted to talk her plan over with someone besides Wade. But who? It couldn't be Nick. Things were strained enough between them already, and he'd insist on going himself. But it was Nick's impetuous actions that had put them on Timothy Sutton's radar in the first place. He'd only make things worse. Her mother would be a better choice, but then she'd be even more stressed about it. Her only child. Her only grandchild. Victoria couldn't burden her with that; she was finally happy.

She was sure the threats were from Sutton. Who else would do something like that? But so far, her investigator couldn't trace them. She had no evidence. Just a gut feeling. But her gut was rarely wrong. No, her mother and Nick meant well, but she couldn't tell either of them what she was up to. They'd only complicate things. She'd have to go it alone.

A slight knot formed in the pit of Victoria's stomach as she drove from her Tarrytown home to her mother's Scarsdale estate. The feeling was so familiar that it was almost comforting. Their relationship had always been a little strained, but she noticed it more now because it stood in stark contrast to the flood of unconditional love that flowed between her mother and Lila. With Lila, her mother could love with total abandon, whereas with Victoria, she always held back. This was the case in most families, but even more so in hers. Plus, Victoria was a terrible liar. Her mother could always see right through her, and she was planning to lie to her today.

She parked her car in the circular driveway,

unfastened Lila, and took her in her arms. She grabbed the baby bag and started walking toward her childhood home. As she took in the sight of the imposing Georgian structure, she wondered when Lila would realize this wasn't how most people lived. How old had Victoria been? School-aged maybe?

When Victoria had decided to go back to work, she'd started to interview nannies. She hired a great one, but still, her mother insisted on watching Lila herself two days a week, and that was fine with Victoria. It meant she could work from home sometimes and have the whole house to herself. A luxury these days. She kept the nanny on full-time anyway. It was the only way to keep someone good. And she was very good.

She'd thought about telling her mother about the threatening text messages but not just yet. Not until she did some more digging to see if she could prove it was him. But her mother had a sixth sense when it came to Victoria. She was fiercely protective, and it was hard to get anything past her.

Victoria wasn't planning on staying long. But when they finished the handoff, her mother started to pry.

"What was that you said earlier, about going away tomorrow?"

"Yes, New Mexico and Arizona. I'm looking for some new artists for the gallery."

"Why now?"

"I mean, it's as good a time as any." It was true. Charles, her business partner, was still running the art dealership, her main source of revenue, and it was booming. With the stock market tanking, people were pouring their money into art. Plus, if he needed her help, she could do those deals from anywhere. Nick was handling the renovations on the storefront in Tarrytown that would become their new art gallery.

He was the expert in the construction area.

But her mother pressed on. "You're planning to branch out to other regions?"

"Well, yes. Why not?"

"You're an expert in the Hudson River School. I thought you'd stick with this region."

"I'm going with an American landscape theme for the opening. The Southwest has great landscapes."

"Okay. If you say so." Her mother gave her a curious look, her signal that she knew there was more to it. But she dropped the subject, secure in the knowledge that Victoria would tell her when she was good and ready. This was their mother-daughter dance. It worked for them.

Victoria kissed the top of Lila's head and hugged her mother.

"I'll see you around four."

"Sounds good," her mother replied. The fact that she didn't push for Lila to stay longer confirmed what Victoria had suspected. Her mother was seeing someone, and she had a pretty good idea who it was. But her mother wasn't ready to talk about it. It took two to tango, so she left it for another day. She needed to get to her office and make some progress if she was going to leave for Arizona and New Mexico the next day. She walked out the door to a perfect fall morning.

―――

Victoria's assistant poked his head into her office and announced Wade Higgins' arrival. The first time she met Wade, he was pounding on her car window like a crazy person. It was hard to believe they'd become friends after a first encounter like that. Well, maybe not friends, exactly. More like friendly business associates.

Wade was a talented computer guy and Victoria's go-to person for information she needed to find without anyone knowing she was looking for it. During the murder case the year before, he'd gotten some flashes that she was in danger—psychic feelings, he called them—and he'd gone to the police. When they didn't take him seriously, he took a more direct approach by pounding on her car window.

She didn't take his psychic warnings very seriously, but when she'd learned of his expert computer hacking skills, she hired him to help with her side investigation: trying to find out who really killed Angie Hansen, hoping to clear her husband of murder. Normally, a victim's real estate agent wouldn't be the prime suspect in a murder investigation—that is, unless he was sleeping with her.

After the case wrapped up and Nick had been cleared, she'd thought back on Wade's warnings: the murderer was a male, he'd done it before, and he'd strike again. It was all pretty vague, but she had to admit, some of it had come true. But she still wasn't convinced. Not only about Wade but about psychics in general.

"Send him in," Victoria called out.

Wade entered her spacious, glass-walled office with its peekaboo view of the Hudson River in the distance. She straightened the folder sitting on top of her tidy walnut desk as he seated himself across from her.

"How's the new place?" she asked.

"I love it. The view is spectacular." Wade had considered buying Angie Hansen's house, the one where she was murdered. That thought made Victoria's skin crawl, so she'd steered him away from it. It was a steal, he said, because of rumors that it was haunted. It was a steal, she countered, because it was a money pit, which was true. As her agent, Nick had even tried to warn Angie, but she hadn't listened to him. So Wade had opted instead for one of the newer condos fronting the Hudson River. They were building tons of them, and it seemed people couldn't get enough of them.

In the area of the Hudson Valley where they lived—Sleepy Hollow Country—people loved a good scare. Haunted houses, psychics, alien sightings. It was all part of the allure, and Wade fit in perfectly. Once the rumor got out about the haunting, the price even went up a bit. Someone bought it and brought in a local ghost whisperer to "redirect" Angie's spirit. The ghost was reportedly gone now, but it was still a money pit. Victoria heard that the new owners had dumped over half a million into it and were still finding issues. Meanwhile, the condo continued to appreciate, and so did Wade's gratitude.

"That's great. I really miss my view," Victoria replied. "I have a view from here, sort of, but it's not the same. We're so far back." Her office was located on the second floor of a low rise building, off Main Street a few blocks from her new gallery, about half way up the steep hill that ran from the river up to Broadway.

"No, it's not the same. I love being right on the river."

She missed her dream home—the one she and Nick had been living in when their lives were turned upside down. It sat on the edge of the Hudson with enormous windows that looked out on its wide expanse. Victoria had loved to sit in her kitchen in the early morning and look across the three-mile-wide river to the steep banks on the other side, which changed with the seasons—the deep greens of summer, the scarlets and golds of fall. Even the sparse winter months had their appeal. The view was everything she'd ever wanted.

But after what had happened in that kitchen, she couldn't stay there. So now they were living in a more spacious but less spectacular home in a kid-friendly neighborhood in Tarrytown near the Irvington border. Yet another reason she resented her husband.

"So, what can I do for you?"

"Have you gotten anywhere on the texts?"

"No. Sorry. All burner phones. I'm trying. Have you thought about going to the police?"

"That's why I wanted to talk to you. I'm going down to Arizona tomorrow. To talk to the police there. In person."

"You think that's a good idea?"

"I have to do something. But don't tell anyone, okay?"

"Sure, but aren't they going to know, Victoria? Like when you're suddenly...not here?" Wade held his hands up and glanced around her office, his eyebrows perched high above his beady brown eyes.

"It's an art-buying trip, Wade." Her fingers flew up into air quotes as she spoke. "For the new gallery?"

"Ah, clever. Your secret's safe with me."

"I know. That's why I pay you so much."

"Really? I thought it was my sharp wit."

"That too."

"Just be careful, okay? If Sutton finds out you're in town—"

"I will. Don't worry!" She wrapped things up with Wade and got to work planning her trip. She needed to tell Charles, her oldest and closest friend as well as her business partner. They'd met back in high school and had been close ever since, although things were a little strained at the moment. She knew they needed to talk. But not now. They'd get back to normal at some point. They always did.

As if reading her mind, he popped his head into her

office. "What's with you and that psychic? It's bad enough I have to share you with Nick. Are you trying to make me jealous?"
"Is it working?"
"Not really. You've never been my type."
"That's right. I forgot. You don't like blondes." They both smiled, and it felt good to be back to their comfortable, casual banter, if only briefly. She proceeded to tell him about her trip, and as expected, he didn't seem to mind. She sensed he enjoyed being in the limelight while she was off learning how to be a mom and opening the new gallery with Nick, and that was fine with her.
"But really. You've been a little distant lately. Is something wrong?"
He knows me too well. "No! I'm just preoccupied."
"Preoccupied with...?"
"Let's leave it until I get back, okay?"
"Sure." He looked a little hurt, and she felt terrible. She didn't want to tell him the real reason she'd grown distant because it was so freaking stupid it was embarrassing. Nick was jealous of their friendship. Or so he claimed one night when they were having it out about his affair with Angie Hansen. She confided in Charles too much, and it made him feel left out and blah, blah, blah. At the time, it had just pissed her off even more. *So I pushed you into her arms because I'm secretly in love with my gay best friend?* She knew it was just a lame excuse to try to justify his affair. But, in the interest of giving the marriage another shot, she'd cooled it on the friendship. But it didn't help her feel any closer to Nick. It just made her miss Charles.

Victoria was in their bedroom packing a bag when Nick came in with Lila in his arms. He'd just returned from their customary evening stroll around the neighborhood. His eyebrows shot up when he spotted her suitcase, and she thought she saw his face go a shade paler. He stood there for a few moments while she continued to pack, his head tilted to one side as he awaited her explanation.

"I'm leaving in the morning." That's how it was between them now. She didn't discuss. She didn't equivocate. She just told Nick how it was going to be. It wasn't healthy—she knew that—but she just couldn't stop herself.

"Leaving for...where exactly?"

"Arizona and New Mexico."

"What?"

"I said Arizona and New Mexico."

"I heard you the first time, Victoria." Nick rolled his eyes.

Maybe he still has some fight in him after all.

"May I ask why?" His taut mouth belied his gentle tone.

"I told you we need more artists. For the gallery we're planning to open? I'm going down to see if I can find some new talent."

"Why now?"

"Why *not* now?" *God, I'm being such a bitch.*

Why couldn't she just forgive and forget? She really wanted to, but it just wasn't working. And marriage counseling made it even worse. It just made her feel like a bad mother. Like she wasn't trying hard enough for Lila to make it work. It wasn't as if she wanted to feel this way about Nick. All she wanted—all she'd ever wanted—was to be a happy family. She wanted to love her husband again. To make herself feel what she'd felt for him before his betrayal. But the more she tried, the more her body resisted, the sharper her comments became, and the more distant they grew from each other. Maybe the time away would do her some good. Nick turned and started down the hall, leaving her alone to pack.

"I'm bringing Lila," she called after him. He just kept walking.

In the bathroom, she took stock of herself as she carefully curated her toiletries, deciding which were essential and which to leave behind. Her honey-blonde hair had more of a wave to it these days, and her skin seemed a bit drier as she ran her hand over her face. She grabbed the richer night cream and plopped it in her cosmetic bag with the other items that made the cut, leaving the day cream behind.

Her body felt weird—foreign, even—like it wasn't really hers. She was still carrying a few extra pounds of baby weight, but it was mostly in her boobs. Her perky, B-cup breasts had matched her petite, taut body perfectly. She wanted them back. But that wasn't going to happen. She didn't even want to think about how they would look after she stopped nursing. Images of deflated balloons came to mind. The rest of her body would never be the same either, and she felt guilty longing for her flat abs as her hand rested on her spongy midsection. She'd waited so long to have a baby. She'd wanted one so badly. How could she be anything but grateful?

But what about the cruel timing of it all? Didn't she have a right to be upset about that? Finding out she was finally pregnant after years of trying just days after she discovered Nick's affair? She would have left him if it weren't for the baby. She knew that. He knew that. Everyone else probably suspected it.

But a baby changes everything—body, mind, and soul. So here they were. Together. For better or for worse, the real meaning of that phrase all too apparent to her now.

TWO

"Hello, ma'am. What can I do for you?"

The front desk officer at the Scottsdale police precinct was on the younger side, but he wasn't *that* young. Not young enough to call her ma'am. She was only thirty-six after all. Victoria wasn't offended, just surprised at how differently she was treated with a baby in tow. There was a time not so long ago when she felt annoyed by the unwanted male attention she received on a regular basis. The flirting. The innuendos. But that didn't seem to be much of a problem these days. She looked down at herself. Jeans, a light-blue blouse, flats. And a baby strapped to her front. What did she expect?

"Do you have a detective I could talk to?"

"A detective for what, exactly?"

"I've been reading about some of your unsolved cases. I think I might have some useful information."

"Which cases?"

She looked around. There weren't a lot of people around the desk, but there were a few. It was also devoid of background noise and chatter, so their voices reverberated throughout the large, empty foyer. "I would rather talk about that in private."

He hesitated for a moment while he sized her up.

What was he thinking? Psychic crackpot? True crime fan?

"What kind of crimes?"

She looked around, hesitant to give up too much. "Sexual assault."

"Let me see if I can get someone." He reached for the phone, and Victoria took a moment to look down at Lila, sleeping soundly in her pouch. That likely helped her case. She was a woman with a baby in need of protection. Who could resist?

"Go through that doorway. Detective Ramirez will meet you there." He pointed to the right.

She took a deep breath, ignoring the urge to run straight out the door and get on a plane back home. The chances of this going well were slim, but she had to try. "Thanks so much."

"You're welcome, ma'am." There it was again.

She walked into the precinct's bullpen and felt a rush of panic as she took it all in. A scruffy man in handcuffs was being escorted to the back, an officer clutching his forearm, dragging him along as he resisted. *Come on! Let's go!*

A female officer was shouting into the phone, her back to Victoria. *"Oh yeah?"* She stood up. *"Oh yeah? Well, not if I have anything to say about it!"* The officer slammed down the phone.

Dozens of officers were scurrying around, looking like they had better things to do than hear about the wacky hunches of some paranoid new mother from across the continent. That's how they'd see her; she was sure of it. Then her eyes landed on a man standing in the doorway of an office to her right. He was tall and lanky, wearing gray pants and a dark blue polo shirt. Striking, but not drop-dead handsome like her husband. Formidable. The sea of people racing around seemed to part for him as his eyes landed on her and he made his way over. His gait was slow and casual, his posture confident but not cocky. Her eyes lingered on him as he approached.

"I'm Detective Randy Ramirez," he announced on arrival. He held out his hand. It was large and inviting, anchored to a slim yet muscular forearm. "I understand you wanted to talk to someone about one of our cases."

A whiff of something hit her and it knocked her socks off. An aftershave? His pheromones? She stood there staring at him while she tried to collect herself. When she realized his hand was still out there, she raised hers and grasped it, in part to steady herself. His hand was warm and dry, his grip firm but not too strong. Comforting. She didn't want to let go.

"Victoria Mancusio. Thank you for agreeing to meet with me."

"And who's this little lady?"

"This is Lila. My daughter." *Of course she's my daughter. Why did I even say that?*

"Let's go somewhere more private, Ms. Mancusio. Over this way." He held a hand out toward their destination and rested his other hand briefly on her back, the warm sensation a pleasant distraction from the chaos. They made their way to a room a few doors down from his office.

"I go by Dr. Mancusio, if you don't mind."

"Dr. Mancusio, it is." He smiled at her as they walked, revealing a nice set of teeth with a slightly crooked one in front that made him look more friendly, less intimidating. Or was it the way his dark eyes lifted at the corners, the smiling crow's feet adding a touch of sparkle? Of all the ways she'd imagined this scenario playing out, this certainly wasn't one of them. After the affair, the baby, everything that had happened, she'd just been feeling numb. Almost asexual. And she certainly didn't need this complication now—this delicious but debilitating feeling stirring inside her. It was probably the post pregnancy hormones. She could block it out. She had to.

"Have a seat," he said.

"Thanks."

"So, what can I do for you, Dr. Mancusio? I understand you have some information for us. About one of our cases."

"Well, yes. But I don't really know where to start." She took a deep breath. "It's all so hard to explain."

"Start at the beginning."

"I've come a long way to talk to you. I'm not from around here."

"I figured. The Northeast?"

"Yes. Westchester. Just north of New York City."

"I know where it is, but I haven't been there."

"There was a high-profile murder case there. Last October. It was all over the news."

"Right! I thought your name sounded familiar. Nick Mancusio is your husband?"

"Yes, he's my husband.

"Your husband was accused of murdering his...client. I don't remember her name."

"The woman's name was Angie Hansen. He was her real estate agent. He was also having an affair with her, but thanks for not mentioning that."

He smiled and gave her a nod.

"He was arrested for her murder, but they dropped the charges."

"Right. It was her attorney, if I remember. Her attorney killed her?"

"Yes, Jeff Malone. He was also a good friend of my husband's. Nick was framed by him. Jeff was angry at Nick for sleeping with her."

"What was the motive again? I don't remember the details." He was likely more familiar with the case than he was letting on. *Does he know that I shot Jeff Malone? In my own kitchen? If he does, what does he think of me?*

"He was representing her in a harassment suit. And as it turned out, she had made up some of the allegations against her boss. Or exaggerated them or something like that. At Jeff's suggestion. To get a bigger settlement," she said.

Ramirez nodded like it was all coming back to him.

"When Nick broke it off with her, she lost it. Told Malone that she was going to come clean and tell everyone she had made up the harassment charges. And that he'd encouraged her to do it. He panicked and killed her. Then he tried to pin it on Nick. He planted her cell phone at our house."

"That must have been a terrible time for you. And a baby in the middle of all of it?"

"She's the light of my life!" Victoria's tone was a bit sharper than she'd intended.

"Of course. I didn't mean anything by that. Just that you have a lot on your plate. But I'm sorry, I'm afraid I still don't understand. What does this have to do with my cases?"

"I'm getting there. Do you have more time?"

"I'll make time. Please continue." He sat back and crossed his arms. No smile this time. Maybe she was wearing out her welcome.

"The short answer is there's a former professor of mine who lives in your area. Timothy Sutton is his name. He was my senior thesis advisor when I was an undergraduate. He's a sexual predator, and I think he's after me. I also think he may be responsible for some of the unsolved assault cases in your area."

Ramirez perked up, leaning forward in his chair. "I

see. And why do you think that, if you don't mind my asking?"

"He sexually assaulted me during my senior year of college."

"I'm so sorry."

"Well, rather, he attempted to, but I was able to fight him off before things went too far. He threatened to kill me if I told anyone, so I didn't. I dropped out of school and went back home. I told my mother, and she advised me not to report it. Then she arranged for me to finish my degree from home. I'm from a well-connected family, as you might know," she confessed.

"Yes, I think I did hear that somewhere." He was being polite. Vander Hofen was a household name in Westchester. They were descended from one of the original Dutch settler families in the area, and she'd always hated the attention. And now, thanks to all the publicity surrounding the murder case, their notoriety had gone national.

"But I have reason to believe he's after me now. And that he's still assaulting women."

"Why would he be after you now? This must have been quite some time ago."

"Yes. Over ten years." She was starting to lose him. Even to her, this was all starting to sound like a stretch.

"Let me explain. I didn't know it at the time, but my mother hired a private detective back then. He obtained information about Sutton pressuring and forcing himself on other students. That got him fired about a year after I left. Sutton didn't know my family was behind it until recently. I had no idea myself."

"How did he find out?"

"Well, when we just started dating, and I told Nick—my husband—what had happened, he and his brother tracked Sutton down and sort of...roughed him up a bit? In my defense?" She shrugged and offered a nervous smile, knowing that it sounded a bit juvenile. "They were young. We were young. I don't think he even knew who Nick was at the time, and I had no idea they did this. But last year, when Nick's face was plastered all over the media..."

"You think he put two and two together."

"Yes."

"Is this just a hunch, or do you have some proof?"

"Our house was vandalized last year. Back when Nick was a suspect. Someone spray-painted *KILLER* on our garage door. When I saw the security footage, it reminded me of him. He's very tall, well over six feet. Wiry. The way the man moved, I immediately thought of him. But I initially dismissed it. It didn't make any sense at the time. Why would he come after me after all that time? I thought I was just being paranoid."

"Right."

"But a few months later, when I found out what my mother and Nick had done, it made more sense. I knew it wasn't Jeff Malone. He was with us at the time of the incident. So I did some research. I found out Sutton was in town when it happened. And for the last few months, I've been getting these threatening text messages. I'll show you. He's baiting me. I don't have any other enemies that I know of. It has to be him." She handed him a printout with all of the text messages and their dates.

"I have a flash drive with the footage of him on the security tape. Do you want to take a look?"

"Sure." He plugged it into the computer. She waited while he loaded it up and watched, and she couldn't help but notice that he wasn't wearing a wedding ring.

"Dr. Mancusio, this all seems very concerning, and I don't blame you for your concerns, but I'm afraid it's all out of my jurisdiction. I can't do much of anything about it. You should go to your local police and file a report. That way, if anything happens, at least it'll be documented. We can work with them if you get enough to file charges for the harassment."

"I know you can't do anything about the text messages, but I also have a file of some unsolved sexual assaults in your area. It could be him, right? I'm sure he hasn't changed. I thought if I told you about him, maybe you could look into it. See if there's something that could put him away for a while? Get him to lay off of me?"

Ramirez looked through the file while she sat there hoping for...what? They both knew she was grasping at straws.

Lila started to rouse, making some babbling noises, bringing Victoria back to the issue at hand. Protecting Lila. The sounds brought a smile to the detective's face as he continued to look over her information. She found herself wondering if he had children.

"You've really done your homework. How did you get all this information?"

"I have my sources."

"Apparently."

"Will you check it out?"

"I'll try. But he doesn't really fit the perp's description for most of these incidents."

"Well, sometimes the description's wrong. Remember the gunman in New York a while back? The one on the subway in Brooklyn?"

He nodded.

"We were all told to look for a young, short guy. About five five, they said. Turned out to be a six-foot-two guy in his sixties."

"I did hear about that," Ramirez replied. "But from what I remember, they had no camera footage for that shooting. But you're right; descriptions from memory can be wrong. Some of these incidents have camera footage; some don't. I'll check them all out and get back to you. And we'll do a workup on him just in case. But I wouldn't hold out much hope. It's a bit of a different profile, psychologically speaking. A guy who uses power to force himself on his subordinates, he's not usually the same guy who jumps out from behind a bush. But give me everything you have on him, and I'll check it out."

"Of course. I know where he works and where he lives. And I wrote out a detailed account of what he did to me and what my family did to him." She gathered all the information she had and placed it on his desk, her hand resting on top. "Here's all of it."

He placed his hand on top of hers, the warmth a welcome sensation in the chilly interview room. It gave her the tingles.

"Dr. Mancusio..." He leaned in and looked into her eyes.

"You can call me Victoria."

"Victoria. You've been through quite a lot. Have you ever thought about...therapy?"

"*Therapy?*" She pulled her hand away and sat up, pin straight, her eyes nearly popping out of her head. She wanted to bolt, but there was too much at stake. *He thinks I'm nuts.*

"You were a victim of a sexual assault. That doesn't just go away. In your state of mind, it's easy to see patterns that aren't there. To want answers to things you can't explain. I promise to look into these cases again. We'll look into him, look at all of this from a different angle, given what you've told me. But it does seem like a bit of a stretch. And you may want to let sleeping dogs lie. Go home and forget all this. Let us do our jobs. If he's as vindictive and dangerous as you say, you could be putting your whole family at risk by poking the bear."

"I don't need therapy, Detective! I need action! *He's taunting me!* And I can't do anything about it. Do you realize how frustrating that is? And what state of mind is it, exactly, that I'm in? What exactly are you insinuating?"

"I'm sorry. I didn't mean to upset you. It seems I've overstepped."

"This isn't about me, Detective. It's about him! He's a dangerous predator. He needs to be stopped."

"We'll check it all out, and I'll get back to you. I promise."

She realized she was glaring at him and tried to soften her expression. She didn't need to prove him right with some crazy-lady outburst. She took a deep breath and tried to calm herself down. "Thank you, Detective Ramirez. I appreciate your time and your concern. Really, I do."

"You're welcome...Dr. Mancusio?" He offered her an apologetic smile.

"I expect my inquiry to be taken seriously, Detective."

"I'm sorry if I offended you. Really, I am." They both took a beat, and he offered her a hesitant smile.

"I'm just really stressed about all this."

"Here. Take my card. And please, accept my apology?" He held out his card as she sat there, arms crossed, feeling like a foolish schoolgirl for letting her hormones cloud her judgment.

"I accept your apology, Detective." She gave him a polite smile, although she was still a bit put out by the therapy comment.

"Good. Let's stay in touch. I'll get back to you after I check it all out. I promise."

Victoria reached over, plucked the card from his

hand, and stood up. "Don't bother to get up. I can see myself out. I've taken up enough of your time. And thank you again..."

She started to walk out the door, feeling his eyes still on her. She turned back to him. "...Randy."

"You're welcome again. Victoria."

Her hand was still tingling as she made her way out of the precinct.

———

Randy was sitting at his desk looking through the information Victoria Mancusio had given him when he was interrupted by an all-too-familiar face.

"Who was that?" Barrett asked, sticking her nose into his office. She'd been on his case even more than usual lately. Seemed he couldn't take a leak without her checking up on him. *Didn't you take a leak an hour ago, Ramirez?* Was that where things were headed? He was still doing penance for pissing her off on a case last year. Going rogue. It had made her look bad, even though he was the one who got the official reprimand. The fact that he'd solved it just pissed her off even more.

"You remember that big murder case last year? Up in New York?" he asked.

"The one with the sordid affair?" Barrett's eyes lit up.

"Yeah." He paused, thumbing through his folder. Then he looked up at her and smiled. Ginny Barrett loved a good piece of gossip, so he let her stew a bit, just for fun.

She gave him a look. *Come on, Ramirez*, it said. It'd be beneath her to actually say it.

"She's the wife. Victoria Mancusio."

"What's she doing here?"

"She thinks some former professor from her past's out to get her. Thinks he might be responsible for a string of unsolved sexual assaults in our area."

"Huh?"

"Have a seat, Captain. I'll take you through it." Randy walked her through everything he'd learned from Victoria Mancusio along with what he could piece together about Timothy Sutton in the twenty minutes or so he'd known about him. He believed her about the reason behind Sutton's abrupt career change. A tenure-track professor at a highly selective college "resigns" in his early forties, moves to a new part of the country, and then starts working at a Barnes and Noble? It had all the trappings of a sex scandal. But there was no proof.

He'd never been officially accused, let alone charged by anyone, as far as he could tell. Aside from a few traffic tickets, his record was clean. He'd kept the same job for years until the store went out of business. Now he was working at an indie bookstore in North Scottsdale.

Victoria Mancusio said her mother had obtained proof of his come-ons to students from a private detective. Enough to get him fired. Maybe he could get a hold of it. It was too late to prosecute any of those cases, but at least he'd get a feel for Sutton's MO. See if it matched any of his open cases.

"Well, don't spend too much time on this wild goose chase," Barrett barked. "We're backed up as it is."

He nodded.

"Understood, Ramirez? I need a verbal this time. Make sure we're on the same page?"

"Affirmative, Captain. Understood."

"Let's hope so." Barrett wasn't really that bad, as far as police captains went. She was just doing her job.

But so was he, and his gut told him to keep digging, even if it was on his own time. Plus, he had to admit, staying in touch with Victoria Mancusio wasn't the worst side gig a guy could have.

THREE

The bookstore where Timothy Sutton worked sat on a dusty street in a small suburb on the outskirts of North Scottsdale. The street looked like a movie set from the Old West, not run-down so much as preserved, suspended in time, surrounded by the timeless desert stretching out as far as the eye could see and much less congested than where she was staying. It was an early October morning, and the temperature was already climbing into the eighties. It was a bit of a drive from where Sutton lived, out of the way, a few degrees cooler at the higher elevation, and quite a bit less congested. Thanks to Wade, she knew he wasn't scheduled to work today.

A bell dinged as Victoria opened the door, alerting the proprietor. She entered, not quite knowing what she was hoping to find.

"Good morning. Can I help you find something?" An older lady behind the counter looked over at her through black-rimmed glasses. Her soft silver hair fell gracefully to her shoulders, flipping up slightly at the ends. According to Wade, the owner's name was Wanda, and she was from Northern New Jersey, but she'd lived in Arizona for over twenty years. She had owned the bookstore for most of that time. Victoria detected a faint New York accent, although her attire was decidedly Southwest—a geometric-print tunic and a thick silver chain necklace with a large red stone in its center.

"I'm just looking, thanks." Victoria smiled, and the woman smiled back, her gaze landing on sleepy little Lila, whose chubby legs dangled from her pouch.

"Okay, just let me know if you need anything," Wanda said.

Victoria still hadn't decided how she was going to play this. She walked around the shop and gravitated to the art books. That could be a good icebreaker. Asking her about local artists. Buying a few of her books. She picked up one of the more comprehensive volumes and started to thumb through it while Lila slowly woke from her nap. Her cooing sounds stirred Victoria inside, and she hoped her breasts wouldn't start leaking.

"She's precious. How old?"

"Almost six months," Victoria replied. *Does Lila really look that girly? She isn't even dressed in pink.*

"That's a great age."

She smiled, reminding herself that she should probably be trying harder to make conversation if she wanted to get anywhere on this little mission of hers. But she still wasn't quite sure just how much she wanted to reveal.

"Yes, it is." She turned toward the woman and started walking over to the counter. "This book. Is it the most recent you have? I'm looking for an overview, but I also need something that showcases more recent artists from the area."

"That's a good one for an overview, but I've got something better if you need something more contemporary—or more local?"

"More local would be great. Thanks!"

The woman walked over to the bookcases and took a smaller book off a shelf. "Try this one," the woman offered, handing it to Victoria.

She looked over the table of contents and paged through it while the owner started to pull out another book. "This one's perfect. I'll take it."

She handed the book back to the owner, who returned to the cash register with it. Victoria lingered at the shelves, her fingers gently gracing the spines lined up neatly on them. There was something about a bookstore that invigorated her. The smell of ink and glue. The rows and rows of books. It reminded her of knowledge, of learning. New beginnings. Endless possibilities.

Then she let out a sneeze, and the proprietor's head whipped around toward her.

"Bless you!"

"Thanks. Sorry about that. I'm not sick. I promise."

"It's the desert air. Ragweed pollen, probably. It happens more than you'd think. People come here thinking it'll be good for their allergies. But it doesn't always work out that way."

"Thanks for the tip." She certainly was a chatty one. That usually bugged Victoria, but in this case, it could work to her advantage.

"Are you looking to buy some art while you're in town?"

"Maybe." Victoria hesitated. She needed to find a way to gauge the woman's relationship with Sutton before she gave away too much about herself. Had Sutton set off any warning bells? Given off any kind of a creepy vibe? Had he rubbed a customer the wrong way? Or was she one of his easy marks, charmed by his intellect and wit?

"Do you know of any up-and-coming local artists I might consider?"

"I know some, but I can give you the name of an art gallery a few towns over. The owner might have more information. He's a great resource."

"That would be wonderful. Thanks so much." She started to place the larger book back on the shelf and then thought better of it. She walked over and placed it on the counter.

"I think I'll take this one too."

Wanda smiled. A big sale for a small shop. "A good one! So you're an art lover?"

"Yes. Well, it's a bit more than that. I'm opening an art gallery. In Upstate New York."

"That's wonderful! What town?"

"Woodstock." Victoria's stomach lurched. What if the woman knew the area?

"I'm not too familiar with that area. But I'm from Ridgewood originally. In North Jersey."

Victoria feigned surprise. "Oh, I know that town. It's so nice there. What a small world! So, how do you like it here?"

"It took a while to get used to the slower pace. But now I love it. And I don't miss the harsh winters at all. But then, you must be an expert in that area."

"I'm sorry?"

"Upstate New York? All that snow?"

"Right! Well, see, I'm so used to it, I didn't even get your...um, drift." They both smiled politely at her lame attempt at humor. *Change the subject, Victoria.*

"So, have you been here long?"

"Over twenty years."

"Wow, and you've had the shop all this time?"

"Most of it."

"I know retail can be challenging. I don't have any delusions about how hard it's going to be. How has it been for you?"

"Oh, you know. Up and down. During the

pandemic it was very hard. But I have a great employee. He's my right hand. A former English professor, if you can believe it. Smart as a whip. He was able to help us pivot to online and curbside sales during the pandemic. He really saved us. And of course, now we have the problem of the labor shortage."

"Right. It seems like a big problem everywhere," Victoria replied. So the woman was a fan of Sutton's. *Good to know.*

"It's quiet now, in the mornings, but we get really busy later in the day. When tourist season hits, I'm not sure what I'll do. I had a young woman working for me who was quite competent. Jenna was her name. But she up and quit with no notice about a week ago. Just left me a message that she wasn't coming in anymore. Something about a family situation, but I'm sure she just got a better offer. I don't think she has much family."

"That's terrible."

"It's life. But it's a shame, really. We were close. And she got on so well with Tim, my other employee. The retired professor? He was helping her with her master's thesis. American literature, I think it was. But that's the reality. I can't afford to pay any more than I'm paying. My rent went up forty percent in the past year. I'm barely surviving. But I'm not surprised that she found something better. So much competition for workers out there."

"I guess it's hard to find good people. I'll take that into consideration."

"It's not such bad timing for me personally. I'm fortunate. I can retire anytime. And my employee is interested in coming in as a partner. Or maybe even buying me out. But I'm going to hold out as long as I can. I love bookstores and the sense of community they bring. And I love being around people. I'm a real chatterbox, as I'm sure you can tell. I'd drive myself crazy at home alone all day!" *Chatterbox* was putting it mildly.

"I'll take that under advisement when I open up. I'm sure it won't be easy, but you're a real inspiration. I'll be lucky if I can make it ten years, let alone twenty."

"Well, you've got a little one to think about. I'd think twice about retail these days if I were in your shoes." She finished ringing up the sale. It was close to a hundred dollars for the two books.

Victoria handed her a hundred in cash, all twenties. "Keep the change."

The woman gave her a curious look, and Victoria hoped that hadn't come across the wrong way. She didn't want to call attention to the fact that she had money. "I mean if it's a problem to make change. It's so close to a hundred anyway."

"Sure. Thanks."

"And thanks for all the advice. I really appreciate it."

"Of course. You take care now."

"You as well." Victoria turned toward the door.

"We do online sales too, so be sure and keep us in mind. Oh, did you want the name of the gallery? In Cave Creek? I've written it here, on my card."

"Oh, right. Sure!" She stopped and turned around to grab the card. She'd already gotten a few new artists in Santa Fe before she came here, and this one wasn't in the plan. But she didn't want to be rude.

"Thank you—" she glanced down at the card "—Wanda."

"Thank you too...uh, what did you say your name was again?"

"Ruth."

"Thanks for your business, Ruth."

"You're quite welcome, Wanda."

It wasn't much, but it was something and well worth a hundred dollars and twenty minutes of her time. A young woman named Jenna, chummy with Sutton, who'd suddenly up and quit out of the blue. She could work with that. Thank goodness for chatterboxes.

She looked at the card again and tucked it in her purse. The gallery in Cave Creek sounded interesting, but she couldn't very well go in there and do business with a fake name.

Ruth. How on earth had she come up with that?

FOUR

Jenna Williams wasn't easy to find, and Victoria guessed that was intentional. She'd given the information to Wade the day before, when she got home from the bookstore, and he'd located her in Sedona, about two hours north of Scottsdale, at an Airbnb, although the lease on her apartment in Phoenix ran for another seven months.

The area was as spectacular as Victoria had imagined. Cinnamon-hued stone monuments rose from the desert floor, revealing their bands of color, giving it a timeless feel. Jagged pinnacles cast dark shadows, the intensity of a cloudless blue sky making them all the more dramatic. It didn't surprise her that the area was a spiritual mecca, and there was a good possibility that Jenna Williams had decided to come here simply for inspiration. It could be a coincidence. She could have decided to quit her job at the bookstore to work on her thesis full-time. Go somewhere a little cooler, out of the sweltering desert heat. But Victoria's gut told her that it was something more. Something like what had happened to her back in college. And if she was right, Jenna was likely just as scared as Victoria had been and just as reluctant to report it.

But what if she was wrong? What if Jenna was still friendly with Sutton? She couldn't very well just walk up to her and ask her straight out if Sutton had assaulted her. But she couldn't do nothing and walk away. She'd have to befriend her somehow. Even that was a risk. But it was a risk she was willing to take if there was any chance of nailing Sutton.

Victoria sat in the café Jenna frequented, a tip she'd gotten from Wade, hoping that she would show up. Wade said Jenna had been there a few times this week, around midmorning. Victoria was working on her computer, and Lila was opposite her in her holder, getting a bit fussy. It was nearing feeding time, and Lila was staring at Victoria's chest. She deflected her with a bottle. *Thank goodness for breast pumps.* She admired women who felt free to nurse their babies in public, but Victoria wasn't comfortable with it, even where nobody knew her.

A young woman walked in who looked like she could be Jenna Williams. Her long chestnut hair from the photos was a bit darker—same length—and her face looked a bit thinner. But she was the right age, late twenties, and the right height. It was probably her.

Victoria stood up, took Lila in her arms, and walked up behind the newcomer in line.

"I'll have a café latte and a blueberry muffin," the young woman said.

"Will that be all?"

"Yes, thanks."

"Jenna, right?" the barista asked.

"Yes, that's right. You have a good memory."

The barista smiled. "I try."

Victoria ordered a latte she didn't really want and waited for her coffee with Jenna, hoping that she was a baby person. Normally it annoyed her when people

made a fuss over Lila, but now she was an asset—the perfect little accomplice.
"She's so cute! How old?"
"Thanks! She's almost six months."
"Is she your first?"
"She is. It's an adventure, I tell you. Nothing prepares you for it."
"I've heard."
"But it's wonderful. I'm not complaining."
"I didn't take it that way."
"Are you from the area?"
"Um, no. I'm just visiting."
"From where?"
"The Phoenix area." She looked down at her feet. "I, uh, wanted to get out of the heat for a bit."
"I can understand that. I'm from New York. It's hot there too, but nothing like this."
As Jenna turned to face her, Victoria noticed a bruise showing through on her cheek that had been covered with thick makeup. Victoria's eyes rested on it a bit too long.
"Jenna! Your order's ready."
"Well, that's me. Take care." Jenna grabbed her coffee, glanced over at Victoria's table, and headed clear across the room. Victoria went back to her table and waited, using the time to look up galleries and artists in Sedona.
After about forty minutes, Jenna got up and left the café. Victoria followed her, keeping a few paces behind. Jenna must have sensed it because she turned around, her eyes wide with something. Fear? Rage?
"Can I help you?"
They stood there for a few moments, sizing each other up.
"I'm actually wondering if I can help you."
"Why would you think I need help?"

Victoria wasn't going to beat around the bush. "I noticed the bruise. On your face? I wanted to make sure you were okay. That you weren't running from something. Or someone."

"It's nothing. I ran into a door."

"You ran into a door?"

"I'm a klutz. It happens."

"Not often."

"Just leave me alone. Please."

"I have resources. I can help you. I know you're scared, but I can help you."

"And why would you want to do that?"

"Because I can. And because I know what it's like to be totally terrified of a man."

"I'm not totally terrified of a man."

"So you're only a little terrified?"

"I didn't say that. That's not what I meant." Jenna's face softened, and her eyes started to tear up. But then she took a deep breath, batted them back, and stood up straighter. Victoria could see her trying to rein in her emotions. Bury them. Like she herself had done years ago. In the bright sunlight, she could see a faint bruise on Jenna's neck.

"Do you want to go somewhere and talk?"

"No. I want to forget about it."

"That's what he's hoping. That's what they all hope. That's how they get away with it."

"Look, it's not what you think. I'm fine. I don't have some stalker ex after me. It's nothing like that. It's nothing. Really."

"It's definitely not nothing. At least think about taking some photos of your bruises. Before they fade. In case you change your mind," Victoria offered.

Jenna let out a sigh.

"Can we please go somewhere and talk?"

"I said I don't want to talk about it."

"I'll tell you what. I'll tell you my story first. And if you feel comfortable, then you can tell me yours. But only if you feel comfortable. What harm could that do?"

"I can't. Not right now, anyway."

"How about later?"

"I don't think it's a good idea."

"Please. Just give me a chance to tell my story. Where's the harm in that? I'm trying to help. And we're both visiting, right? We can keep each other company."

Jenna seemed to be mulling it over, and Victoria let her sit with it for a bit.

"I guess I can meet you later. But only to hear your story. You seem like you need someone to talk to. That's all I'm committing to for now."

"Understood. Anytime. What works for you?"

"How's lunch? Unless you already have plans?"

"No plans. Lunch sounds great. Any suggestions?"

"The Prickly Cactus?"

"Sure. How about noon?"

"That's fine."

"What did you say your name was?"

"Jenna."

"I'm Victoria. I'll see you at noon, Jenna." There was no turning back now.

Victoria arrived right before noon and got a quiet table in a far corner, a rounded booth. She'd have a good view of Jenna's face, but they wouldn't be directly facing each other. She hoped that the sense of privacy would get the young woman to open up. But as noon came and went, she prepared herself for a no-show. *Maybe she left town.* That would be the end of it. Victoria couldn't very well keep showing up everywhere Jenna went, stalking her.

And then she showed. About fifteen minutes late.

"Where's your baby?" Jenna asked on arrival.

"With her nanny. She's traveling with us." Victoria had gotten a hotel room for the day, even though she planned to be back in Scottsdale that evening for her early morning reconnaissance mission the next day.

"Must be nice," Jenna replied.

It was an odd comment, but Victoria let it go. *Maybe she was raised by a single mother.* But she made a mental note that Jenna might have a chip on her shoulder about money and censored herself accordingly.

They spent the first half of their meal getting to know each other. Victoria didn't lie, but she was careful about how much she disclosed. Jenna was guarded, but she started to open up a bit when Victoria told her she'd gotten a master's and then a doctorate. That seemed to be pretty safe territory, giving her pointers on how to finish up her thesis and get her master's. Victoria was an English major as an undergraduate, so she was familiar with Jenna's topic. That helped to warm things up a bit. When there was a lull, Victoria tried to steer the conversation where she needed it to go.

"I had a great advisor for my doctorate. A woman."

"Oh?"

"I was adamant about working with a woman. After an earlier experience I had."

"Does that have something to do with the story you wanted to tell me?"

"Yes. It does." Victoria hesitated, not sure how much to say. The whole truth might freak Jenna out, but it was the only approach that could get her to see what was at stake.

LITTLE LOOSE ENDS

"I was sexually assaulted. By a professor of mine. My senior thesis advisor. Back when I was an undergraduate."

"I'm very sorry to hear that."

"I was actually able to fight him off before things went too far. I have my father to thank for that. He insisted on self-defense classes. He was adamant that I learn to protect myself."

"Good advice. Sounds like you had a great dad."

"Yes, I did. But you see, I didn't really defend myself. Not in the bigger picture. He threatened to kill me if I told anyone. So I dropped out of school. I never filed charges. And I never reported it. And now it's too late."

"That must have been terrible. I can't imagine."

"Can't you?"

"No, I can't."

"He was an English professor."

Jenna's face went a shade paler, and she froze in her seat. *This very well might backfire. But I can't stop now.*

Victoria continued. "I wasn't his only victim, you see. And I'm responsible for that. Eventually, he was fired from his position. But it could have stopped with me if I'd been strong enough to do something about it at the time."

Jenna's eyes widened. "Who are you? And what do you want from me? You didn't just run into me in a café. What the hell is going on?"

"I told you. I'm someone who wants to help."

"And I told you I don't need any help. Sounds like maybe you're the one who needs help. Seeing things that aren't there. Approaching strangers in a café. It could get you into trouble."

"What happened to you, Jenna? What did he do to you? Please tell me."

39

"Nothing happened!"

"I know you're scared of him, Jenna. That's how Sutton operates. That's what gives him the power. But I've been to the police. They're looking at him for a string of unsolved sexual assaults in this area. I know you worked with him, and you don't seem the type to quit your job out of the blue. Please. Go to the police. Tell them everything. Make him pay for what he did. Before it's too late."

"I told you. Nothing happened." Her voice was calm now, almost mechanical. "And I have absolutely no idea what you're talking about. I'm going to go now." She'd shut down. Fear does that to a person.

"Please. Jenna. Take this. Think about it." Victoria held out Ramirez's card.

"Detective Randy Ramirez. Sutton's on his radar. You might change your mind. If you do, he can help you. And my number's on the back."

"You stay away from me!" Jenna spoke at low volume, her eyes narrowed on Victoria. She grabbed her purse and stood up. "And if you come near me again, I'll call the police on *you*." She snatched the card from Victoria's fingers and left.

Well, that could have gone better. At least she took the card.

Leading a double life was exhausting, so Victoria actually didn't mind some downtime. She took her time finishing her meal in preparation for her afternoon gallery appointment. Then it was a long drive back to Scottsdale for her early morning mission.

FIVE

The streets were quiet in the predawn hours. Wade had done his best to give Victoria a rundown on Sutton's routine, and she was hoping he'd stick to it this morning. Sutton lived in an area called Kierland, a mixed-use residential and commercial area of Scottsdale that offered a convenient walking lifestyle for young, trendy professionals. His place sat a few blocks from its center in an area adjacent to a string of resorts and walking trails. From what Wade could deduce by hacking into Sutton's Strava feed, he went for a walk almost every morning around six. Victoria waited for him beside his townhome, perched behind a bunch of palm trees and a giant saguaro cactus, hoping to get a glimpse of him. *And then what?*

Of all the risky things she'd done since her life had been forever altered by Nick's affair, this was by far the most dangerous. Too dangerous to bring Lila, so she'd left her with her nanny, who, up until today, had mostly been enjoying a free vacation in Arizona. She could barely admit to herself what she was contemplating. But here she was, stalking Timothy Sutton with a loaded weapon in her possession. Her senses were heightened with anticipation, waiting to see if he would show. She knew this was a crazy move.

That's why she hadn't even told Wade about it. What if someone saw her? What if he saw her?

She wasn't planning to kill him. At least not yet. This was a trial run of sorts. But she had thought about it. A lot more than a normal person probably would have, especially after the latest text, the one that had put her over the edge.

Most of his texts were ambiguous. Not directly threatening. Sutton was too smart for that. Even if she could prove he'd sent them—which she couldn't yet—he hadn't said anything that could get him arrested. Even a restraining order would be difficult. That's why she hadn't told anyone. There had been no direct threats. There was nothing actionable. And they weren't constant, just every now and again. Little reminders to let her know he was watching. To let her know he was still calling the shots. That he'd always be calling the shots.

How's the new place working out, Victoria?
Maybe I'll pay you a visit soon.
You're home alone a lot, Victoria. Is that safe?
Tell Nick it's not wise to jog in the dark.

She had been waiting him out, hoping he'd tire of it and move on. The texts had tapered off a few months after Lila was born, and she'd started to feel hopeful it all might just fade away. But about a week ago, he'd crossed a line with the one that set her off.

You're a mother now, Victoria. Be careful. The world is a dangerous place.

Veiled threats against her or Nick, that was one thing. But to threaten Lila? He really had no idea what she was capable of. She'd been reading up on a famous case from back in the nineties. A mother had walked into court and shot and killed the man who had sexually assaulted her young son. The man had previously served time for sexual assault and gotten out, and she didn't trust the system to protect her son. The boy's mother had done time for the murder, Victoria knew, but not that much time. About three years. Surely Victoria's lawyers could do better.

If it came to that, Victoria was willing to follow that example—kill Sutton and go to prison to keep Lila safe. It wasn't an ideal solution, killing him, but at least they'd be free of him once and for all. Nick and her mother could raise Lila just fine. They had all the money in the world. It wasn't that big of a sacrifice, going to prison to make sure your child was safe.

She hadn't laid eyes on Sutton since that night over ten years ago when he was curled up in a ball on his apartment floor as she raced to get out before he could recover from the kick to his groin. She could still hear his threat in that low rumble of his. *If you tell anyone about this, you're dead!*

Then his front door started to open, and she froze. A moment of self-doubt hit her like a ton of bricks. Her heart started to race. Could he see her over in the shadows? This was dangerous. Crazy dangerous. Foolish. A big mistake. What if he had a weapon too? Many people did in this state. It wasn't New York. *What was I thinking?*

He came into view as he stepped down from his stoop and into the wash of the streetlights. He'd lost the hipster look and the ponytail. His hair was cropped, and he looked neat. Clean-shaven. A bit thinner, but he had the same gait. She'd know it anywhere, like on their security tape. He paused for a moment, taking in the fresh air, and it suddenly dawned on her that she had a clean shot.

She felt for her gun, tucked safely in its holster. It would be so easy. This wasn't the plan, to kill him now. But what if this was the only chance she would get? She'd left all the important numbers with the note she'd left the nanny: *I should be back in an hour or so.* If she didn't come back, they'd figure it all out. Sutton would be dead. And Lila would be safe. It wasn't such a big sacrifice, was it? Prison? Maybe she'd even get away with it. It was tempting. So very tempting.

She'd imagined this moment many times. Wondered if she could actually pull the trigger. Now she was pretty sure she could. But she wouldn't. Not yet. She'd give the wheels of justice a chance first. But she kept her hand resting on her weapon for a few moments, just in case.

Then he cocked his head in her direction, and she felt a rush of panic. Had he sensed her? Smelled her? She stayed still. Very still. Her heart was beating so hard that she wondered if he could hear it pounding in her chest. Sweat beads formed at her temples. She pulled out her Glock 43 and kept it by her side.

Her nose got itchy, and she felt like she was going to sneeze. She forced herself to stifle it, wiggling her nose ever so slightly. Sutton stood there, his head tilted toward her but not looking in her direction. She didn't dare to move a muscle.

Then, just like that, he turned and walked away from her and out of sight. She breathed a small sigh of relief. Then she holstered her gun, scratched her itchy nose, and made a mental note to take some allergy meds if she ever decided to stalk someone in the desert again.

Back at her hotel suite, she sat on the spacious deck looking out at Camelback Mountain, finally able to reflect and relax. The midday sun was straight overhead, and the view was impressive. The colors

LITTLE LOOSE ENDS

here were so different from home. They were much more subtle. There was color; but you to look harder to see it. The desert had its own stark beauty, but the landscape seemed so stagnant to her. The Hudson, it flowed. It reinvented itself every day. She loved to look out on it as it moved past her. She never got tired of the way the sun sparkled on the water or of watching the occasional ship float by, adding a sense of motion. The desert, it just sat there under the punishing, blazing hot sun, day after day after day. Waiting for something new to happen. But it never did.

If she ever left the Hudson Valley, she'd need to be near water. She thought of Hawaii and the perfect romantic week she'd shared there with Nick nearly a year ago. She could still picture the gentle blue sea and the rolling whitecaps outside the window of the luxurious oceanfront suite that became their sanctuary for that long, lovely week. They'd exhausted themselves with steamy lovemaking punctuated by runs and swims and room service for two. They hadn't even left the property. It was the last time she'd felt truly happy, the last time she'd felt totally in love. She liked to think that Lila was conceived there. And then he ruined it all by sleeping with Angie Hansen less than a month later, so that sweet memory was forever tainted by his betrayal, but Lila remained as a testament to the love they once shared.

She was leaving in the morning. In the three days since she'd arrived, what had she actually accomplished on her mission? Not much. But not nothing, either. It was possible the little seeds she'd planted would mature into something more. Maybe Jenna Williams would come forward and file charges. Maybe Detective Ramirez would find some way to connect Sutton to one of his unsolved cases. It was possible, but not probable. In all likelihood, nothing would happen as far as Sutton was concerned.

What then? Would he keep on taunting her forever? Or would it eventually just fade away? Was this all a mind game to him? Or would he act on it? Should she take action before he had the chance, or should she wait it out? Wanda had mentioned he was talking about buying into her bookstore. That meant he had some money. That might make him less likely to do anything crazy. If the sale went forward, maybe it would mean he was moving on. She'd have Wade look into it.

Then she thought about the text messages again, looking for a pattern. They'd stopped for a while and then started up again. Could that have had something to do with his relationship with Jenna Williams? His latest text came about the time Jenna quit. That could mean something. They looked nothing alike. Jenna was a busty brunette, and Victoria a petite blonde. But both were young scholars. Eager for knowledge; intellectually, his type.

She considered what Ramirez had said. Let sleeping dogs lie. He had a point. It was a big risk, poking around in his business. It could very well backfire. Maybe she should think about some therapy. But then, she couldn't even tell a therapist the whole truth about her backup plan. They'd lock her right up.

Randy Ramirez. She felt all girly just thinking about him. It was so ridiculous she actually started to laugh. But it also made her face what she'd been dreading to admit, even to herself. She didn't feel the same way about Nick anymore. She cared about him. She really did. She wanted to be in love with him. It would be so much easier. But she didn't feel the same anymore.

She assumed many couples went on like that for

years. Decades, even. How many people were really in love during their entire marriage? Maybe they had affairs. Maybe they stuffed down their feelings for other people. Maybe they busied themselves with other things until so many years went by the familiar habits of the person became such a welcome comfort that it was worth more than passion. She could live with that.

She thought back to that night at Angie Hansen's house, the night when she'd followed Nick. The night Angie Hansen was murdered. She remembered the feeling like it was yesterday. Seeing them locked in an embrace. Their kiss. The gut punch that followed, when all of her suspicions were proven right. How she had to pull over to the side of the road on the way home, her body racked with sobs. And the funny thing was, she longed for that feeling. That terrible ache in the pit of her stomach. Because back then, she knew she was in love with her husband. And now, she just felt numb inside. Was it her way of blocking out all the pain he'd caused her, or was she falling out of love with him?

That reminded her that she needed to call Nick. They'd missed each other yesterday, and it was her turn to try him. She grabbed her phone and noticed there was a message from a Scottsdale number from over an hour before. Maybe Jenna had changed her mind.

She listened to the message. It wasn't Jenna, but she wasn't too disappointed, because it was Randy Ramirez, and she started to feel all tingly in spite of the fact that she knew it was ridiculous. He didn't say what he wanted, just that he had some follow-up questions from her visit the other day. It was Saturday. *Do detectives work on Saturdays?*

Then a wave of panic hit her, canceling out the

hormone surge. What if someone saw her at Sutton's house? What if he was calling to investigate her? It brought back the memory of how she'd felt when she was a suspect—briefly—in Angie Hansen's murder. Sitting in the interrogation room. The bright lights. The claustrophobic feeling.

She checked the number against the one from the precinct. It was different. Was it his personal cell? Lila was napping, so it was a good time to talk. She might as well get it over with. If someone had seen her there, gun in hand, what exactly would the charge be anyway? Open carry was legal in Arizona. She punched the call back button.

"Hi, this is Randy."

"Hi...Detective...um, Randy. This is Victoria. Victoria Mancusio?"

"Oh! Hi, Victoria! Thanks so much for calling me back. Is this a good time for you to talk?"

"Sure. Lila's down for a nap. What can I do for you?"

"I've been looking into Timothy Sutton. I was wondering if you might have access to that evidence you mentioned. That your mother got from the private investigator when you were in college? I know it was a while ago, but it would give me insight into his MO. Sorry, his pattern of behavior. I want to see if it matches any of my cases."

"Oh, right. Sure. Did you find something?"

"I can't really comment on ongoing investigations."

"Of course."

"So, do you think you can get hold of it?"

"I'm pretty sure I can." *But I don't want to.* To get that information, she'd have to out herself to everyone about what she was up to. Her mother. Sam Coleman, the PI who'd handled the job back then. The PI she'd also hired to help clear Nick of murder. The one who may or may not be her biological father. She was still reeling from her mother's bombshell revelation about that. She'd been stalling on finding out the truth, but she had to face it soon. If only for Lila's sake, she had to find out the truth about her lineage.

"That would help a lot."

"I'm still in Scottsdale, but I'm leaving for home in the morning. I can probably have something for you early next week."

"That would be great, thanks. I can't expend a lot of resources on this. We have a backload of cases we're trying to clear. But I promise I'll check it out. Even if it's on my own time. This is my personal cell. Contact me here for the time being. Until we get some solid evidence."

"I appreciate this very much." There was a lull in the conversation, and she wondered if he would move things into the personal realm.

"Okay, then. So, have a safe trip back, and I'll look to hear from you early next week?"

"Yes, Randy. Thanks again."

"Of course, Victoria. Bye now." And that was it.

She was dying to tell him about Jenna Williams, but she couldn't. It was Jenna's story to tell, not hers. Jenna was right to be scared. Sutton was dangerous. Plus, she knew from Nick's case that detectives didn't look too kindly on amateurs inserting themselves in their business. No, Randy Ramirez was intrigued right now—with her, with the case—and she needed to keep it that way. But without a victim to press charges, they'd be nowhere. He was the curious type; he'd probably find Jenna on his own. And she was also hoping that if Sutton found out the police were poking around in his business down here, the texts would stop. Maybe he'd move on, and they could both get on with their lives. If not, she always had her backup plan.

As her mind lingered on Randy Ramirez and the sexy sound of his brawny twang, she remembered that she needed to call Nick and felt a twinge of guilt. But then Lila woke up with a screeching cry that jolted her out of her dreamy state. She put her husband on the back burner again and went to get Lila.

It was late afternoon, and Victoria was settling in for the night. She was looking forward to an uneventful evening after all of her adventures. Maybe she'd take a bath. Watch something on Lifetime. Forget about her problems.

Then she heard her phone buzz and went to grab it. An unknown caller. It didn't look like an Scottsdale area code, so she almost didn't answer but then thought better of it.

"Hello. This is Victoria." The caller didn't say anything. Maybe a robocall? Then she felt her stomach tense up. What if it was Sutton? What if he knew she was in town? What if he'd seen her at his house? Followed her? He didn't live that far from her hotel. She waited, and her heart started to race. Finally, someone spoke.

"It's Jenna."

"Jenna? How are you?" Victoria was shocked. Even though she'd been hoping for this call, she wasn't expecting it to come so quickly.

"I'm fine." An awkward silence followed.

"I'm glad you called." She heard Jenna let out a sigh. "Really, I am."

"I'm not so sure about this."

"That's okay, Jenna. We can just...talk. Nothing wrong with talking."

"I think I want to tell you my story."

"That's good. I know that's a hard first step, Jenna, but I'm here for you."

"Yeah, sure. But I have some conditions first."

"Conditions?" Victoria already had some reservations about Jenna. Now what?

"I've been doing some research on you."

"What kind of research?" Victoria leaned into the call, wondering if she'd made a grave mistake tracking the young woman down.

"I know you have money, Victoria. Lots of it. Which is something I don't have. I'll tell you what. I'll go to the police about Sutton but only if you can get me out of here. Relocate me somewhere. Away from him."

That caught Victoria off guard, but she played it cool. "We could talk about that. It's understandable you're afraid of him, Jenna. But the police could offer you protection too. Have you thought about that?"

And how do I know you won't just take the money and run?

"The police won't do anything, and you know it! Why didn't you report him to the police when it happened to you, Victoria?"

"That's a fair question."

"And you had all the resources in the world at your disposal."

Victoria's silence spoke volumes. What could she say to that? As if reading her mind, Jenna continued.

"Look. I'll meet you in person. Before you leave, if it's not too late. And I'll tell my story. You can even record it if you want. For insurance purposes. Then you know I won't screw you over. You'll have my story. But I won't go to the police until I have the resources to get away from him."

"Can you meet me first thing in the morning tomorrow at my hotel?"

"Sure." They worked out the details.

Victoria knew she was moving into some bizarre and disconcerting territory. She was pretty sure Jenna wouldn't make up a story about Sutton assaulting her. The bruises were real, and she had quit her job rather abruptly. But this did feel like a bit of a shakedown. And Jenna could very well screw her over anyway, even if it was all true. Take the money, not file any charges, then disappear. If she was that desperate, Victoria could hardly blame her.

It was a risk Victoria was willing to take to hear Jenna's story and get the truth, to find out how dangerous Sutton really was these days, to vindicate her hunches about him, and reassure herself she wasn't some crazy woman with an unjustified vendetta. She could certainly afford to help Jenna. And then there was the guilt. Maybe if she'd filed charges against Sutton ten years ago, Jenna wouldn't be in this position in the first place. She felt a responsibility to protect her.

Victoria aimed the TV remote, clicked, and started scrolling through the guide. *Nightmare PTA Moms* aired at six. Perfect. She went to draw her bath, relishing a night of calm before the storm.

SIX

Jenna arrived at Victoria's room at nine o'clock sharp the next morning dressed in jeans and a plain black t-shirt, her eyes hidden behind a pair of dark, sporty Ray-Bans. She wore her dark hair in a ponytail, which stuck out the back of the baseball cap on her head. She took off the glasses when she came in but not the cap. Her face was bare, which made her look younger, more vulnerable. The bruises had faded a bit, but they were still visible, even more so without the makeup, and Victoria felt the urge to protect her, like a big sister.

"Can I get you some coffee?"

"Sure."

"How do you take it?"

"Milk. No sugar." Jenna stood near the entrance, sizing up the place. It dawned on Victoria that it was a pretty impressive suite, two bedrooms, well over a thousand square feet. She hadn't really given it much thought, but for someone used to a standard hotel room, it might be a bit of a shock.

"Please. Have a seat." Victoria put out some croissants and fruit along with the coffee on the dining table off to the side of the living area.

"Nice place," Jenna remarked, grabbing a croissant

and digging into it.

"Thanks."

"Is Lila sleeping?"

Victoria was surprised to hear Jenna use her daughter's name. "No, she's over with her nanny."

"The nanny has her own room?"

"Well, yes. She likes her privacy, and so do I."

Jenna nodded and sat down, and Victoria followed. Neither of them knew how to begin. Jenna was still scanning the suite.

"We're certainly from different worlds," Jenna remarked with more than a hint of resentment.

"I can't help where I come from, Jenna. But we do have one major thing in common, so can we maybe just focus on that?" Victoria was getting annoyed by Jenna's little digs, so she pushed back a bit.

"Sure. I didn't mean anything by it. It's just an observation. Oh, and thanks for breakfast. I drove down from Sedona and didn't have time to eat. I'm starved."

Victoria was absolutely sure Jenna did mean something by it, but she let it go. "So, you said you wanted to tell me your story. What made you change your mind?"

"Cards on the table?"

"Sure."

"When I found out who you were, I saw a way out. I'm still afraid of him. I had to quit my job. I want to move away, but I have a lease. Student loans. A pretty worthless degree until I finish my master's. I had to quit my job. I have like three hundred dollars in the bank, and my rent's due. I need a new start, but I'm broke. I'm in debt. Not from doing extravagant things. Just from—life." She paused and looked away, letting out a sigh. It wasn't a dig this time; it was her reality.

"That's quite a bind to be in. I can't even imagine

how you feel." Victoria felt for her; she really did. She'd always taken her wealth for granted, even rebelling against it at times. But she'd always had it to fall back on. What would it be like to start with nothing and then have something like this happen? These days, it was harder and harder to get ahead. She knew she was fortunate, and it filled her with guilt. It's why she had started a nonprofit offering college scholarships to talented young art majors. It's why she lived in a home that was modest in proportion to her wealth. Helping Jenna wasn't really so different. And she reminded herself, once again, that if she'd reported Sutton to the police back then, maybe Jenna wouldn't be in this position in the first place. Perhaps she was a bit of an opportunist, but she was still a person in need of help. And Victoria was in a position to help her.

"So, what do you think? Can you help me get away? Can we help each other?" Jenna asked.

"That's what I'm hoping. I know I can help you get a new start. Can you help me bring Sutton to justice?" Victoria was doing the math in her head while Jenna munched on some honeydew melon. *A hundred grand. That's my limit.* But she wouldn't start there, and nobody could know the full extent of what she was doing. More secrets. More lies. She didn't like it, but this was the only way to get Sutton. *Well, not the only way. But the least insane way.*

"I think I can do it." Jenna sat up straight and looked her in the eye.

Victoria nodded.

"I think I want to do it."

"How do you want to start?"

"I told you I'd tell my story. Should we start there?"

"Sure. If you're ready to start?"

Jenna took a deep breath. "Yeah, I'm ready. And I

want you to record it. Like I said. For insurance. And in case something should happen to me." The young woman's hand went to the bruise on her neck. *Jenna is truly frightened; I'm sure of that.*

Victoria pulled up the recording app on her phone, but Jenna held up her hand in protest.

"Wait. Let me give you some background first, okay? I'll tell you when to start recording. It'll make me less nervous."

"Sure."

Jenna started in. She told Victoria about how it was when she first met Sutton. He was charming, brilliant, witty. He made her laugh and impressed her with his wealth of knowledge. He had a girlfriend at the time, he'd told her, a woman around his age she'd never met, so she didn't really take his attention for anything more than friendship. He was a big help to her as she was trying to finish her online master's degree. The admissions team had made a lot of promises about how much attention she would get, but in practice, her advisor was rarely available, and she had racked up a ton of student loan debt. She needed to finish and get a real job. Her plan was to teach community college and leave herself time to write novels, and he was helping her with that too. Sutton was nothing more than a mentor to her, a colleague, maybe a friend, and she thought he felt the same way.

"I'm getting to the incident. Do you want to start playing it?"

"Sure." Victoria took a sip of her coffee and then started the recording.

"He asked me to go out for drinks near where he lived after work. We'd done it before, so I didn't think much of it. I was dating someone, and I was going to meet him after, for dinner, so I stopped at home and changed. I was dressed up a bit more than usual. Maybe he got the wrong idea. He said he had some books that could help with my research over at his town house. So after the drink, I walked with him over to his place." Jenna paused and took a sip of her coffee, then she continued.

"I remember I said something about his girlfriend as we were walking over, but he told me he'd broken up with her. He said she was too boring. Lacked a sense of adventure, I think were his exact words. Something like that. I remember 'cause I got a bit uncomfortable with the word 'adventure.' I almost decided not to go, but then I didn't want to offend him. We worked together, and I liked my job. So I went." She took a deep breath.

"When we got inside, he started looking at me differently. I could tell he had the wrong idea. It made me nervous but only because I didn't want to hurt his feelings. I didn't want things to get awkward if I rejected him. I had no idea he'd get violent. I liked my job. Wanda, my boss, she's like a mom to me. And she thinks he walks on water. I didn't want to have to quit. When he went to get the books he asked if I wanted another drink. I told him I couldn't. That I had plans."

"When I told him I had a date that night, that I was meeting the guy after, that's when he started to get angry. 'You little tease," he said or something like that. 'You think you can just get away with this? Flirting with me? Using me to help you finish your work? Then giving it away to your real boyfriend?' I'm not sure if that's exactly what he said. But it was something like that. Accusing me of leading him on. Using him."

Jenna paused for a moment, and Victoria noticed a faraway look in her eye. Was it guilt? Was she second-guessing herself? Or was she just trying to remember? "Then I got pissed. Really pissed. I guess that was the wrong way to play it. But, like I said, I thought he was harmless. We started arguing. He said I led him on. I told him I didn't lead him on. That it was all in his head. 'Stop playing hard to get, Jenna,' he said." She recounted that he'd forced himself on her, tried to kiss her, and started to grope her, but as with Victoria, things hadn't gone too far. She pushed him away, and he stopped, which had surprised her.

"Then I told him he wasn't going to get away with it. That's when he punched me in the face and grabbed me around the neck. And then the panic hit. I thought he might kill me. I tried to knee him in the nuts, but I couldn't quite do it. I was trying to elbow him. And then his grip started to loosen a bit. I was wearing him down, I think." Her eyes started to tear. "I was getting tired too. But I knew if I stopped fighting..." She paused and took a few breaths.

"And then he let go for some reason. So I shoved him. Really hard. He fell back on the floor. I was surprised. He's a big guy. Well, not muscular, but tall."

Victoria remembered thinking Sutton was unexpectedly strong for a thin man, but then she had no real basis for comparison.

"But I guess with my adrenaline surging, my shove was pretty powerful. He was down, so I got out of there, and I never looked back." Jenna put her head in her hands.

Victoria stopped the recording, got up and stood behind her, placing her hand on Jenna's back while she sat there in silence, gentle tears running down her face in a rare moment of vulnerability. "I'm so sorry for what you went through, Jenna."

After a moment or two, Jenna sat up and leaned

forward, pulling away from Victoria's touch. "I'm fine," Jenna said, holding up her hand. The tough girl was back, and Victoria reseated herself across from her on the other side of the table.

Although they were from completely different backgrounds, it made sense that he would go after both of them. They were both strong and independent women, beautiful and generally out of his league. Both of them were young scholars hungry for knowledge, which gave Sutton an in as a mentor. There were similarities in the incidents too. The drinks, the "come up to my place for the info" ruse, the accusations of being a tease. Was it possible that Sutton was delusional? Did he really believe he'd been led on? What would that make him? A narcissist? A sociopath? She needed to read up on that. Consult with a psychologist or maybe a profiler. She needed some framework from which to predict his next move.

"And then I just blew off my dinner date. With a text message! I never even had a chance to explain to him why I didn't show. He seemed like a good guy. I really liked him, but I had no choice. I didn't know him well enough to tell him about it."

"After you report it, you could contact him again," Victoria offered.

"No, it wasn't serious at all," Jenna said. "He's moved on, I'm sure. That's how it is these days with dating apps. Nobody loses any sleep over things like that. They just pull up their phone and swipe."

Victoria thought it sounded dreadful. She'd hated dating and enjoyed being married. The security. The routine. She hadn't dated that much before she met Nick, and she certainly didn't want to start now.

"You said he let go of you for some reason. Do you think he regretted it? Came to his senses?"

"I have no idea. But I got the feeling that he

stopped because he had to not because he wanted to."

"Because he had to? What do you mean?"

"I can't explain it. There was this look of defeat on his face. I guess it could have been regret. It all happened so fast. But that's not what my gut told me. I was surprised that he fell back so hard too, but then, like I said, my adrenaline was pumping. You hear about people lifting up cars and stuff, you know?"

"Right. Well, I guess it really doesn't matter. It was a horrible experience, and you're safe now."

"Am I?" Jenna asked.

"Yes. Let's figure out how to get you out of here."

Victoria made her an offer. She would secure Jenna a lease on an apartment somewhere up near her, month to month. She'd give her the funds to terminate the lease on her current apartment and cover her moving expenses. She'd pay off her grad school loans, around twenty-five thousand. And she'd give her some money for living expenses since Jenna's part-time gig tutoring online wasn't enough to live on. They settled on another forty thousand over the next year, giving her time to finish her degree. The payments would have to be kept secret through an offshore account to avoid any complications with Sutton's prosecution. But first, Jenna had to report it.

Jenna countered. She wanted to go back to Sedona since she'd already paid for the Airbnb and the rental car for another week and wait until all of it was in place before she went to Ramirez. That was too risky for Victoria. She wasn't going to give a stranger all that cash with nothing in return.

They settled on a compromise. Victoria would give her the money to get out of her lease and move. Jenna would file the report right before she left for New York. Once she was there, Victoria would give her the funds to pay off her loans. Then she'd give her the

spending money in four payments, quarterly, all via an offshore account.
"I can have the move secured within the week, Jenna. But I need one more concession from you. Can I have your permission to tell Detective Ramirez you'll be in touch in the meantime?"
"I don't know about that."
"I won't tell him your name. I'll only tell him the basics. Then he might take me a little more seriously. He can also tell me what you can do to cover your bases legally. That reminds me, can I take some photos of your bruises?"
"I already did. But fine. Go ahead."
Victoria took out her phone and took a few close-up photos.
"So, do we have a deal?" Victoria asked.
"Yeah, Victoria. We have a deal." They shook on it, and Jenna headed out.
Victoria felt good about it—even though she knew it was a risk—because she felt vindicated. She knew now that she wasn't just paranoid. Sutton hadn't changed. He was still a danger to her and others. He needed to be stopped. And the fact that she now had a reason to call Randy Ramirez was icing on the cake.

SEVEN

Randy's phone rang—a New York number that he now recognized—and he felt a rush. *That was fast.* Had Victoria already gotten the information he'd requested? He'd only talked to her yesterday. But he didn't really mind the call, even on a Sunday, and that wasn't good. He was divorced, but he wasn't the type to covet another man's wife, especially after what had happened to him. He'd never act on his attraction to her, but still. It wasn't productive.
"Hi, Victoria."
"Hi, Randy."
"Are you back home?"
"No, but I'm leaving for the airport shortly."
"What can I do for you?"
"I have some more information. About Sutton."
"Oh?"
"I did some investigating. On my own."
"Ah, we don't generally recommend that sort of thing, Victoria."
"I know. Trust me, I know. But I found something, and I wanted to tell you about it."
"What?"
"Sutton assaulted someone. Recently. A young woman in her twenties. Someone he already knew.

Just like what happened to me. A very similar MO."

"Who?" He thought it was cute that she was using detective lingo. *MO.* Normally something like that would annoy him.

"I can't tell you who she is right now or how he knows her. She told me her story. She's going to come see you soon. Within the next week, she said."

"Victoria, this is pretty dangerous territory you're heading into. Why don't you just let us do our jobs?" This seemed a bit much, a bit obsessive, even. Tracking down a potential victim? How had she even found her? And who was feeding her all the information? Maybe his attraction to her was clouding his judgment. Was she a victim or a woman out for vengeance? Or was she a little of both?

"I have photos, Randy. Of the bruises he gave her. She told me her story. I recorded it. She said I could play it for you if I didn't tell you her name. Do you want to hear it?"

Randy was hesitant. He knew it wasn't a good idea, but curiosity got the better of him. This was an unofficial investigation, and it was on his own time. What if a friend called him with something like this? He'd probably listen to the recording. But that didn't mean he should follow a relative stranger down some rabbit hole. He decided to do it anyway. Getting justice wasn't always compatible with playing by the rules.

"Okay. Play it."

"Hang on a minute." He waited while she did whatever it was she was doing. "I'm ready," she said.

"Let it roll." He listened as Victoria waited quietly on the other end for the recording to finish. The woman sounded young, maybe in her twenties. Her voice was steady, if a bit halting. It was hard to tell without looking at her face, but his gut told him she was telling the truth. Still, it was worthless in terms of an arrest or prosecution. No name. No date. It could be a passage from a piece of fiction for all anyone knew. And if it ever came to an arrest, it could easily look like Victoria had put the woman up to it. He wished Victoria had just let him do his job. But would he have? He had to admit, before listening to this tape and before what he'd found out on his own about one of his cold cases, he'd thought she was grasping at straws.

"So you see? He's still doing it. He's still a danger. And the text messages to me started up again right about the time this incident happened. There has to be a connection."

Randy knew he should reprimand her. Tell her what a mistake this was. But Victoria was a victim too. She was afraid of Sutton, and the threat wasn't only in the past. It was also in her present and targeted not only at her but at her daughter. He had a six-year-old son, and he'd do anything to protect him, so as a parent, he understood, even respected her. But as a professional, he knew this was a bad idea. If this mystery woman came forward, he'd take it to Barrett. She was a fierce protector of victims' rights and a champion feminist. But if she found out what Victoria had done, it wouldn't look good.

"I'll keep digging, I promise. But until she comes in, there's nothing I can do officially." *And you may have given Sutton reasonable doubt.* He didn't have the heart to lay that on her now. "But you have to promise me one thing. Go to the police when you get home. Tell them about the texts and your suspicions about the security tape from last year. Give them my information. Then we can all work together."

"I'm planning on it."

"And get me everything your PI has on him."

"I will. Oh, there's something else. After I shut off the recorder, she told me one more thing. I'm not sure if it's important, but it seemed odd to me."

"Anything could be important. What was it?"

"She said when he released his grip, he had a weird look on his face."

"A weird look?"

"Yeah. And she said she felt like he stopped because he had to, not because he chose to."

"Hmm. Any idea what she meant by that?"

"No, not really. But I thought I should tell you. She said he looked defeated. Or maybe tired."

"I'm glad you did. It could be important or could be nothing. Maybe he came to his senses?"

"Maybe."

"I'll factor that in to my analysis."

"Great."

"And, Victoria?"

"Yes?"

"Be careful. And take care of yourself. Please."

"I always do. Bye, Randy. And thanks."

"Bye, Victoria. Text me when you get home." *Why the hell did I say that?*

"I will. Bye, Randy." She hung up, leaving him alone with his thoughts.

Randy's son was with his ex this weekend—a custody arrangement Randy hated—but it had given him time to do some investigating of his own. He'd been dying to tell Victoria what he'd already found out, especially in light of what she'd just told him. But he couldn't. Between talking to Victoria and this new information, he was charged up. He needed to go for a run, let all the new information settle. He liked it when the seemingly disparate parts of an investigation started to add up to something. It gave him a buzz and made him feel alive. Most of the open assault cases

Victoria brought him were dead ends as far as Sutton was concerned. Wrong MO. Wrong race. Too fat. Too short. All except one.

It was a case from two years ago from the downtown precinct. An "escort" had been roughed up by a client. She'd reported it, but nothing had come of it. She was a high-end call girl, not a streetwalker. Attractive. Classy. Pricey. The type important men might frequent or men who just thought they were important—like Sutton. She'd given a good description, one that fit Sutton. They'd hired a sketch artist. The drawing was still in a file somewhere, and he could dig it out. But the case had gone cold. No DNA hit. The victim claimed she'd never seen him before. She'd never followed up. He had no idea if the victim was even still around.

He had the rest of the day free, so he figured he'd keep digging, even into tomorrow. Captain Barrett had said not to work on Victoria's case, but this wasn't her case. It was theirs. A cold case that he might possibly crack open, and Barrett certainly couldn't argue with that. Randy lived for a good collar, and he wasn't about to stop now, no matter what his captain said. He changed into his running gear to work off some of his excess energy, then it was full speed ahead.

Victoria got the last of her things packed up. The car service was due in a few minutes, and she was looking forward to going home. Except she knew that she'd have to tell Nick and her mother about Sutton soon, and she was regretting that she'd kept it a secret for so long. Nick would not take this well, and she could hardly blame him. Had she kept it to herself in an effort to punish him? Did she really not trust him? Or was it simply that she didn't want to rock the boat?

The bitterness she felt toward Nick lately had been a bit of a delayed reaction. In the midst of the murder, the pregnancy, and the fear of her child's father going to prison, her emotions about his infidelity had been too much to process at the time. The feelings of resentment took a while to surface, but they hit her a few months after Lila was born. She was hoping it was a phase, because she was tired of feeling that way. And although her attraction to Randy was a pleasant distraction from her problems, it was also confusing. And ridiculous. His life was here; her life was home with Nick and Lila, and she needed to try harder to make her marriage work. She'd have to start by coming clean about her trip, the threats, all of it.

And the thought of that put her stomach in knots.

EIGHT

A few days passed and nothing else came of Victoria's detective work. She'd returned with three new artists worth pursuing—one from Sedona and two from Santa Fe—and that had satisfied Nick. Things had been better between them since her return. Her sharp edges had softened a bit because of the guilt she felt about her crush on Randy Ramirez. And because things were going so well, she still hadn't gotten up the courage yet to tell Nick about the texts. She knew it was wrong, but the feeling of normalcy was so comforting she needed to live in that space for a while.

No calls from Ramirez or Jenna. But no further texts from Sutton either. She'd told Ramirez she'd get back to him early in the week with the information from the PI. She was behind schedule because in order to do that she had to tell her mother what she was up to.

She pulled up to her mother's house to drop Lila off. *First my mother, then Nick.* She shut off the engine, stepped out, and made her way to the house.

Victoria handed Lila to her mother, took off her coat, and draped it over her arm.

"You're planning to stay awhile?" Her mother looked more surprised than pleased. That was odd.

"Not long. Why? Going somewhere?" Victoria asked.

"No. Of course not. But I thought you needed to get to work."

"Not right now. I own the place, remember? I'll get there when I get there." Then something dawned on Victoria. Maybe someone was coming over. Someone her mother didn't want Victoria to know about. Her mother hadn't even offered her coffee, a sure sign that something was up. She could have a little fun with this.

"I know that, Victoria. I just thought, given your time away, you'd need to get going, that's all."

"I have time for some coffee."

"Well then, I'll go get some for us." She left Victoria to get Lila settled and rushed into the kitchen to get the coffee. She didn't offer any food. Another sign that something was up.

Victoria hated the thought of putting a damper on her mother's newfound zest for life. Part of the reason she was hesitant to tell her mother was to protect her. Since Lila had come along, her mother seemed so happy. So full of life. But Victoria was sure there was more to it. She hadn't seen her like this since her father was alive. He'd died when Victoria was in college, and a sadness had washed over their home, like a part of it had died with him. It had always felt so lonely and empty when she visited. But these days, the home was full of energy again, and so was her mother. She'd attributed it to Lila and the freshness of her new little life. But a budding romance would also explain it. Whatever it was, Victoria felt terrible for what she was about to do—fill her with worry and sap her joy.

Her mother returned with the coffees.

"So, what did you want to tell me?"

"Why don't we sit." Victoria motioned to the sofa,

and her mother sat down, followed by Victoria. "I've been getting some threatening text messages. I think they're from Timothy Sutton. I'm not certain, but I'm pretty sure they're from him."

"What?" Her mother's eyes widened and her hand went to her mouth. "Since when?"

"Since about a month after the case wrapped up."

"And this is the first you're telling me about it? Victoria!" Her jaw was tight, and her voice was a few decibels louder.

"We don't have time for that, Mom. Here. Look." She handed over a printout of his texts with the dates, and her mother sat there, her eyes scanning the page, as Victoria continued.

"I went to the police in Scottsdale when I was there last week." She proceeded to tell her mother most of the story but not all of it. She told her about Wade's investigation, meeting the bookstore owner, the unsolved sexual assaults, and meeting with Ramirez. She didn't mention her trial run stalking Sutton or her interactions with Jenna Williams. She'd wait until Jenna actually made good on her end of the deal. Then she asked her mother for the background information on Sutton's actions at the college.

"So, do you have the information Sam gathered? Or do we have to call him?" She and her mother hadn't talked about Sam Coleman since the day her mother had come clean to Victoria about their fling. Victoria didn't even like bringing him up, but in this case, it was unavoidable.

"I have copies of everything. But I think you should leave it, Victoria. If you poke around and get them to start investigating, Sutton might connect you to it. And then he'll really be after you. I wish you had told me about this. We could have taken a more subtle approach. But I guess it's too late for that now." What exactly did her mother have in mind?

"Subtle? Like last time?"

"It worked, didn't it? He suffered the consequences. He was fired. He didn't get away with it. If it hadn't been for Nick, he'd never have known it had anything to do with you."

"He didn't get charged! He didn't end up with a record! It left him free to do it to other women. And that's all my fault."

"None of this is your fault, Victoria."

"I've already gone to the police. I can't turn back time. And it's my decision. So please, Mother. Just give me what you have on him so I can get it to the police in Arizona. At least I'll know I've done all I can. Let me make my own decision this time. I'm an adult now."

"I'll get you what I have. But I don't like this, Victoria. I don't like it at all." Her mother turned from her, and Victoria could already see the weight of the world back on her delicate shoulders as she walked away. The dancing-on-air look had vanished. And it was all her fault.

"Can you stay? Jack Stark's coming to pay me a visit. He'll be here soon. We can go over it with him. Together." And now she'd robbed her mother of the chance to tell her about her new romance on her own time. As Victoria had thought, she was seeing Jack Stark. Former Detective Jack Stark. The man who'd arrested Nick for murder.

"So you and Stark are..."

"*Friends*, Victoria."

"Friends." She smiled. "Right."

The phone rang, and her mother picked up.

"No, it's fine. Come in, Jack."

Jack hadn't seen Victoria in months, although he'd been seeing Sandra Vander Hofen off and on for a while now, ever since his retirement. He figured he'd quit while he was ahead, regarding his career. Take the victory on the Angie Hansen case and call it a day. Like many former detectives, he'd set up a private investigating firm, but he hadn't taken any paid clients yet. He was also doing some pro bono work on some of his past cold cases. He thought he'd be bored, but he wasn't. Not yet. He kind of enjoyed being a regular person for a change.

He was surprised to see Victoria's car there. Sandra had insisted they keep things on the down-low, so he called her to see if he should maybe come back later. But she told him to come in. *Does that mean she thinks things are getting serious between us?* He wasn't sure he was ready for that. And it wasn't like her to spring something like this on him. Maybe something else was up. He made his way into the house, curious to see if he was right.

"Hey, Victoria," Jack said. "Long time."

"Hi, Jack. Congratulations on your retirement. How's it going?"

"Good so far. Your mother's keeping me busy. Getting me back into golf."

"We've got a problem, Jack," Victoria's mother said. "Sit down."

So much for small talk. "No coffee? You know I work better with coffee, Sandra." He flashed her a grin, but her face stayed stone-cold, his effort to lighten the moment falling flat.

"Victoria's been getting threatening text messages. For months! Instead of telling us about it, she went on a wild goose chase to Arizona. *With Lila!* What if he comes after her, Jack?"

"What if who comes after her?"
"Sutton!"
"Who's Sutton?"
"Mom, go get Jack some coffee. Please. I'll explain it to him."

Sandra looked like she was about to object, but then she let out a sigh of exasperation. "*Fine!* I'll get you some coffee," she huffed and headed off to the kitchen.

"Light and sweet, Sandra. Sweet," Jack called after her. She never made it sweet enough, and he guessed it was intentional. She'd been on him lately about his diet.

Victoria ran Jack through a slew of information. The text messages. Her theory. She showed him the security footage from when their garage door was vandalized. She talked about her recent trip to the police station in Scottsdale. After he'd been briefed, he fully understood Sandra's concerns. He'd be frantic if his daughter had done something like that. The last time Victoria had taken matters into her own hands, it had almost gotten her killed.

"Victoria, first off, why didn't you report the text messages to the police here? Why are you putting all your faith in this Higgins guy?" Jack remembered Wade Higgins all too well. His psychic "feelings," his smug attitude. He wasn't a fan.

"I don't know. I guess I didn't want to worry everyone. I hoped it might just...fade away?"

"Let me run it past Detective Sanchez. See what she thinks." Sanchez was his old partner, and she was not a big fan of Victoria's.

"Sanchez hates me."
"She doesn't hate you."
"She doesn't like me."
"She doesn't need to like you to do her job."

Victoria sat there, her head tilted to one side, mulling it over. Then she let out a deep breath. Jack felt like she was still hiding something. "Sure, run it by her. It can't hurt."

"Maybe it's not Sutton sending the texts. Have you thought about that?"

"I'm sure it's him. Who else would it be?"

"One of Angie Hansen's relatives? Or one of Malone's?"

"No, it's him. He vandalized my garage door last year, and he sent the texts. I'm sure of it."

Sandra returned with Jack's coffee, a bit less frantic now but still rattled. Tinkering around the house seemed to soothe her nerves. Jack noticed that, like her daughter, she rarely sat still. They were a lot alike, which kept things between them lively, to say the least.

"What do you make of all this, Jack?" Sandra asked him.

"I wouldn't get too riled up yet. Sutton sounds like he's got a strong self-preservation instinct. Just because he sent a few text messages, it doesn't mean he'll come after her. The bookstore owner told Victoria he was thinking about buying the business from her. Maybe he came into some money. I can look into it. If that's the case, he's got a lot to lose."

"But what if he finds out what she did? Going to the police? Trying to get him arrested?" Sandra said.

"How will he find out?" Jack replied.

"I don't know! He's clever, Jack." Sandra put her head in her hands and shook it back and forth.

"Mom. Calm down. Jack's right. Sutton's not stupid. He doesn't want to go to prison. I was thinking if I went to the police and they started investigating him for something down in Arizona, he might stop with the texts. It might deflect him."

"It's possible," Jack said, nodding his head. "Good thinking, Victoria."

Victoria smiled, seeming happy about the compliment.

"Why not block him? Or get a new number?" Sandra countered.

"All my clients have that number! I'm not changing my number. And blocking him? What good would that do, Mom? He'd be sending me threatening texts, but I wouldn't know about it?"

"I agree with Victoria, Sandra. Keep your enemies closer, you know? We need to know what he's thinking. Where his head's at. He came here once already. We need to be prepared," Jack said.

"So you think it was him? On the security tape?" Sandra asked.

"Yes, I really do. It would fit his profile. Once he found out it was Victoria who ruined his life, he was probably at the height of his anger. He'd want to do something. The action he took, it's in line with what we would expect. It's a little risky—even brazen—but it's not something that would land him in prison. The text messages are a step down from that. It might just be his way of processing the realization that your family was behind it all. But it does seem odd that they stopped for a while and then started again out of the blue."

"I was thinking that too," Victoria said. "I guess we have to wait and see."

"So where does this leave us?" Sandra asked.

"We wait. Let the detectives in Scottsdale do their thing. I wouldn't hold my breath, though. I agree with Ramirez. The profile is really different in most of those unsolved cases. Unless he's escalating for some reason, it doesn't really fit his MO. Let's hope the garage door and the texts were his way of getting back at you and that he'll just move on. And you're right, Victoria, even a cursory investigation of him might be enough to put him off you once and for all. I agree that he doesn't want to go to prison."

Victoria looked at her watch as if she were going to leave. "I'm running late. But there's one more thing. I may have found another victim of his. A young woman I located in Scottsdale. She told me he assaulted her. She wasn't going to report it. But I encouraged her to think about it, and now she might do it."

"Well, that could be good. Right, Jack?" Sandra asked.

"Define 'encouraged,' Victoria." Jack didn't like the sound of that.

"We just talked. I told her about how bad I felt that I didn't report it. That he'd done it to her. To other young women."

"How did you find her?" Sandra asked.

"Look, I've got to get going. I'll explain later. She might not even go through with it, so let's wait on that."

"Victoria, what about the fact that—" Jack began.

"Not now, Jack. Thanks for the info, Mom. I'll get it to Detective Ramirez. And Mom, I haven't told Nick about any of this yet. I will. Soon. But don't mention it. Okay?" Victoria went over and kissed Lila, and then she headed for the door.

"When would I mention it? I never even see him these days." Sandra shook her head and shrugged.

"Still. Just don't say anything. To anyone. Nice to see you again, Jack. It's nice that my mom has a new...*friend*." Victoria smirked.

Jack felt his face flush, much to his surprise. "Nice to see you too, Victoria. Try to stay out of trouble."

"I'll try. You two do the same." Victoria flashed

them a sly smile as she made her way out the door.

"So, what do you think?" Sandra asked.

"I think she's not telling us everything."

"That's exactly what I was thinking."

"Great minds think alike, you know."

"I've heard that. Do you know what I'm thinking now?"

"I think I do." He leaned over and gave her a proper kiss hello.

After all the drama in her life, it was nice to feel some joy for a change. Victoria had picked up on the chemistry between the two of them months ago, and she was sort of hoping it was Stark her mother was seeing. He was honest. Smart. And he also had a good sense of humor. Her mother needed that. He was a good guy, even if he had arrested her husband for murder. But he was also the one who'd kept digging, not convinced that Nick was guilty. He was the one who figured out it was Malone, right about the time he was in her house, trying to kill her.

Stark hadn't rescued her, because he arrived after she'd already shot Malone. But he had kept her from taking the final kill shot, Stark's gun drawn on her as she stood there with her weapon pointed down at Malone, wounded and moaning on her kitchen floor. "Don't do it, Victoria. You don't want his death on your conscience. It's a terrible burden."

Malone was knifed to death in prison; he was no longer a threat to them. And the truth was she'd lost no sleep over shooting him. Was that because she hadn't killed him? Or was there something wrong with her? One thing was for sure; Sutton wasn't the only one with a strong self-preservation instinct, and hers was even stronger now that she had Lila to worry about.

She felt terrible for leaving out the part about moving Jenna Williams up to New York. The connection between them was going to come out if Jenna filed charges, but Victoria still didn't fully trust the other woman to go through with it. And there was no sense in telling them that part until Jenna went in to see Ramirez. Moving her up to New York could be a mistake, but she was banking on the fact that once she got Jenna up to New York, she'd be easier to manage. *Keep your friends close and your frenemies closer.*

If it came to a trial, Sutton might use the fact that she'd helped Jenna relocate as part of his defense, allege that Victoria had put her up to it. But it was a chance she had to take. She'd let him get away with it once, back in college, and other women had suffered as a result. She needed to be brave this time. And she agreed with Stark; Sutton was a survivor. If they arrested him for assaulting Jenna, he'd lawyer up. Try to make a deal. Lay off of her. He wouldn't come after her family and murder them. *Would he?*

She fastened her seat belt and checked the time. Nearly ten o'clock, and she needed to get going. She forced the negative thoughts from her mind and focused instead on her mother and Jack Stark—the way he was able to calm her down and the way they looked at each other. They were good together, she could tell, and they seemed only too happy to get rid of her, like a pair of teenagers. She found the role reversal endearing. As she prepared to drive away, Victoria stopped to look back at Stark's car in her rearview mirror and smiled. *Sandra and Jack, sittin' in the tree, k-i-s-s-i-n-g.*

NINE

Back at her office, Victoria walked into a flood of issues she hadn't anticipated, mostly due to transportation snafus. There was a problem with a painting Charles was trying to procure for one of their best clients. It was held up in customs, but he needed it—pronto. Some of the materials for their gallery renovation hadn't arrived; they were sitting on a freighter somewhere in the ocean. The gallery was scheduled to open in a few weeks, and they were a little behind schedule. With laser-like efficiency, she sliced through the pile of material on her desk and cleared her email inbox, firing off directives, finding solutions.

For the first few hours, she didn't think about Sutton or Jenna or her trip. She blocked it all out and charged ahead. She could do that—compartmentalize her life. It was a valuable skill and one that had allowed her to achieve phenomenal success as one of the top art dealers in the Tri-State area. Victoria didn't even need to work; she was born into money. But she was driven to succeed for some reason even she didn't fully understand. She liked the challenge, the feeling of accomplishment, the security of knowing she could take care of herself if it all went to hell.

They lived well off of what she and Nick earned—very well for someone with an art history degree—although since Nick had sold off his real estate brokerage to open a gallery with her, their income had gone down. They'd hardly ever used the money in her trust until recently. Although she treasured her time with Lila, she needed to get her head back into her career. She'd worked too hard to let it go, and the new gallery was an important milestone to her, the achievement of a lifelong dream to combine her passions for art history, education, and commercial success.

After she put out the immediate fires, she turned her attention to the Jenna situation. She'd already wired the money the woman needed to terminate her lease in Phoenix and pay for the move. Then she'd set her up with an apartment in Ossining, a nearby town. Victoria didn't want to see too much of her, just enough to keep her under control. Now the ball was in Jenna's court. She was supposed to go see Ramirez, but so far, Victoria hadn't heard anything.

When she had a moment to herself, she closed her office door to call Randy and tell him she had the information he'd requested. But then Charles popped in, and she put it on the back burner. She informed him that she'd placated the disgruntled client and made some progress on the painting shipment, and he seemed pleased. He was about to leave, then he turned back to her with a curious look on his face.

"Wait. What's going on? You look different," Charles said.

"Different how?"

"Perkier."

"Perkier? Is that a word?"

"It is indeed." Then he took a seat in the white leather armchair across from the desk, leaned back, and folded his arms like he had all the time in the world. "Now tell me. What is going on?" He leaned in, his eyes wide and curious. He could read her like a book.

"Well, I do have some gossip if you're interested." Victoria thought what good timing this was. She could deflect him with her mother's new romance. Hopefully, that would placate Charles for the time being.

"If I'm interested? Spill it, Victoria."

"My mother's seeing someone."

"Oh wow! That's great! Anyone I know?"

"Jack Stark."

"The name sounds familiar but—"

"Detective Jack Stark," Victoria interrupted.

"The guy who arrested Nick?" His jaw dropped.

"Yeah." She continued to tell him about it, hoping it would throw him off her scent. Then her assistant, Nate, called in to her.

"Victoria, a Detective Ramirez is on the phone for you. He said he tried to call your cell, but you didn't answer. He says it's important. Do you want to take it?"

"Yes, I'll take it. Give me one minute." She looked over at Charles. "Can we table this and pick it up later?"

"Another detective? What are you up to now?"

"Nothing."

"Wait. You're blushing, Victoria. I guess your mother's not the only one who's got a thing for detectives."

She widened her eyes and motioned to the door. "Just go! I'll explain later."

"This isn't over. I'll be back." Charles wagged his index finger and flashed her a smug smile as he got up and made his way out of her office.

"Close the door? Please?" She flashed him a cheesy smile as he closed it behind him.

Randy had made some progress on a cold case that fit Sutton's profile. He located the file from two years ago, but he had yet to track down the victim. She seemed to have vanished. It was an assault and battery case, not really a sex crime. From what he could tell from the report, she'd seen a man looking at her in a hotel bar, and she went over to talk to him. Then the man went with her to her hotel room for what she thought was a routine business transaction. They started into a "heavy make-out session" as soon as they entered the room. But when she stopped and asked for payment before things went any further, he got angry and confused, like he didn't know she was a professional or thought he was entitled to a freebie. They started to argue. Then he assaulted her, not brutally, but enough to leave some bruising on her face and arm. Then he stormed out the door.

From the sketch in the file, the man could be Sutton. It was a pretty close match to the photos Randy had of him. But he wanted to show it to Victoria. It seemed to fit his profile, the profile of a narcissistic personality. A beautiful woman came on to him. It fed his ego. But when she asked him for money, he retaliated against her for the insult. It was very similar to what had happened to Victoria and the mystery woman on the tape. But without a victim to press charges, he was still stuck. He was waiting on hold to talk to Victoria.

"I'll put you through now," Victoria's assistant said.

"Hi, Randy. Sorry to keep you waiting."

"It's fine. Sorry to call your office number. It's just I think I might have found something from one of the cold cases, and I need your help."

"Really? What case?"

"I can't tell you that right now. Sorry. But I texted you a photo of a drawing a sketch artist did a while back. Can you look at it? Tell me if you think it could be Timothy Sutton?"

"Of course." He waited while she pulled up the photo.

"Got it?"

"Yeah."

"What do you think?"

"It certainly could be him. The eyes are right and the shape of the face. It has the right look, if that makes any sense. I haven't seen him in so long. His hair is different. It resembles him, for sure. But I can't say for sure it's Sutton."

"A sketch is not like a photo. It's more subtle, more like a feeling of familiarity. But it might be enough to get us to open an investigation into Sutton. That would give me more resources. It would be even better if your mystery woman would come in. Any progress on that?"

"Not yet. I'll try to check in with her today." They wrapped things up, and they hung up, leaving him to his work.

He felt that Victoria's demeanor was a bit different today. The conversation wasn't as fluid; she was more professional and more formal, maybe because she was at work. That was probably a good thing, he reminded himself, although he'd be lying if he said he didn't feel a bit disappointed. But there were a lot of great women out there who weren't married. Maybe it was time to start putting himself out there again. His friend kept bugging him about this woman his wife knew who was "perfect" for him, but he hadn't pursued it. The divorce had nearly killed him, and he was still holding out hope for a reconciliation, even though he knew it was futile. His ex-wife had moved on. So could he. If he could feel a spark for Victoria Mancusio, then he could feel something for someone more available. That's all this was, a harmless flirtation, an indication that it was time to get on with his life.

He picked up the phone and texted his friend. Told him it was a go on the blind date. It was time to get back in the game. Then he started to head out on his "lunch hour" to pay a visit to the bookstore where Sutton worked. He hadn't told Barrett about any of it yet. If she found out, she'd be upset. But she'd forgive him. She always did. They were on the same side, and deep down, he knew she actually appreciated his willingness to bend the rules a little. At least, he hoped she did. Then he got a call from the front desk officer.

"Ramirez?"

"Yeah?"

"A Jenna Williams is here to see you."

"She asked for me, specifically?"

"Yeah."

"I'll be right there." If this was who he thought it was, there was no turning back. He'd have to level with Barrett. And soon.

He went out to the lobby to find a young woman, late twenties, maybe, with long, wavy charcoal hair, full lips, and deep, dark eyes. She was on the taller side, curvy and fit, wearing jeans that hugged her body. Her smooth, tawny complexion was marred by a slight bruise on her left cheek that showed through her makeup. He brought her into an interview room and got started. She spoke to him in a voice that seemed older than her years—seasoned by a rough, if brief, few decades of life, if he had to guess.

"I want to report an assault." Jenna recounted the story he'd already heard on the tape as Randy filled out the report. Her demeanor was a bit different from a typical assault victim. She had an edge to her, but her body language didn't give off any indications that she was lying. Her tone was even. She looked him in the eye. She didn't fidget with her hair or smirk, or even smile. But she lacked a certain aura of vulnerability, which didn't necessarily mean she wasn't frightened. If he had to guess, she was the kind of person who'd been hardened to it all, and he wondered what Victoria had done to convince her to come forward.

"I'll put you in touch with victim services. They can help you with getting counseling. Do you have any medical bills from this incident?"

"I didn't go to the doctor."

"If you do, keep receipts. You could ask for compensation."

"I don't need a doctor. Or counseling. I want to see him in prison. What happens until then? Can you protect me?"

"Well, first, I have to see if we have enough to get an arrest warrant. And we'll go from there."

"And if you do?"

"Then you'll have to testify. He has the right to face his accuser."

"Can you protect me then?"

"We'll do what we can."

"Which is?"

"Truthfully, there's not too much we can do with the resources we have. We can get a restraining order. But I don't expect he'll come after you for a relatively low-level offense like this. He's got too much to lose."

"Yeah, well, what if you're wrong?" She gave him a hard stare, and all he could do was shrug. "Well then, I may leave town for a while."

"You have someone you can stay with?"

"I'll be fine."

"I'll be able to reach you at this number?" Randy pointed to the form.

"Yes, of course."

They wrapped things up, and Jenna Williams went on her way, leaving Randy with more questions than answers. He didn't think she was lying, but he had a strong suspicion there was more to the story than she was letting on, and that made him wary. He went to find Barrett and fill her in before things got too far along.

Victoria called Jenna and it went to voicemail. She was starting to get concerned. Maybe Jenna had decided to quit while she was ahead. Wade had done some background on her before Victoria wired her the money to move, and Jenna's hard luck story had checked out. She'd been raised by a single mother who had died of cancer a few years back. Her father didn't seem to be involved in her life at all. She had an older sister in Florida. And she was broke. As far as resources, Jenna had almost nothing in her checking account. She'd gotten some life insurance money when her mother died but not much. It all seemed to be gone now. She owned her car outright, had only a few hundred in credit card debt and a pretty high credit limit at her disposal, but over fifty thousand in student loan debt.

It was hard to see how she could start over with the little bit Victoria had given her so far, but it wasn't impossible. Jenna was resourceful. Scrappy. And scared. That much Victoria was sure of. Maybe it was all too much for her. If Randy could get Sutton another way—with the new case he'd uncovered—maybe that was even better all around. Then, for sure, none of this would lead back to her. She was starting to wish that Jenna would just disappear. Then maybe Randy could get Sutton on his cold case, and none of it would lead back to her.

Charles came back, as promised. "So, should we pick up where we left off?"

"Where exactly did we leave off?"

"Some detective guy was on hold for you. And you were blushing."

"I wasn't blushing, Charles."

"If you say so."

"There is something going on, but it's not what you think. I haven't even told Nick yet. And I can't really tell you about it until I tell him. It's nothing to do with the business."

"You're divorcing Nick for a hot detective named Ramirez?"

"No! Stop. Look, I know I've been a little distant lately, and I owe you an explanation for that."

"I'm not taking it personally. I figured you were busy."

She let out a sigh. She needed to level with him.

"No. That's not the reason I've been distant. It's got to do with Nick and our efforts to give things another chance."

"I don't understand. What's that got to do with me?"

"He's...jealous?" She offered him a hesitant shrug.

"Huh?"

"Of you. Of *us*."

"Of *us*? There's no us."

"I know. But that's what he claimed. It came out when we were having an argument, back when I found out about his affair. He said our relationship made him feel left out. Our friendship. Our closeness. The constant texting. The inside jokes. He said he couldn't compete with it. Our long history, our similar backgrounds. I know it sounds ridiculous, but he seemed sincere at the time." When she said it out loud, she realized how stupid it sounded.

"Are you kidding me, Victoria?"

"I know how it sounds, Charles. But I'm trying to make it work with Nick. For Lila."

"Look, Victoria. This is me. And I love you. I care about you. You're like a sister to me. Do what you need to do regarding the marriage, for Lila's sake, if that's what you think is best. But I can't sit here and watch you kid yourself! That's a pathetic attempt to try to rationalize what he did! So you're not allowed to have close friends? If I was a female friend, would he still feel that way? At best, it's a pathetic excuse. At worst, it's dangerously controlling!"

"I know! Believe me. I got angry at him at the time. But I've been so busy with Lila and everything else that's going on. And I want to make the marriage work. I didn't intend to cool it off so much with our friendship. But with Lila and my being away from work, it just happened. And I let it. But cooling things off with you hasn't helped at all with me and Nick. It's only made me feel more alone."

"Is that why you're opening a gallery with him instead of me?" She knew Charles wasn't crazy about that, but up until then, he hadn't said anything about it.

"I don't know. Maybe? And I'm sorry I sprang that on you. It seemed like a way to bring Nick and me closer. To save our marriage. To keep our family together. We had so much fun on our home remodel years ago. I thought it could bring us back somehow."

"I get it, Victoria. I'm a dad. I'd put up with a lot from Roger for Chloe's sake. I mean, we all do it to some degree. But love without trust? I'm not sure it's possible. Do you love him still, Victoria?"

"I don't know. If I do, it's buried under layers of resentment. But I'm hoping that maybe I will. In time."

"Maybe." Charles got up to leave. "Okay. Look. Just let it sit. Let it all settle. You don't have to make any decisions right now." He started to walk out the door.

"Charles?" she called after him.

"Yes?"

"Has Roger ever said anything? About our friendship?"

"He's noticed that it's cooled off, if that's what you mean."

"No, like, does he get jealous?"

"Jealous? No! He's grateful for it. Gives me someone else to bother. You know how I can get and how quiet he is. I think he misses you more than I do." Charles smiled.

"Okay."

"Victoria, whatever you decide, I'll be here for you. I told you that. And nothing's changed. You don't have to explain yourself to me. Take your time on the Nick situation. We can keep our friendship on the downlow while you sort it all out. But I will need a rundown on the hot detective, or all bets are off."

"How do you know he's hot?"

"Oh, he's hot," Charles said.

"Yeah, he is." Victoria smiled. "Now get out of here and let me get back to work."

"You're blushing again." And Charles went on his way.

It felt good to get all that off her chest. She pulled out her phone to see if Jenna had responded. Nothing yet. She silenced her phone and continued to bury herself in work, letting fate take its course. After about an hour, she checked her cell and noticed there was a new message. She listened as Ramirez relayed the fact that Jenna had come in and filed charges after all. She should have felt triumphant, but now that she was having second thoughts, she felt her stomach lurch. She'd have to tell everyone how she was paying for Jenna's relocation, and she'd have to tell Nick everything.

TEN

Jack had tried to play down the threat the day before at Sandra's house for her sake, but in truth, he was pretty concerned. He felt like this was a long time to hold a grudge. It seemed like Timothy Sutton was a clever guy, and he obviously had some agenda. What was his long game?

Victoria called yesterday and said she didn't want to file a formal report regarding the threatening text messages yet because she didn't want to call attention to her family, especially since they were making an arrest soon down in Scottsdale. At this point, Sutton still had no idea she was involved. But Jack still wanted Lexi and the Tarrytown PD in the loop and on the lookout, just in case, so Jack set up an informal meeting with his old partner and mentee Detective Lexi Sanchez.

Jack waited as Lexi reviewed the security footage Victoria's house the year before. Then he watched in comfortable silence as Lexi sat at her desk, staring down at the texts, her head cradled in her hands, trying to keep her dark bangs from falling over her eyes as she processed everything. Although relatively new to the position of detective, she had a lot of training as a profiler, and it came in handy. He could see her wheels turning.

"They're making an arrest today?" Lexi asked, looking over at him, her head still cradled in her hands.

"That's what Victoria said."

"What charge?"

"Assault and battery and attempted sexual assault."

"It's not anything that will get him put away for a long time, but it might be enough to get him to lay off the Mancusios. I agree; he seems like he's got a strong self-preservation instinct. From the text messages, it seems like he's playing with her head. Most people, if they're going to come after you, they just do it. They don't send warning signals."

"True. What are your thoughts on his pathology?"

"Best guess? Narcissistic personality disorder. Exaggerated feelings of self-importance. Excessive need for admiration."

"It fits."

"And someone like that wants to stay out of prison."

"Let's hope so."

"What did you find out about his finances?" Lexi asked.

"He came into some money about two years ago. Close to a million. His father died and left him everything. Most of the money came from the sale of his father's home on the outskirts of Philly and his life insurance. Looks like Sutton invested it. Mostly mutual funds. Pretty liquid."

"So that's what he was planning to use to buy into the bookstore."

"Looks that way."

"It could mean that he's got some incentive to play it conservatively. Lawyer up. Take a plea," Lexi said.

"Or he could disappear. It's not a lot of money, but

if he left the country, it could last a while. No kids. No family. Nothing to tie him down."

"I guess we just wait and see," Jack offered. He was about to make his way out of the room and get on his way, but Lexi continued.

"So, how's retirement?" Lexi asked.

He turned back to her. "It's not as bad as I thought it would be. I'm keeping busy."

"If that's what you kids are calling it these days." Lexi smirked.

"What's that supposed to mean?"

"I'm a detective, Jack. And I 'detect' a little more pep in your step."

"I'm sleeping better these days."

"I'll bet!"

"Stop it, you." He couldn't suppress a sheepish smile.

"So it's true."

"Shut up."

"I think it's great, Jack. It's nice to see you looking so happy," Lexi said.

He actually was happy, more than he'd been in a long time. As his former partner, she knew the sordid story of his messy divorce. Most everyone on the force did. But Lexi was the only one who knew how he'd really felt about it—devastated. And she was also the only one who could get away with teasing him. Even though she was young enough to be his daughter, she'd come to be more like a kid sister to him. And kid sisters busted chops.

"Thanks."

"Just don't let it cloud your judgment."

"Don't let what cloud my judgment?"

"The fact that you're seeing Victoria's mother and also helping her with the case."

"How did you know?" Jack's eyes widened.

"Ha! I didn't. I only suspected it. Until now, that is." She flashed him a smug smile.

"Damn."

"That's interrogation one-oh-one, Jack. You're slipping."

"A lucky break, Sanchez."

"Right." She winked.

"I gotta run. Golf date. Sleepy Hollow Country Club."

"Must be nice."

"Yup, it is."

"Keep me posted."

"You got it, boss."

Randy wasn't too optimistic about this case going their way, but he did think that rattling Sutton and letting him know he was on their radar might be enough to keep him in check. He would have preferred to file charges against Sutton for both cases, but it was only going to be the one. He'd tracked down the victim from the cold case, and she was dead. From what he could deduce, it seemed like she had died from some sort of medical condition. No signs of foul play. But with no complaining witness, the case was of limited value. Since the victim was deceased, he'd given Victoria more detail about the case. As he'd expected, she agreed that it sounded like it fit with what had happened to her and Jenna. He was hoping that if he found something to tie Sutton to the case, he could find a way to introduce it.

They brought Sutton in without incident, about three in the afternoon. And now that Timothy Sutton was sitting across from Randy, looking him in the eye, he understood Victoria's concerns. He could see how people could find the man charming—and juries were made up of people.

He didn't present as a criminal, and he was more attractive in person than Randy had expected. Neat, well-groomed. Charismatic, in a bookish sort of way. His mannerisms might have come off a bit effeminate on a smaller man, but with his stature and his large, slender hands, which he casually waved around as he spoke, he seemed cultured, cosmopolitan, the kind of guy you'd expect to have a British accent. Maybe that was because he spoke with such precision, choosing the exact words to show off his pedigree and then delivering them with perfect articulation. But somehow, it didn't come off as smug. It seemed like it came naturally to him. Maybe it was the eyes. They were warm and inviting, not what he'd expected, and that made him all the more dangerous.

Randy already knew this wasn't a case they should take to trial. They had no forensic evidence to connect Sutton to the assault. He had hoped to rattle him in the interrogation because Sutton wasn't fooling him. He knew there was anger seething right under the surface, but he also knew it would be almost impossible to bring it out here. Sutton had self-control, and he was under a microscope. He certainly wasn't stupid enough to lose it here. After some brief small talk, Randy got to it. As expected, the conversation was short and sweet.

"So why am I here, Detective Ramirez?" He even used a proper Spanish accent, rolling his *r*'s ever so slightly.

"Jenna Williams. Tell me about your relationship with her."

"I don't have a relationship with her."

"You worked together, no?"

"Are you asking me to confirm something you

already know?"
"Answer the question."
"We worked together."
"You don't work together anymore?"
"Jenna resigned."
"Why?"
"I have no idea."
"Maybe it had something to do with you?"
"I want my lawyer." And that was it. After the lawyer arrived, it was mostly formalities. The lawyer insisted that Sutton not spend the night in jail. They had no evidence, the lawyer proclaimed, and they would never get an indictment.

Randy apologized for the fact that it was already too late in the afternoon to hold an arraignment—and thus impossible to avoid a night in jail—even though he had planned it that way. Sutton was trying to play it cool, but when he realized his fancy lawyer couldn't find a way to send him home for the night, he flashed Randy a death stare. *If looks could kill.* But looks couldn't kill, so Randy went home to his nice, comfortable three-bedroom townhome, and Sutton went off to his cell to await his arraignment the following morning.

Things had been better between Victoria and Nick the last few days, but she knew they were about to get worse. She needed to tell him what was going on, and she had planned on doing it that evening. But it was so nice to feel normal again. But the more she waited, the bigger a deal this would become. But as they sat at the dinner table, she just couldn't find the words to tell him. *After dinner*, she told herself.

Instead, she let them enjoy a nice dinner together.

They talked about the gallery. Nick had found a workaround for the supplies. His family ran a large construction business and were able to supply what they needed. They were back on schedule. He was in his element during this part of the venture, but she wondered what would happen when it was completed. He didn't have much interest in running an art gallery. It was her dream, not his. He really was trying to please her these days, though, and she vowed to try harder.

Lila had fallen asleep early. It was a good opportunity. She was about to start telling him when he started in.

"There's something I need to talk to you about, Vic."

"What is it?" Had he figured it out, or had someone told him? It would be way worse if he didn't find out from her. But then he'd be angry, and he didn't seem upset; he seemed nervous. Contrite, even.

"It's about the gallery."

"Okay. What about it?" She breathed a sigh of relief.

"Well, it's sort of about me, too."

"Just tell me, Nick."

"There's an opportunity in the city. In finance."

"Oh?" She was so relieved it wasn't about Sutton or her little plan she had to stop herself from grinning and feign a modicum of displeasure.

"I know you had your heart set on us running the gallery together, but it's not really my thing, Victoria."

"Oh. Well, Nick, that's okay. Really it is."

"Of course, I'll see it through the opening. But running a gallery, isn't that more of a you-and-Charles thing?"

"Well, yes, but I thought you weren't too keen on the me-and-Charles thing."

"I was an idiot. I'm sorry. He's like a brother to you. I wasn't making it up, Victoria. About how I felt. You two have your thing, and I'm not a part of it. But maybe I don't need to be. We're from different worlds, and Charles is from yours. I'm close like that with Mark. And you're an only child. It's good you have someone from your world you can talk to, with all the shared memories. I'm sorry I even brought it up."

"I think he'd love to run the gallery with me. He was a little upset about being sidelined."

"So you're not mad? About my bailing on you?"

"No, not at all. I couldn't have done the renovation without you. And that's almost done."

"You sure?"

"I'm sure. So, tell me about this finance job." This was actually the best news she'd heard in ages. Nick went on about the new job, and it was the first time she'd seen him so lively and so engaged in anything since all the craziness started. It was a midlevel position at a newer hedge fund. Ironically, a competitor of the one Angie Hansen had been at when she'd accused her boss of sexual harassment. It sounded perfect for Nick, and she didn't have the heart to derail the evening with her confession.

"You want help with the dishes?" Nick asked.

"No, I've got it. Can you check on Lila?"

"Will do." He kissed the top of her head, and she sat there for a bit, thinking about how much fun it would be to get back to normal, with Charles running the gallery and Nick doing his own thing. Then she started in on the dishes, a task most people hated but one that, for some strange reason, relaxed her. Maybe everything would work itself out. Sutton would get charged. He'd back off of them and nobody would be the wiser. But what about Jenna? She was moving to New York, and Victoria expected some rough patches before this was all behind them. She went about her evening cleaning routine in her methodical manner—rinsing and stacking the dishes just so, wiping down the maple cabinets, spritzing a special cleanser on her Sub-Zero stainless fridge to remove the smudges, cleaning and patting dry the white granite counter—in a compulsive effort to bring order to her life as best she could while events beyond her control continued to spiral.

ELEVEN

Victoria had been waiting over two hours for Nick to wake up. The evening had been nice and easy, finishing off with a lazy but comfortable roll in the hay. But she'd still had trouble sleeping, anticipating how he would react to her revelation. She finally heard him coming down the stairs. Lila was up, fed, and playing in her rocker. She had to tell him about Sutton. *Now*.

When he came into the kitchen, she let him get his coffee. Then she started right in.

"There's something I have to tell you, Nick."

"First thing in the morning? Must be serious."

"It is."

He sat with his coffee, a somber look on his face. "Is it about us?"

"No, it's not about us. Not in the way you mean." She bit her lower lip, stalling.

He let out a sigh of relief. "I'm a straight shooter, Victoria. Don't beat around the bush. Just tell me." He sat at the kitchen island with his coffee.

"Okay." She sat down next to him with a printout of the text messages in her hand.

"About a month after the case wrapped up, I started getting some vaguely threatening text messages. Not often, just every once in a while. I'm pretty sure they're from Timothy Sutton. I've got them here, with the dates."

She handed him a printout, and he scanned it, his eyes widening.

"I'm also sure he's the one who spray-painted *KILLER* on our garage door back when you were a suspect. He was in town when that happened."

"*What?* When? Why didn't you tell me this sooner?"

"I didn't want to worry you, Nick."

"You didn't want to worry me? I'm your husband!"

"And I didn't want you to do anything rash. I know how you can get."

"What the hell is *that* supposed to mean?" He stood up, hands raised in the air as his volume increased, full-on Italian style. He started pacing around the kitchen. "You didn't want me to do anything *rash*? When someone was threatening my family?" His voice was getting louder and louder, his body language more menacing.

"Nick, please calm down."

"*I'm not gonna calm down!* What the hell were you thinking, Victoria?" He was stomping around the room, his fists as tight as billiard balls, his jaw clenched, breathing through his nose like a bull about to charge.

This wasn't anger. It was rage. She was pretty sure he'd never hurt her, but her body reacted as if he might. Her heart started to race. Her palms started to sweat. Lila felt it too. A loud wail emanated from deep in her diaphragm, reverberating through their home. Victoria picked her up and held her close.

"You're shouting, Nick, and you're scaring me! You're scaring Lila!" Victoria's tone was hushed but firm, her lips pressed tightly together in a vain attempt to compress her emotions. "Please! Take a deep breath and calm down."

Nick started running his hands through his hair, trying to calm himself down, but he was still pacing around in circles, waving the paper around. "I can't believe you didn't tell me about this!"

"I know this is a lot, Nick." Victoria continued to rock Lila, who was starting to settle down.

"Stop handling me, Victoria. I'm not a mental patient." His lips were pressed together and his jaw was still tight, but at least his voice was back at seminormal volume.

She waited as he processed all of it, not wanting to fuel the fire.

"Have you gone to the police?" Now his look had turned cold. Stone-cold.

"Yes."

"When?"

"On my trip. I went to the police...in Scottsdale."

"So you *lied* to me? About the trip? It wasn't an art-buying trip?"

"I didn't lie, exactly. I just didn't tell you everything."

"Stop it, Victoria. Just stop it."

"I'm sorry...I —"

"*Stop!* And you didn't think to warn me, even?"

"I've been keeping tabs on him. I know where he is all the time. If he was ever headed our way, I'd tell you."

"How? How have you been keeping tabs on him?"

"Wade Higgins."

"The psychic computer guy? The one who tracked down Angie's boss for you?"

"Yeah."

"So that guy knows my family's being threatened before I do? Your own husband? We said no more secrets, Victoria. A fresh start. Is that what you call this?"

"I'm sorry, Nick."

"Who else knows? Your mother? Charles?"

"I told my mother yesterday. And Stark knows." This didn't seem the right time to tell him about their budding romance.

"So, I'm after Higgins, Stark, and your mother but before Charles. I guess I should be flattered, no?"

"Nick, can we put all that aside for a minute? I have to get you up to speed on everything. They're arresting him soon." Victoria put Lila back in her rocker and sat back down.

Nick sat next to her. "For the text messages?"

"No. There's nothing in the messages that could even get a restraining order, even if we could prove it was him, which we can't. But I did some investigating when I was there. I found out there was a woman who worked with Sutton who quit with no notice, and I tracked her down. She told me Sutton assaulted her. She didn't want to report it at first, but she contacted me before I left and said she'd be willing to go to the police. And she did. I also gave them a file of unsolved cases in their area. They found another case, a cold case, that they can maybe tie to Sutton."

"What if Sutton figures out it was you who started all of this?"

"He won't." This wasn't the time to tell him she was moving Jenna up here. *One step at a time.*

"What if he does? Did you even think about that?"

"Look who's talking! Why do you think I didn't tell you?"

"What's that supposed to mean?"

"How do you think he figured out it was my family who ruined his life? He'd never even be after me if it wasn't for you, Nick! You and Mark? What you did?

Roughing him up back then?"

Nick's jaw dropped. This stopped him in his tracks and he stood there, glaring at her.

"And then he saw your face splashed all over the media last year. I'm sure that's how he figured it all out. Why else would he come after us now? I couldn't risk you doing something like that again."

"That was over ten years ago, Victoria! I was practically a kid! I'd never do something like that now! Give me some credit. We could've handled this together. Pops has connections. I would have taken care of it. But you're such a goddamn control freak, you had to do it all yourself. And then you throw the blame back on me. It's my fault! Again!"

"I don't want to assign blame, Nick."

"Oh, yes you do, Victoria. Yes. You. Do! It's my fault our marriage is in trouble. It's my fault Sutton's after us. And it's my fault Angie's dead!" He was yelling again, but this time, his face was twisted in pain. He stood up again, pacing around and into the living room. His hands were pulling at his hair like some medieval form of penance.

Victoria's eyebrows shot up. "Nick! No! Is that what you think? It's not your fault she's dead. It's Jeff Malone's fault. You had no idea he was telling her to lie. You had no idea he would snap. None of that is on you, Nick. None of it. You hear me?"

Nick took a deep breath and sat on the sofa, his head in his hands, looking down at the hardwood floor. He was quiet now. Strangely still. A hush washed over the house. She sat next to him and put her hand on his knee. He looked over at her. They were silent for a few more moments. And then he spoke.

"No, it is on me, Victoria. You're not the only one holding back on something."

"What are you saying?"

"There's something I never told you. About that night." He looked away from her, his hand on his forehead cradling his head.

"About the night she was murdered?" Victoria felt a chill race up her spine. She remembered the feeling, wanting to believe Nick was innocent, but a part of her wondering if he could have done it. Wondering if she was living with a murderer. If the father of her child was a murderer. But Jeff had confessed. *This doesn't make any sense.*

"Yes. About that night. About the second time I went up there."

"The time you lied to the police about in the beginning?"

"Yeah. The lie that got me arrested."

"Okay."

Nick turned toward her. "I told them I went up there again because I thought I saw your car. Remember? I was worried you might be confronting her."

She nodded.

"That was all true. But when I saw you weren't there, I felt like something was off. She wasn't answering my texts. I didn't think she'd go to sleep that early."

"And?" Victoria was riveted to her seat.

Nick stopped and took a deep breath. "I didn't just drive up to her house and leave when I saw you weren't there like I told everyone."

"Huh?"

"I parked, Victoria. And I went to the door. And I opened it." He started to shake, gulping in breaths of air. He could hardly get the words out. "I opened it! And I...I saw her...lying there, in a pool of b-blood."

He was trying to suck back the tears so he could get

the story out. He took a deep breath and steadied himself. Another deep breath. Then he continued.

"But I didn't call for help. I just wiped the doorknob and left. I didn't kill her, Victoria. But I may have let her die."

Victoria felt confused, the implications still not really sinking in.

Nick hung his head, and she could see him trying to stuff it all back down, but his pain was visceral. But why? Why didn't he call for help? Then it hit her, the full implication of what he was telling her, and she felt the ground shift beneath her feet.

"Wait. It's because of me. Isn't it? You didn't call anyone because of me? Because you thought I might have killed her?"

"I thought there could have been a struggle. Yes, Victoria. I thought you might have been responsible for what happened. So I left. And I'll have to live with that for the rest of my life."

"Oh my God. I'm so sorry, Nick. I'm so sorry you had to go through this alone. Does anyone else know?"

"Father Patrick." Nick sat once more with his head in his hands, looking down at the floor. She was surprised when Nick had asked that they raise their daughter Catholic. Nick was raised Catholic, but he hadn't practiced in the time she'd known him. She'd assumed he'd done it to please his mother. But now she could see there was much more to it.

"Nick, the ME's report said she likely died instantly. So did Stark. You know that. In all likelihood, there's nothing you could have done."

"But I'll never know that for sure, will I?"

"No. Not a hundred percent." She reached over and hugged him tight. It was too horrible. All of it. She couldn't leave him now, could she? After what he'd done for her? The fact that it was all his fault to begin with was kind of beside the point.

She knew that he'd covered for her once, early in the investigation, when he thought she might have done it. He'd been prepared to go to prison for her back then. And now this. The guilt he was carrying around. For her.

Then his body stiffened, and he wrestled himself free from her embrace. He stood up, calmer now but distant. "I need some time alone. I'm going up to our room. Give me some space?" He turned from her and started walking toward the stairs.

"Okay...but there's more I—"

"Not now, Victoria!" And then he stomped his way up the stairs.

Victoria grabbed her phone and went to check on Lila, trying to assess the damage, her perfect little nuclear family in total meltdown.

———

About an hour later, Nick came down. He was carrying what looked like an overnight bag.

"I'm going to Brooklyn."

"Now?"

"I need to talk to my father. And not over the phone. We don't have much time."

"Nick, please, just..." She tried to grab his arm, but he pulled away. She knew what he was up to. Nick's father had connections. He could get to Sutton. She'd always suspected his family was behind the prison hit on Malone. But if they took Sutton out now, it would surely land back on them.

"Just let me do this! Stay out of it. Will you, please? I won't do anything 'rash.'" His eyebrows shot up, and his fingers flew up into air quotes as he continued to the door. He turned back to her. "We need a backup plan, Victoria."

"Be safe, Nick."

"I'll see you later." He didn't stop to look back at her again as he walked out the door. After a few moments, she heard his car start up and drive off, leaving her questioning everything again. Was she being too hard on him? Would she have covered for him if the situation had been reversed?

She grabbed her phone to call and check on the arrest, but Randy had beaten her to it. She looked down at his text with mixed emotions.

Sutton in custody. Arraignment later today. I'll keep you posted.

She was about to call Nick and tell him, when another call came in. She picked up.

"Hi, Victoria. I held up my end of the deal. Now it's your turn." *Oh yeah. Jenna.*

Jenna went on to say that she wanted the first installment of cash. She explained that Randy expected Sutton to make bail after the arraignment, so she was headed for the airport. Victoria told Jenna the cash would be in her account by the time she arrived, and she'd deliver the paperwork the next day. That seemed to satisfy Jenna, and they hung up.

Everything was falling into place, and it seemed like her plan might work as long as they could make the charges stick. Jenna would have to go back for the trial if Sutton didn't take a plea, but Randy was hoping he would.

This was the first time in almost a year that she felt completely safe. Sutton was in a jail cell for now. He couldn't harm them—at least not today—so she tried her best to keep that thought front and center. Then she left Nick a voicemail to bring him up to speed, including the part about Jenna moving up to New

York. *Might as well get it all out in the open.* And then she went about her day, trying not to think about Jenna Williams or Sutton or any of it, at least for a few hours.

It was late afternoon, and Randy was sitting in his office. The arraignment had gone as expected. He'd figured they didn't have enough evidence to hold Sutton in pretrial detention, but Randy was still disappointed when he'd made bail. It wasn't even that much—fifty thousand—but Sutton had to report in daily and wear an ankle monitor, so at least that was something. The indictment would be in a few weeks, at the earliest, and the women would be pretty safe until then. He texted Victoria and let her know. So now they just waited.

Jenna had called earlier and said she was going up near Victoria for a while until she was needed. Randy found that a little concerning, but then maybe they had bonded. Jenna would also be safer there, and she had seemed pretty skeptical of his ability to protect her. She said Victoria offered to help her relocate. It wasn't such a bad idea, getting out of town. But it didn't look good. What did that mean? Help her? He needed to check in with Victoria about that.

"Ramirez?" Barrett had taken a sudden interest in his case and not just to micromanage him. He wasn't surprised that she was being supportive. But this seemed like more than that. Even a bit personal. And she was still watching him like a hawk.

"Yes, boss?"

"What's this I hear about Jenna Williams going up to New York?"

"Yeah. I think she left already."

"Did Victoria Mancusio have anything to do with this? Financially speaking?"

"Jenna said Victoria was helping her relocate. That's all I know."

"Helping her how?"

"I don't know any more than what I just told you."

"This doesn't look good for our case, Ramirez."

"Yeah, I know. But it's a free country. I can't stop Jenna from going." He realized he might have come off a bit snotty. "I mean, you know what I mean."

"Start digging into it. Find out exactly what kind of help she gave her. We need to get ahead of this."

"She's safer up there. It's not a bad idea—"

"That's beside the point! It could look like a payoff. Like she paid Jenna Williams to make the complaint."

"Are you saying you think Victoria put her up to it? Like it didn't really happen? I saw the bruises. They were real. Something happened to Jenna."

"I get that. But maybe they're not from him."

"I guess that's possible." Truthfully, that hadn't crossed Randy's mind.

"Maybe she's just playing Victoria. Or maybe she saw an opportunity to get away from someone else. And even if she's not, if the defense can make it look that way, it's game over." Barrett wasn't telling him anything he didn't already know.

"I'm hoping we can just make a deal and be done with it before it comes to that. We don't want to take this to trial."

"Are you in touch with the detectives up there? Are they working on the threatening text messages?"

"Yes, Captain."

"Keep me posted on all of it."

"Will do."

"All of it, Ramirez. Are we clear?"

"We're clear, Captain."

LITTLE LOOSE ENDS

Victoria was in her office finishing up for the day. Lila was home with the nanny, so she didn't need to pick her up from her mother's house, and she was glad about that. She didn't have the bandwidth to discuss this with her mother after the blowout with Nick. She still hadn't heard from him, and she wondered if he'd be home when she got there.

It was an unsettling feeling, having Nick leave suddenly like that. She'd been the one to call the shots in the relationship most of the time, and it caught her off guard, the feeling of abandonment. Now, she had to face the possibility that it might not be up to her whether their family stayed together. But she understood his reaction, and she wasn't surprised. It was a big breach of trust, not telling him about everything until last night. And he was the protective kind; it was in his blood. It was all such a mess. How much worse could it get?

She heard her phone buzz with a text alert and hoped it was Nick. She grabbed her phone and clicked. It was an unfamiliar number again. Her stomach sank.

You don't look like a Ruth.

TWELVE

This time, Victoria headed straight for the Tarrytown police station. She called Jack Stark, and he said he'd meet her there. Then she called her mother and asked if she would please relieve the nanny. She walked down from her office—a few steep blocks—to the precinct, a quaint brick building that sat across from the Tarrytown train station fronting the Hudson. This time of year there could be twenty-degree swings from one day to the next, and today it was cold and blustery.

The decorations from the Halloween festivities were still up in the trendy shops and restaurants that lined Main Street. Halloween was the biggest holiday of the year in Sleepy Hollow Country. The year before, the murder of Angie Hansen in the midst of peak tourist season had upped the tension but hadn't impacted business too much. This year it was pretty much back to normal—harmless, spooky fun grounded in centuries of American traditions and legends.

Victoria and Nick had skipped the Halloween parade this year. Last year, they'd gone with the Malones and returned home to find the word *KILLER* spray-painted on their garage door. It made her shudder to think that Sutton had been in town then, maybe even watching them as they strolled around. She blew right by their new gallery as she raced to the station, but it reminded her that she needed to check in with Nick.

She met up with Stark in the parking lot of the precinct, and they walked in together, both of them silent and somber. They checked in at the front desk and went to meet Detective Sanchez. Victoria hadn't seen her since the murder case had wrapped up, and she knew Sanchez didn't particularly care for her or her husband.

She remembered how hard Sanchez had been on Nick when she found out about his affair, and Victoria was sure the detective didn't approve of her choice to stay in the marriage. But Victoria considered her to be fair and competent. A valuable asset to the case. And, as Stark pointed out, Sanchez didn't need to like them to do her job.

Stark started right in as they got seated. "Walk us through the encounter at the bookstore. What exactly did you disclose about yourself to the woman?"

Sanchez shot Stark a look. "How about I ask the questions, Jack? Or did you forget you don't work here anymore?"

"Sorry, Lex. Of course." Stark offered a shrug of humility as if he actually *had* forgotten he didn't work there anymore.

"Now, Victoria, walk us through the encounter at the bookstore." Sanchez flashed Stark a smirk, and he gave her a nod. Victoria remembered Sanchez being a bit reserved last year, but she seemed to have grown into her new leadership position.

"The owner was really friendly from the start. We were the only ones in the store, and she asked me if I was from out of town. I told her yes and that I was in town looking for artists for a new gallery I was opening."

"Did you mention anything about Tarrytown?" Sanchez asked.

"No. I said it was in Woodstock."

"Did you ask a lot of questions about her employees? Anything that would make her suspicious?"

"No, not at all. The woman was a talker. Wanda's her name. A self-proclaimed chatterbox. I've got her card here." Victoria handed it to Sanchez, and the detective placed it on the desk between them.

"She just kept going on and on—I hardly got a word in—about how Sutton had helped her survive during the pandemic by moving the store online. About Jenna quitting with no notice. About how close Sutton and Jenna were. I got the feeling she really liked Sutton. He can be very charming."

"I'm sure. That's what makes him so dangerous," Sanchez said.

Stark was holding back, taking it all in, but he was on the edge of his seat, and Victoria could tell he was dying to jump in.

"Did you make any purchases?" Sanchez continued to her line of questioning.

"Yes. Two art books."

"How did you pay?"

"Cash."

"That in and of itself is a red flag."

"I guess. I probably should have just left without buying anything. I just felt bad, leaving empty-handed."

"What's done is done. Don't beat yourself up." Sanchez bit her lip as she tapped her pen on her notepad, a pensive look on her face.

Victoria was appreciative of her generosity. Maybe

she'd misjudged the detective. Or maybe it was just different when you were the victim, not the suspect.

"How much were the books?"

"Close to a hundred dollars."

"That's a big sale for a small store. She probably said something to Sutton about it the next day. If she rattled on to you, a complete stranger, imagine how she is with her employees. She probably gives him a play-by-play every time he comes back from a day off. It's not that hard to piece together. She tells him about a big sale. A woman with a baby, from New York, into art. It's not that hard to figure out once they'd picked him up on Jenna's case."

"I guess I could've picked a better cover. But I'm a terrible liar, so I figured the closer to the truth, the better."

"Like I said, what's done is done. So, what's your take on all of this, Jack?" Sanchez asked.

"I tend to agree. When they brought him in to question him about Jenna Williams, it probably clicked. He's been sending you these taunting texts, Victoria. It's not a stretch to think that you would take action. And it's not good that he sent this new one, because it's obvious that it was him."

"It's not good at all," Sanchez agreed, "because it means he doesn't care that we all know he sent it. And he wants you to know that he knows you were at the bookstore. It doesn't make much sense. I'd expect him to keep that close to the vest. You don't usually make bail and then fire off a threatening text."

"What's the implication?" Victoria asked.

"He's getting bolder for some reason. It'll help the prosecution if they can prove he sent the text messages," Stark said. "And now it will be easier to do that. There was nobody else who knew you used the name Ruth?"

"Nobody except Wanda, the bookstore owner."

"Unless…" Sanchez sat for a moment with her elbows on the table, her chin resting on her fingertips.

"Unless what?" Victoria asked.

"Unless he's going to claim that you put Jenna up to it. Maybe that's their defense. I mean, you're the one who found her and encouraged her to come forward. And now she's moving up here, and you're helping her. Maybe it's his way of telling you he's on to you, and they're going to try to prove you engineered all this because of some paranoid and baseless vendetta you have against him."

"Her bruises were real," Victoria said. "She wasn't making it up."

"That just means that someone assaulted her. It doesn't mean it was Sutton. Maybe she wanted to get away from someone else, and she saw you as her ticket out of town."

Victoria nodded. She had to admit that was a possibility, and it hadn't even occurred to her. What if Jenna was running from someone else, and she just blamed it on Sutton to get Victoria to move her away from Scottsdale when she found out she had money?

"Still," Stark added, "why not just keep that for the attorney? Let him use it behind the scenes? Why lay his cards on the table now?"

"He's a narcissist," Sanchez replied. "Maybe he has to let her know that he's the one who figured it out. He's probably furious too, so he might be feeling a bit more impulsive right now. Maybe it was a way of acting out, and he regretted it right after he sent it. Who knows? I'm sure his attorney is having a fit about the text, if he even told him about it."

"So what do we do now?" Victoria asked.

"Let me get our computer forensics team on this and see if we can get a trace. I'm glad you brought it in

LITTLE LOOSE ENDS

right away. The sooner, the better. And I'll call that detective down in Arizona. Let him know what's up. See if there's any news on their end. Ramirez, is it?"

"Yes. Detective Randy Ramirez." Victoria sat for a moment, looking at the two of them, waiting to see if they might offer her anything remotely comforting. They didn't.

"We'll take it from here, Victoria." Sanchez stood up, cuing them in to the fact that the meeting was finished.

Victoria said her goodbyes and let them get to work before they could ask her any awkward questions about Nick and his whereabouts. She planned to stop at the gallery to see how things were going on the renovation and see if they'd heard from Nick since she hadn't as of yet.

"So, what do you think?" Jack asked as soon as Victoria was out of earshot.

"I think Nancy Drew's at it again." Lexi shook her head.

"Nice of you to hold back on that little dig until she left. I was beginning to think she'd grown on you."

"What's that supposed to mean?"

"I didn't get the feeling you were a big fan of hers. When we were on the case last year."

"I have nothing against her. My beef was with you. The way you just seemed to dismiss her as a suspect right off the bat."

"Well, the fact that I was right doesn't excuse my lack of suspicion. I was right about her, and you were right about me. So can we call it even?"

"Sure. And look, I get why she's so hell-bent on getting this guy. I'd feel the same way, and I'd love to see him pay for what he did to her. To those other college girls. It's too bad nobody pressed charges ten years ago. But just like last time, she has to go and interfere and try to do it all herself. And then we have to clean up the mess. She may have given him reasonable doubt if they can make it look like she orchestrated this accusation from Jenna."

"I know. But like you said, what's done is done. What are your thoughts on the Jenna Williams situation? You think she's telling the truth about Sutton?" Jack asked.

"Who knows? I want to interview her when she gets into town. I'll be able to tell more then. And I'll consult with the detective in Scottsdale."

"I'll talk to Victoria about that. Have you tried Ramirez yet?"

"We've been playing phone tag. I'll try again. As soon as you get on your way." Lexi gave him a hard stare. He got the hint. Subtlety wasn't her thing, and Jack accepted that.

"Okay. I'm heading out. Check in with me if you get anything, okay? I am a licensed PI, you know."

"I heard that somewhere. How's business, by the way?"

"Slow until recently. And that was intentional. I wasn't really looking. But then this one sort of dropped in my lap." Jack shrugged. "I'm working a cold case, though. In between my golf rounds."

"The missing persons from twenty years ago?"

"Yup. The father passed away last year, but I'm still in touch with the mother."

"Anything yet?"

"Nope. But you never know."

"Right. You're a trouper."

"Sure. I'll get out of your hair now."

They wrapped things up, and Jack checked his

phone messages as he exited the station. There was a text from Sandra to meet him at Victoria's house. Not exactly the kind of exciting evening he'd had in mind, but then the buzz of a new case was a different kind of excitement, and he had to admit, it was nice to be back in the game.

Victoria stopped at the gallery and found things were coming along just fine. She could actually start hanging the artwork in a few days, although not all of it had arrived yet. But it concerned her that nobody had heard from Nick all day. She stopped at her office afterward to take care of some other business and started out for home, obsessively checking to make sure her ringer was on.

She came into her home to find Stark and her mother playing with Lila on the living room floor. Normally, it would be a heartwarming scene, but today it was problematic. What would she tell them about Nick? She had to think of something, and fast. She wondered if Stark had told her mother about the new text message from Sutton. She should have told him not to. It would only make her more frantic, and none of them needed that.

"So, you moved that other girl up here? Jenna what's her name?"

"Yes, Mother."

"Victoria, I really don't think that's—"

"Mom, I really can't do this right now. Okay? What's done is done." Victoria gave her a look she used only sparingly, and her mother retreated.

"So, where's Nick?" her mother asked as if reading her mind.

"He's in Brooklyn."

"Brooklyn? Why?" Her mother's face took on a look of concern, and Victoria realized where her mind had gone. Nick had moved to Brooklyn for a while after the affair before they had reconciled, and she was probably concerned that they were on the rocks again. *If only that were the reason.* Marital problems. They seemed so trivial to her now.

"Oh, he just went to get some construction supplies from his father. Some of our stuff got stuck in the shipping bottleneck, so they're fronting us some materials. For the gallery renovation."

"I see. And that's the only reason?"

"Yes! Nick and I are fine, Mom. Don't worry." But Victoria *was* worried. What if he actually had gone to Arizona? What if he decided to kill Sutton and take the consequences to keep them safe, just like she'd almost done at his house that morning in Arizona?

What Victoria really wanted was to be alone with Lila. She didn't want to seem unappreciative of the free child care, but she needed them to leave.

"Hey, Sandra, what say we get out of here and go for a nice dinner? Just the two of us? Maybe River Market?"

"I thought you'd never ask," her mother replied.

"I'd invite you to eat with us, but—"

"Victoria, I hate to break it to you, but Jack's offer is a lot more tempting. I love spending time with Lila, don't get me wrong, but I could use some grown-up time. You, Jack?"

"I serve at your pleasure, Sandra."

"Smart move. Victoria's not really known for her culinary prowess, you know."

"Hey!" Victoria didn't really mind about the dig. It was true. She wasn't that great a cook. She wasn't horrible either, but she wanted them to leave, so she didn't counter. They said their goodbyes and went on their way. As soon as they were out the door, she pulled out her phone to see if Nick had called. There was a text from him but no voice message. *In Brooklyn still. I'll be home late tonight. Don't wait up.* Don't wait up? What did that mean? She fired off a text to Nick about Sutton making bail and Jenna moving up to New York. Then she tossed the phone aside and took Lila in her arms.

"Hi sweetie, I missed you!" She held her daughter close and took in her scent, letting all of her worries fade away as she cuddled her. Then she held Lila out at arm's length and marveled at her greatest creation. It really was something to celebrate, especially with all the trouble she'd had bringing a pregnancy to term.

"Hello, my little miracle! Hell-o!" She bounced her up and down as Lila smiled. "Where's Daddy, Lila? Is your daddy in Ar-i-zo-na?" Lila babbled at her, full of smiles.

"You don't care? Well, I don't care, either. Let's go get some dinner. Who wants dinner?" She made a funny face, and Lila let out a belly laugh. She remembered the first time her daughter had laughed like that. It was directed at her daddy, and it was the best sound in the world, the sound of her child experiencing pure joy. Then she balanced Lila on her hip and went into the kitchen to make herself a mediocre but perfectly adequate dinner.

She ate dinner and got Lila to bed, and she thought about having a glass of wine but then opted for herbal tea. She wanted to stay up and wait for Nick, but she was exhausted. She saw there was a voice message from Jenna reconfirming for tomorrow. She'd almost forgotten Jenna was in town now and wasn't looking forward to seeing her. There was something about the young woman that made her uncomfortable. But a deal is a deal, and she'd promised to keep her safe until Sutton was behind bars.

Victoria headed up to the bedroom with her tea, trying not to think about where her husband could be. She pulled down the covers and crawled into her cold, empty bed with a steamy romance novel, longing for a little more of both in her life. Maybe in her dreams.

THIRTEEN

Victoria woke up a bit later than usual. She'd tried to wait up for Nick, but she must have dozed off somewhere near midnight. It was now close to seven, and Nick was in bed next to her, sound asleep. She hadn't heard him come in, but at least he was home. She didn't want to think about where he'd been or what his mood would be like when he got up.

She went to check on Lila, who was just starting to wake. She changed her and brought her downstairs. She was eating some solid foods now and was weaned off of breast milk, so they were all sleeping better these days. It could have been a nice, lazy Saturday. But she knew better than to hope for that. It was going to take some effort to try to repair the damage from her shattering reveal. She should have told him sooner, and she really had no good explanation for why she hadn't.

The sun was just starting to rise, but it was hard to notice it through the thick trees that framed their yard, keeping them insulated from the outside world. When they'd moved there after the case wrapped up, the home felt cozy and safe, especially in contrast to their home near the Hudson. But for some reason, on this particular morning, it dawned on her that the trees in her yard weren't just a protective buffer against the outside world. They could also serve as the perfect hiding place for an intruder, and the dark shadows they cast started to prey on her imagination.

She needed to go see Jenna today, first thing, and look her in the eye. See for herself how the young woman was holding up. The possibility that Sanchez raised gnawed at her. Could she have been duped? Might Jenna be running from someone other than Sutton? If she was frightened enough to do something like that—lie about Sutton just to get away—Victoria could hardly blame her.

She heard Nick coming down the stairs and was at a total loss for how to smooth things over, but she knew that flat-out asking him if he'd flown to Arizona and killed Sutton was probably not the way to go. There hadn't been any news from Randy about Sutton being dead or missing, so that was a plus. And it would be difficult—but not impossible—to go out and back from Arizona in the time he'd been gone.

"Morning," she said.

He gave a nod in her direction, and then he went over and kissed Lila on the head. "Good morning, angel. Are you Daddy's little angel?" Lila wore an ear-to-ear smile at the sight of her father. She adored her daddy. She was also a nice buffer for their marital issues. He got some coffee and was about to leave the kitchen. She had to start somewhere.

"Nick?"

"What?"

"Don't you think we should talk?"

"What do you want to talk about?"

"Come on, Nick."

"Everything's fine with the gallery supplies. All good. I got it sorted out yesterday, so don't worry." This passive-aggressive act wasn't typical of him, and she didn't like it.

"That's not what I meant. Did you get my text?"

"Yeah. So, he's out on bail now?" Nick asked.

"As far as I know. But he's wearing an ankle monitor. And he's required to check in daily until his indictment."

"I guess that's something."

"Are you going to tell me where you went yesterday?"

"I told you where I went. Brooklyn. Mom and Pops want to see more of Lila. I'm going to take her over there this weekend."

"You know that's not what I meant." And she knew him well enough to know that was all she was going to get out of him, so she didn't press it any further.

"Victoria, I already told you all you need to know. We needed a backup plan. In case he doesn't get convicted. Or even indicted. The evidence is pretty thin. Now we have one. That's all you need to know." He turned from her and made his way out of the kitchen.

Would he be shocked to know that she also had a backup plan? That she was willing to go to prison to protect Lila? For all of their marital issues, they were certainly on the same page about one thing. They were both willing to do anything to protect their daughter.

It was midmorning, and Randy was in his office mulling over the information he'd gathered trying to connect Sutton to his cold case. He was stalling on Barrett's directive to look into Jenna's connection to Victoria. Jenna was a victim, not a suspect, and she had a legal right to go wherever she wanted, so he wasn't spending much time looking into her or the money trail. If Victoria had done anything more than provide her with a safe place to live while they waited for the case to play out, he didn't want to know about it. Let the defense team look into it. That was their job, not his. He had more important things to do, like looking into the cold case he hoped to pin on Sutton, seeing if he could find a way to get it to be admissible in court. He had to find some way to place Sutton at the scene, and he'd finally found something, a credit card receipt that placed him at the hotel on the night the woman was assaulted. It wasn't much, but he'd give it to the DA and see if they could use it.

"Ramirez?" A uniformed officer came in with a panicked look on his face.

"Yes?"

"I think we've got a problem."

"Yes?"

"It's about Timothy Sutton."

And suddenly, everything else went on the back burner.

So far, Victoria's meeting with Jenna was proving to be as awkward as she'd imagined it would be. The apartment she'd rented for Jenna was in a two-story garden apartment complex, and hers was on the second floor. A large one-bedroom, fully furnished. Nothing spectacular, but safe and clean.

"So, how's it going, Jenna?"

"How do you think it's going, Victoria?"

"It's temporary. Things will get better."

"It doesn't feel that way. My life's been turned upside down."

"I know."

"Do you?" Jenna stood in the living room, her arms

crossed snugly in front of her.

"Yeah, Jenna, I do. If there's one thing I know after last year, it's how it feels to have your life turned upside down."

"I guess you probably do. Sorry." She turned away from her.

"So, how do you like it here so far?" Victoria asked.

"How do I like it? I don't like it. It's freezing here. And the colors of the trees. The fall colors. It's all so...different." Jenna let out a sigh.

"Nice different?"

"Maybe if I was here on vacation. But given the circumstances, it just makes me feel homesick."

"Can you try to pretend it's a vacation?"

"Sure, Victoria. I'll pretend it's a vacation." Jenna rolled her eyes, and Victoria was starting to wish she'd just gone ahead and shot Sutton that morning in Arizona. Three years in prison might be preferable to months on end of dealing with Jenna and her attitude.

"How do you like the apartment?" Victoria asked.

"It's...adequate, I guess?"

"Rents are very expensive here. It's actually a pretty desirable apartment, by most people's standards."

"Most people like me, you mean?"

"I mean most people."

"But not by you?"

"If you have something to say, Jenna, just say it."

"I thought with your resources, it would be a little more...upscale."

"And how would that look, Jenna?" Victoria was concerned that Sanchez wanted to dig further into Jenna's story. What if the detectives found out about the additional money she'd given her?

"I guess not that good."

"It's bad enough that I've done this much. I'm hoping that the fact that we've been relatively transparent about it will work to ensure it doesn't help Sutton's case. It can't look like I'm bribing you. You didn't take it like that, did you?"

"What? No. What are you even talking about?"

"Never mind." Victoria reached into her purse and took out an envelope.

"Well, a deal's a deal. You delivered on your end, so I'm delivering on mine." Victoria handed over the envelope. Jenna looked at her, and Victoria nodded at her to open it.

"Thanks."

"In here is all the information you'll need. It's got the number to an offshore account with the funds to pay off your student loan and the first installment for your living expenses, minus five thousand."

Jenna shot her a look and opened her mouth like she was going to protest, but before she could say anything, Victoria pulled out another envelope, a much thicker one.

"And here's five thousand in cash to tide you over until your online job starts to bring in some money."

"Oh. Thanks." Jenna took the envelope with the cash.

"And don't pay off the student loan now. You know how it would look."

"I'm getting a master's degree, Victoria. I'm not an idiot. I know how it would look."

"I didn't mean it that way, Jenna."

"What other way could that be taken?"

"I'm sorry if I offended you. I just don't want to end up in prison."

"Prison?"

Victoria knew that Sanchez wanted to interview Jenna, that the detective had her doubts about the whole story. And although she was also curious, Victoria didn't really want the truth to come out in a police interrogation in the event she'd been played. What else might spill out? Maybe it was better to give Jenna a heads-up about Sanchez.

"When I told the detectives I was helping you move up here, they floated the idea that I'd put the idea in your head. About Sutton. And you'd made the whole thing up."

"Why would I do that?"

"To get away from someone even more dangerous."

"That would be a very stupid move. You think Sutton would lie back and take a false accusation? Then I'd have two people after me, wouldn't I?" Jenna said.

Victoria gave Jenna a hard stare, sizing her up. What she said made sense, and it did give her some comfort.

"But you see how it would look if they found out how much money I'm giving you? And they might ask you about it. So keep that in mind."

Jenna nodded in a rare gesture of deference. "I see how it would look, Victoria. I'll be careful. Don't worry. I want to get Sutton as much as you do."

"Okay. Is there anything else you need from me before I get going?"

"No, I'm good."

"Good." Victoria started to walk away.

"Wait," Jenna said.

Victoria turned back around.

"Thank you, Victoria. I do appreciate what you're doing for me. But it's still hard. And it's just starting to hit me. How my life will never be the same."

"It can be, Jenna. Don't let him rob you of that. Once he's convicted, you can go back home."

"No. I don't think so. He knows I filed charges. I need to be far away from him. Whatever happens, I'll always be worried. Until the day he takes his last breath."

"I know how you feel because I feel the same way." She found herself thinking about Nick and was starting to wish he had made it all go away. *I really should have gone to him earlier.*

"Be strong, Jenna. And let me know if you need anything else. I'll be going now. Maybe use the time to focus on your work."

"My work?" Jenna scoffed. "Sure. I'll start on the next great American novel or something." She shook her head.

"What more do you want from me, Jenna?"

"I'm sorry. I know you don't mean anything by it, Victoria. But I swear, you can be so clueless sometimes. People like you have 'their work.' People like me just have 'work.'"

"Got it. Thanks for the clarification. I'll be going now."

"Bye, Victoria. And I'll be fine here. Don't worry."

"Good to know. Bye, Jenna." *And for the record, I wasn't worried.*

FOURTEEN

Victoria ran some errands and then drove to her office in Tarrytown. She was planning to catch up on some work while Nick and Lila enjoyed some father-daughter time, and the office was quiet. She stopped downtown at her favorite coffee shop—The Hollow—to treat herself to a latte and a pumpkin scone. The taste of fall was in the air, and she needed a break from all the tension, a sense of normalcy in the face of all the stress and worry.

She walked in to the whir of the grinder and the smell of freshly brewed coffee and warm pastry, and she realized she was very hungry. The new gallery was a few blocks down from the coffee shop, and she was hoping they could do some cross-promotions. Tarrytown was one of the few areas of New York that had withstood the onslaught of national chains, and most of the businesses were independently owned—trendy shops and restaurants that reflected the eclectic vibe of the area. It was nice to walk down a street that didn't look like an airport lobby, and most people wanted it to stay that way. It's also what made it a tourist destination—that, and its famed reputation for spirits and ghosts in conjunction with its neighbor town, Sleepy Hollow.

The town was still crowded with tourists, although the main Halloween festivities had already ended, so she had to stand in line a bit longer than usual for her coffee. She pulled out her phone to check her messages while she waited. There was one from Randy Ramirez, but she didn't want to listen to it there. It upped her anxiety, though, and she tapped her foot as she waited, annoying the man in front of her, who turned around and gave her a look.

"Sorry." Victoria offered a nervous smile, and he smiled back. Why would Randy call her now? It seemed odd, and the more she thought about it, the more she started to panic.

Finally, she made her way to the front, ordered, and waited, savoring the smells and resisting the urge to check the message from Randy. Her name was called, and she grabbed her coffee and scone and walked outside.

It was a perfect fall day. Not too cold. A slight breeze was in the air. An undercurrent of chill warned of the long winter ahead, but it was tempered by the crimson and gold leaves still clinging to the tree branches and the warm sun overhead. She took in the Halloween decorations and strolled along Main Street, thinking about her gallery. The opening was in a few weeks. She knew they would make the deadline but was nervous that it wasn't finished yet. Still, there wasn't much she could do until all the artwork arrived.

Choosing to ignore Randy's message and live in denial a bit longer, she popped into her favorite jewelry store for some retail therapy. The shop, Shaylula, was more than a jewelry store to her. It was a landmark of sorts in Tarrytown, a gathering place for chitchat and laughs, and the owner, a fellow proprietor, was closer to a friend than a business associate.

"Victoria! How've you been?"

"I'm hanging in there."

"How're the plans for the gallery going?"

Victoria filled her in on the plans for the opening and offered her an invitation to the VIP event. She reported that business was going well. The town was still buzzing with activity, and Victoria hoped that the opening of the gallery in mid-November, with her exhibition about the Hudson Valley, would help keep it that way even as the Halloween tourism dropped off.

"This necklace. It's amazing. It reminds me a bit of the Southwest. The design." She thought back to her recent trip there, when all the trouble had started, and she was filled with apprehension.

"Those colors are perfect for you."

"It's so unique."

"Want to try it on?"

Victoria allowed herself to enjoy a few more moments of self-indulgence and decided to treat herself to the necklace. They wrapped things up, and she walked outside. It only took a few seconds for her problems to come rushing back. *The phone message from Randy. Right!*

She listened to it, and her head started to spin. *Is this a nightmare? Is this really happening?* She listened once more and had to brace herself against the building and crouch down to keep from passing out.

"Timothy Sutton is in the wind. He vanished into thin air. Call me."

The rookie officer stood before Randy staring at the floor, looking like he was about to be sick. Randy had gotten the news about Sutton a few moments ago, and he'd already called Victoria and Jenna to let them know. But he was still missing most of the details.

"How the hell did this happen? How?" Randy punched his desk with his right fist so hard he thought he might have broken something. He gave it a few shakes, rubbing it with his left hand, his anger mitigated by the searing pain.

The young officer's eyes lifted up toward him as he spoke, but his head was still tilted down toward the floor.

"I don't know, sir. We didn't see anyone leave his place."

"His car's still there?"

"Yes. We put out an APB."

"Well, I would hope so."

Why would Sutton risk something like this? It made no sense. This meant their entire profile was off. Best-case scenario, Sutton was leaving the country. Worst-case scenario, they were missing something. Something really big.

"Ramirez! What the hell is going on?" Barrett was about to explode. This was a total embarrassment to the department.

"I wish I knew."

"It doesn't make any sense."

"I know."

"Get security footage from the area from the last few weeks. We need to see his normal pattern. Where he goes, what he does on a regular basis. Maybe it can give us some clues as to where he might go."

"We think he exited out the back in the middle of the night sometime. I'm not sure why we didn't get an alert. They're investigating. Maybe he used a Faraday bag to block the signal and then hacked it off or let the battery die." Randy bristled at the thought, annoyed that it was so easy these days to outsmart the technology, but then they counted on the fact that most people wouldn't take the chance and disappear for a relatively minor offense.

"Why would he risk it? We've totally miscalculated his profile. I feel like we're missing something."

"No idea. But his money's been moved somewhere."

"Damn it. They took his passport, right?"

"Yeah, but that doesn't mean much. The underground market's pretty prolific around here. It's not that hard to get fake papers."

"What're you thinking? About his motivations?"

"I think he spent one night in jail and decided it wasn't worth it to roll the dice. He can live a pretty good life with the money he's got."

"You don't think he'll go after them?"

"I don't think so. But I can't say for certain. It's a suicide mission if he does. And right now, he's holding all the cards. Nobody knows where he is. Maybe that's enough for him. Just making them sweat."

"Unless he's a murdering psychopath, and we don't know it. Look into all the unsolved homicide cases, will you? Starting when he first moved here. See if anything fits his profile. If we're missing something, we better find it—fast."

"Will do," Randy replied.

"And don't forget to dig into the Victoria Mancusio connection with Jenna Williams and her move up there. This whole thing is starting to stink." Barrett marched away and left Randy to sort out the whole stinking mess.

Victoria was beginning to feel like a regular at the Tarrytown PD, and that wasn't a pleasant thought. At least she wasn't a suspect this time. When she arrived at the station, Detective Sanchez had already been briefed by Randy and his team in Arizona. It seemed like everyone was just standing around scratching their heads, which didn't give her much confidence. They'd sent a uniformed officer to check on Jenna, who was reportedly fine but frantic, and Victoria had already set up a security detail at both of their residences, sundown to sunup. This felt all too familiar.

To Victoria, it was virtually impossible to believe that Timothy Sutton would just up and disappear of his own volition, so her first thought went to Nick. *Could he have gotten down to Scottsdale and back in one day?* Probably not. But then, he could have hired someone to get rid of Sutton. And that was the best-case scenario because any other explanation was far more dangerous for her and Lila. She needed to talk to her husband. Look him in the eye.

"So where does this leave us?" Victoria asked.

"I'm afraid until we get some kind of hit on his whereabouts, it doesn't leave us with much to go on." Sanchez was not making her feel any better.

"How did he disable the ankle monitor?"

"It's not actually that hard to get it off. A savvy person can block the signal with a device and hack it off, or let the battery die. It's just most people don't do it, for obvious reasons. From what Ramirez told me, it looks like it stopped transmitting around two in the morning. He could be anywhere by now."

This wasn't making Victoria feel any better.

"I don't see anything about it on the news. Why isn't it getting more media attention?"

"It's more of a local story. I don't think the national media will pick up on it."

"They might if they know we're involved."

"True. Is that what you want?"

"What's your thinking on it?"

"Keep a low profile. Don't call attention to yourself. You're not connected to this case in any official way. Just keep your security team in place and hold tight. A media circus just attracts more crazies. Presents more complications."

Sanchez was right. Victoria knew that firsthand and didn't relish the thought of a repeat of last year, with reporters swarming her everywhere she went.

"What's your best guess? About Sutton?"

"From what I know, he's got a big ego and a strong self-preservation instinct. If he is at all concerned about the possibility of jail time, he's got enough money to live pretty well in certain parts of the world. Maybe he just decided to cut his losses and bail."

"I'd love to believe that, but it doesn't sound like him. If he knows I urged Jenna to come forward, which he seems to know, based on his last text, he'll find some way to get back at me. Maybe not now. But eventually," Victoria replied.

"Maybe just the thought of that is enough for him."

"What do you mean?"

"Maybe he knows that you'll never have peace of mind this way. Never knowing when he might strike. Maybe that's his way of getting back at you."

Victoria's stomach sank, and she felt a bit dizzy. She had to rest her hand on a chair back. She hadn't even considered that. But what if what Sanchez was saying was true? If they never found him, then every day for the rest of her life she'd be worried. About herself. About Lila. She'd never have any peace. Had he found the perfect way to torment her? Make her wonder, every day of her life if that was the day he would strike? She couldn't live like that. If that was the case, she'd just have to go on the offensive and find him herself. Nobody wanted to find him more than she did.

She wrapped things up with Sanchez and went on her way, thinking about how she could step up her efforts. She needed to hunt him down before he got to them, or he drove her stark raving mad because, from her vantage point, those were the only two possibilities—and neither was acceptable to her.

PART TWO

FIFTEEN

One week later

Jenna knew the walls were closing in on her. Her only choice was to run. Take the money and run. And that's exactly what she was doing.

She longed for her desert home with its blazing hot crimson sun and indigo sky. It was only early November, and it was already freezing in New York. How did people live like this? She wished she'd never gone down this road, but she had, and she couldn't go back. The only way was forward—and fast.

As she stood atop the staircase of the deserted Scarborough train station, looking down at the tracks on a dark, cold Saturday morning, headed for her new life, she froze—reacting to the sensation of a presence behind her. She felt a hand on her shoulder and turned around to face him.

"Hi, Jenna. What's your rush?"

It was too late.

A week had passed, and nobody had a clue about Sutton or his whereabouts. Victoria and Nick were at home waiting for Sanchez to come over with some kind of breaking news. Stark was on his way over too, at their request, to see if they could all put their heads together and try to make some progress.

Victoria hadn't grilled Nick any further about what he'd been doing the night he was in Brooklyn, but she'd given up hope that he had somehow miraculously gotten rid of Sutton. There was something he wasn't telling her, though; she was sure of that. But she didn't think it had to do with Sutton's disappearance. If that were the case, he would have found a way to let her know they weren't in danger anymore. Plus, she could tell that he was still very much on edge. Nick said he'd made a backup plan that night, which likely meant doing something in the event Sutton wasn't convicted. Neither of them had considered the possibility that he'd just go on the run, and in that case, Nick's backup plan was worthless, as was hers.

She knew Sutton had a strong self-preservation instinct. It was possible that he just decided to cut his losses and not risk any jail time. He had close to a million dollars and no real ties that she knew of, but it didn't seem like that much money to live on for the rest of his life. But it also made no sense to her that he'd risk his entire future just to get back at her. Maybe what Sanchez suggested was true. Maybe just leaving her wondering for the rest of her life about his whereabouts was enough for him, and then he got the added benefit of knowing he wouldn't serve another day behind bars. What she needed was insight into his pathology, and she was frankly disappointed in the detectives' inability to accurately profile him. To her, that was a critical piece of the puzzle. How far would he go? And how could she stay one step ahead of him?

"Hey." Nick came into the kitchen, just having

finished up his Peloton session. Things had settled down a bit between them, but they were nowhere close to normal.

"Hey back. Detective Sanchez is on her way over. She said she had some news."

"Wasn't Stark coming over too?" Nick went over to get some coffee.

"Yeah."

"Just like old times. Maybe they've got another murder they can try to pin on me."

"Stark's on our side now. Remember? He works for us."

"We'll see about that. Maybe that's why he's seeing your mother. Gets him on the inside. Then they can bring down the whole family."

"Very funny."

"And why all the drama? Why couldn't she just tell you over the phone what was up?"

"I have no idea, Nick. I know as much as you do." Lila started to fuss, and Victoria went to pick her up. Nick grabbed his coffee and went up to shower, and she went to put Lila down for a midmorning nap. She didn't have a clue about where Nick's head was at. He was hot and cold and a bit distant today, and she didn't like it. Sure, she should have told him sooner. But so what? It wasn't nearly as bad as his betrayal, and she needed to keep reminding herself of that.

It felt a bit like déjà vu to Jack, driving over to the Mancusios' home in a professional rather than social capacity. Lexi was on her way there with some new information, and Victoria had asked him to stop by. She'd retained him as a PI, against his better judgment, which was no match for Sandra's persistence. The family was getting restless. A week had passed, and nothing had come of the manhunt for Sutton.

These days, the Mancusios were living in a spacious and tasteful home on a desirable cul-de-sac, but it was hard to believe this place didn't feel like a major step down to them from their last home—a stunning modern structure with large windows perched on the edge of the Hudson. As Jack started toward the door, he realized this was the first time he'd be seeing the two of them together since they were at the station the day they arrested Jeff Malone. And it would be the first time he'd be seeing Nick Mancusio in a new context. It might be awkward.

Mancusio answered the door. "Hello, Detective Stark. It's nice to see you again, but I sure wish it were under different circumstances." He seemed more composed than he had the last time they'd met, but then that wasn't a very fair comparison.

"Same here, Nick. And why don't you call me Jack?"

"Jack, it is." So far, he seemed fine.

"Please come in." Mancusio escorted him through the door. "So, what's going on?"

"I have no idea. I just know that Detective Sanchez called Victoria and said she was coming over with some news."

"Can I get you anything, Jack? Coffee, light and sweet? Isn't that how you take it?" Victoria asked.

"Sure. That would be great, Victoria." Maybe the woman couldn't cook, but she sure made a great cup of coffee. He remembered that much. Velvety smooth.

Victoria left him alone with her husband, and it was less awkward than he'd imagined it would be. He supposed it was probably good to get it over with. If he continued seeing Sandra, they'd need to find a way to relate to each other in some way other than as detective and suspect. Right now, Nick Mancusio was his client, and that seemed like a good interim step.

"Would you like to have a seat, Jack?"

"Thanks." Jack sat on the sofa, and Mancusio followed suit. This house felt warmer than their last one. Not stunning and modern, but comfortable. The decor was still sparse, with everything in its place. The fireplace had a spectacular painting of the Hudson at sunset over it, and some family photos sat atop its mantel.

"I haven't been able to find out too much. Most of Sutton's money is gone, more than half a million, but I don't know where he moved it. With the money being gone, it could really be that he's left the country."

"I'm sure we'd all like to believe that. But I wouldn't bank on it." Mancusio offered him a friendly smile, and it reminded Jack that Nick was a pretty affable guy—as long as his back wasn't up against a wall.

"I've been in touch with Detectives Sanchez and Ramirez. We're working on a few theories. But Sutton was kind of a loner. There aren't many people we can interview to get a read on him or where he might have gone."

Victoria came walking in with his coffee. "Or what he might do next. What about the bookstore owner? What was her take on all of this?"

The smell was delightful, a little slice of heaven. Sandra claimed he was a coffee addict, and it was contributing to his occasional insomnia. Perhaps, but if that was his biggest vice, so be it.

"At first, she found it all very hard to believe. But then, when they showed her the photos of Jenna's bruising and gave her more information about his past employment termination, she went to pieces. She feels guilty for leading him to you. And for being fooled by him."

"It wasn't her fault. I should have had a better cover."

Mancusio's eyes widened. "Is that your takeaway, Victoria? You should've had a better *cover*? What are you, a CIA agent? *Jesus Christ!* Maybe you shouldn't have gone in the first place. Did that ever occur to you?"

Victoria glared at him and then took a deep breath through her nose. Jack could tell she was steaming. Then she redirected her gaze toward the floor, fiddling with her hair and avoiding both of them, attempting to calm herself down, if he had to guess.

"Let's all take a step back here, okay? The last thing we need is you two turning on each other."

"You're right, Detective...uh, Jack. I'm sorry. This is all just a lot to process." Mancusio's words were at odds with his tense jaw, and Jack sensed this wouldn't be the last Victoria heard of it. Which was fine with him, as long as he didn't have to get sucked into their marital drama.

There was a knock at the door, and Victoria got up to answer it, leaving the two of them sitting in an uncomfortable silence.

It was Lexi. She walked in with a look he'd seen before, eyes wide and nostrils flaring, that he'd come to interpret as a mixture of anger and worry.

"Hi, Lex."

She shot Jack a curt look.

"I mean Detective Sanchez." He flashed her a smile, but her look stayed stone-cold. Something was up.

"Jenna Williams is missing."

"*What?*" Victoria's hand went to her mouth. "I mean, how do you know she's missing? Not just...out?"

"All her stuff's gone. I got a call from the unit that

was patrolling her house. They hadn't seen her in a while and got concerned, so they went and knocked on the door, and she didn't answer. Then they went in. What time does the security detail usually leave her place?"

"They're supposed to stay until seven. She didn't have much stuff. Just one suitcase and a carry-on bag. It wouldn't be hard for her to slip out unnoticed."

"We'll check security footage in the area. There was no sign of foul play. But if it was voluntary, if she just decided to bail, how the hell could she pull off something like that in her financial situation?" Lexi looked over at Victoria, and Jack thought he saw her face blanch a bit.

"She has a sister in Florida. Maybe she's helping her," Victoria offered.

"We called the sister. She hasn't heard from her in ages. Says they're not very close. Have you heard from her at all?" Lexi asked Victoria.

"Not a word."

"Any sign that Sutton got to her?" Jack asked. He'd been digging into her social media feed, doing some background on her for the family, and from what he could deduce, she didn't have any financial resources. No family, no boyfriend she could turn to for help. Either Sutton got to her, or she came into money somehow.

"No signs of a struggle. Nothing so far from security footage around her building. But we're looking into all angles. I have to go. Look, if you can afford it, I'd keep the security round the clock until we have more promising information to report." Lexi's phone buzzed, and she picked up, moving off to the side as she took in the information.

"Anything good?" Jack asked.

"Sort of. They caught some security footage of her

from another complex. It looks like she took her stuff and caught an Uber. No signs she was being forced. We're trying to track it to see where she went. But it seems for now like she may have just bolted after she found out Sutton was on the loose."

"Have you gotten anywhere on his profile?" Victoria asked.

"We're working on it, Victoria. I've got to get back to the station."

"I should get going too," Jack said. "I'll wrap things up here, and then I'll meet you over at the station, Detective Sanchez."

Jack finished up his business with the Mancusios, snuck a long last sip of his smooth dark roast, and went on his way. He had a pretty good idea where Jenna Williams might have gotten the money to disappear, but he planned on keeping that to himself for the time being.

"So you're saying you think there's a connection there?" Victoria asked, biting her lower lip, playing her cards close to the vest. She had to keep reminding herself to look at the computer camera and not the other woman's face.

"Of course there's a connection. Everything that's happened in your past is connected to who you are now. It's just a question of what kind of a connection. And how it's affecting you now. But then, you're a smart woman, Victoria. I'm sure you know that on some level."

Victoria did know that, but she preferred to throw the therapist a bone now and then. "So you think the incident, it's causing an inability to let myself be vulnerable?"

"Well, yes. The 'incident' was an assault, Victoria. It had an impact."

The therapist was using a background on her computer screen that made Victoria's head spin. She was finding it hard to focus on what she was saying. Why couldn't she just call in from an office like a normal person?

"But what happened to me with Sutton. It didn't go that far. I fought him off." Victoria knew that, technically, what happened to her was an assault, and she'd referred to it that way at the police station, but she had trouble thinking of it like that. She'd fought him off after all. Things hadn't gone that far. She didn't feel like a victim or even a survivor. People had survived far worse, and it seemed unfair to them for her to claim that status.

"It doesn't matter. You trusted him. And he betrayed that trust. He was your mentor. He was supposed to look out for you. It's a grave violation."

"What kind of person would do something like that?"

"I know. It's terrible, isn't it? And not very uncommon, unfortunately."

"No, I mean, I'm asking you in a clinical context. Wouldn't he have to have some kind of disorder? Normal people don't do things like that."

"No, they don't."

"I've been reading about narcissistic personality disorder. Do you think he has that?" Victoria was hoping to get some insight into Sutton's psyche in order to try to predict his next move. But she didn't want to be obvious about it, especially with what she was contemplating.

"I can't really diagnose someone without having them in front of me. But from what you've told me, it's possible. But let's bring the focus back to you."

"Right." *Let's start with how I stalked Sutton and thought about shooting him. About how I'm still thinking about it. What would you say to that? Is that normal, Doctor?*
The therapist continued. "Add that to your upbringing. Your father's fears that were layered onto you from a young age, and then one of his fears actually came true."

"It's thanks to my father's very valid *concerns* that I was able to fight Sutton off!"

"I'm not judging your father, Victoria."

"Look, I can see that there could be a connection between the incident and the fact that I may have some issues getting close to people."

"Good. And it's not like making the connection suddenly cures you. It just that having an awareness of it, of the way the 'incident' affected you, it sort of starts to take its power away, if that makes any sense."

"I guess it does."

"You're making progress, Victoria."

I'm not a child. "I've got to run now."

"Same time next week?"

"Ah, I'm not sure. I'll get back to you."

Victoria closed her laptop and went back to work, trying to shut out what happened in the past and stay focused on the present. It seemed like a luxury to her, with their lives possibly in danger, to sit around and mull over something that happened over a decade ago, even if her therapist had made some good points. She needed to stay focused on finding Sutton since the detectives didn't seem to be getting anywhere. What were they missing about him? Why was he going off script? And what would he do next?

SIXTEEN

Randy was sitting at his desk replaying the video footage over and over, hoping it would somehow look different to him the next time around. But it didn't. It looked the same, and he had to tell Barrett right away. The longer he waited, the worse it would be for him. For his case. He picked up the phone and called Barrett in.

"What's up? Did you find something on Sutton?"

"Sort of."

"Don't keep me in suspense, Ramirez."

"Take a look at this, Captain." Barrett stood behind him, preparing to watch the video he'd cued up. Before he jumped to any conclusions, he wanted her to view it, to see if she would have the same reaction.

"Is that Sutton's house?" she asked, pointing to the screen.

"Yeah." They watched as the door swung open and Sutton walked out, looking like he was going to veer off to his right. Then they watched him stop and tilt his head back the other way. Then they watched him walk away.

"Okay? So, the guy likes to go for walks. This is weeks before his arraignment. I don't get it. Is this connected to his disappearance?"

"Watch it again, but this time don't look at him. Look over here." Ramirez tapped on a dark spot on the screen. "Right here." He played it again and waited for her reaction.

"Oh my God. Is that who I think it is? Is that Victoria Mancusio?"

"Sure looks like her. She was in town during this time. She left the next morning. I wanted to show it to you right away."

"Well, isn't that a strange coincidence? She comes to town, finds a new witness, stalks Sutton, and then gets him arrested. Sounds like someone with a vendetta to me."

"She wasn't in town when he disappeared. And maybe it's not even her."

"Even if we can't prove it's her right now, she strikes me as the type who would rattle easily. Send this over to the Tarrytown team. Get them to bring her in and shake her up a bit. See what falls out."

"You got it."

"Anything on the money trail yet?"

"No, but I'm working on it."

"Maybe you should take a trip up there. Meet with them in person."

"I think that might be a good idea. I'd like to look over Jenna Williams' place myself. See if anything looks off. I'd like to question the husband too." Randy thought it seemed a bit too convenient that Malone had been knifed to death in prison. He'd heard rumblings about the Mancusio family having some reach and thought it might be good to question him about Sutton. "I know Victoria wasn't here the day Sutton disappeared because I talked to her that day, but I don't know about the husband."

"Good plan. For all we know, they're in on it together."

"I guess anything's possible." That was an interesting thought. A very interesting thought. Maybe she was just flirting with him as a tactic to throw him off their trail. *Now, who was getting paranoid?*

Victoria got a call from Sanchez asking her to come down to the station for a few questions. Her mind went to the money she'd given Jenna. Had they tracked it? All of it? She wasn't too surprised with the way Sanchez had looked at her earlier. But so what? It wasn't illegal to give someone money.

Still, she wasn't taking any chances. She called Sylvia Murray, the attorney who'd represented Nick when he was charged with murder. She was the best in the business if you were looking at life in prison. Perhaps she was overkill for a situation like this, and it took quite a bit of persuading to make something this inconsequential worth her while, but Victoria felt confident Murray was the right person for the job.

They met at the station and walked together to meet Detective Sanchez. Victoria didn't have much time to get the attorney up to speed. She told her about the money, and Murray advised her to keep it to herself. She'd done nothing illegal, and even if they found out about it and accused her of bribing Jenna, they'd never be able to prove it.

Murray stopped her just as they were about to enter. "Is there anything else I need to know?"

"Nothing I can think of."

"Say nothing unless I tell you to answer. Otherwise, let me do the talking."

"Got it."

"Okay then, let's keep this short and sweet. I've got

LITTLE LOOSE ENDS

accused murderers waiting for me in lockup." They checked in and were escorted to an interrogation room, where Sanchez was waiting for them.

"Have a seat." Sanchez directed Victoria and Murray to one side of the table, and they seated themselves. Sanchez sat across from them, notebook open and pen in hand, with a laptop to the side of the notebook. "Do you know anything about Jenna Williams' disappearance?"

"Go ahead and answer, Victoria."

"No. I already told you that."

"Let me switch gears. Victoria, can you run me through your trip to Arizona again? Where did you go? Who did you meet with regarding the Sutton case?"

"My client has nothing further to say on this matter. We're going now."

"Just one minute. I want to show you something."

They all stared at each other for a few long moments.

"If you'll indulge me, Counselor. Please?"

The usually unflappable Murray flashed Victoria a momentary *What the hell?* look but then quickly recovered her composure. "If my client has no objections."

"I have no objections." Victoria suddenly felt claustrophobic, like she couldn't breathe. *What does Sanchez have?*

The detective flipped open her laptop and turned it around toward them. She had a video cued up, and Victoria's stomach sank when she saw the screen. It was Sutton's house. Sanchez started it up, and Sylvia Murray watched, looking a bit perplexed. It took a second viewing for Murray to see what Victoria already knew was there in the shadows. They had video of her stalking Sutton in Arizona.

"What's this?" Either Murray was clueless, or she had a great poker face.

"It's your client, stalking our missing perp."

"Prove it, Sanchez. Come on, Victoria. We're going." And they stood up and left.

When they got outside, Sylvia pulled out her phone to make a call as she entered her Lexus, looking over at Victoria with a face that said *Stay put*. She ended the call and walked over to her client. "Was that you?"

"So what if it was?"

"I don't like being blindsided, Victoria."

"I didn't think it was relevant," Victoria replied.

"I'm on your side, Victoria. Is there anything else I need to know? I can't do my job with one hand tied behind my back."

"No. Nothing. And I didn't deliberately withhold that piece of information, Sylvia. I just didn't think it had any relevance to the issue at hand. Can they even prove it was me?"

"I highly doubt it with just that video footage, but now that they have it, they can maybe get your rental car data and see if you drove there."

"And what if I was there? What could they even charge me with? It's not a crime. To stand by someone's house." *Thank goodness my gun wasn't visible in the video.* She'd kept it to her side as she'd been trained. At least that was something.

"No, but if you're trying to make a case that you had nothing to do with his disappearance and that you didn't bribe Jenna Williams to make a false accusation—because that *is* a crime—it doesn't look good."

"I didn't bribe Jenna! She told me Sutton assaulted her."

"Then you have nothing to worry about."

"Sylvia, I absolutely did not bribe Jenna Williams,

and I had nothing to do with Sutton's disappearance. And I'm paying you to make that clear to the authorities. Are we clear?"

"We're clear, Victoria. Don't worry. I'm on your side. I just needed to hear you say it—with conviction—so I know what I'm dealing with. I work for you, whatever the circumstances. Maybe we can threaten to file a countersuit for harassment if they don't let up."

"I'd love to but not now. I need them on my side until we find Sutton."

"Let me know if you change your mind."

Many women might crave a day at the spa after a day like she'd had, but Victoria knew what she needed to do in order to feel better. After Sylvia Murray left, she pulled out her phone and called her contact at Patriot Shooting Center. They said they didn't have any appointments that weekend, but when she floated them a figure—a very generous figure—for some off-hours private lessons they acquiesced to a Sunday date and not just to brush up on her shooting. She was going full-on tactical training. Real-world scenarios. This was war, and she needed to be prepared.

Next she called Wade Higgins and told him to free up some time for her the next afternoon. They were all missing something regarding Sutton, and she was tired of watching everyone sit around scratching their heads, wondering why their profile was so wrong. She knew him better than any of them. If they were missing something, she'd find it. And then she'd find *him* and bring this insanity to an end once and for all.

Narcissists can be charismatic, confident, competitive, and great manipulators, which also makes them successful and able to win people over.

Inward signs: a sense of entitlement, using sarcasm, resentment, righteous indignation, passive aggression, the silent treatment.

Outward signs: sudden fits of anger or rage, screaming and yelling, becoming verbally or physically aggressive, trying to inflict emotional or physical pain.

Many narcissists are also paranoid and vindictive. They aim to punish and destroy the source of their frustration and pain.

"So what's the plan?" Nick asked, popping his head into her home office.

"Sylvia said to just let it be. They've got nothing." Victoria wasn't in the mood to talk about the run-in with Sanchez. She still wanted to prod Nick some more about where he was that night, but right now she had more pressing issues.

"Are they doing anything to find him besides harassing us?"

"They're being pretty tight-lipped about it if they are. Sylvia said she could file a civil suit if they keep bothering us."

"What do you think?"

"Let's wait and see." Lila let out a piercing cry that came screaming out of her baby monitor, startling both of them. She'd started teething, so she was a bit fussier lately.

"I'll get her," Nick offered.

"Thanks. I've got a lot to do for the opening." Victoria got back to work. She was looking over her notes, trying to connect the little she knew about Sutton's behavior to the research she'd done.

Many narcissists have been known to disown and abandon their victims in response to a solid challenge to their authority. Thus, a narcissist may leave town, change a job, avoid friends and acquaintances, or even get a divorce to secure relief from the pressure and save face. It really could go either way. What she really needed was more information about his past behavior from someone who knew him better than she did. From the literature, it seemed like when confronted, they could flee—or they could get violent.

Often, violent behavior was triggered by frustration, toward actions perceived to be a threat to the self. The key link between narcissism and aggression was provocation.

She'd looked over most of the criteria for different disorders, and narcissistic grandiosity fit him the best, although the literature noted that the disorder could be comorbid with other disorders such as sociopathy, psychopathy, or substance abuse. Many men with this disorder, research confirmed, engaged in sexual harassment, sexual coercion, and even sexual violence based on their sense of entitlement and inflated sense of self, especially in casual situations, as if they actually believed that all women wanted them. In relationships, they often started out charming, but then often devolved into controlling behaviors like passive-aggressive tactics, gaslighting, and isolation. They could escalate into anger, rage, and intimate partner violence. But she didn't see much evidence that they crossed over into first-degree, premeditated murder.

When he'd been called out about his behavior at the college, he'd gotten divorced. Moved to a new area. Started over. It was quite possible he was doing the same thing now.

But then she'd provoked him. Not once, but twice.

So which is it, Sutton? Did you leave town to find your next victim and continue your pattern, or are you coming for me?

SEVENTEEN

Victoria's lesson at Patriot Shooting Center the next day went well. Very well. Her trainer claimed she was a natural. But then what would he say, given how much money she was throwing at him? She couldn't have a weapon with her every second of the day, so they worked on disarming tactics and hand-to-hand combat moves. Evasion. Distraction.

She was a bit leery about asking him to teach her the offensive moves. What if he got the wrong idea? But it seemed to be just part of the routine, so they worked on that too. How to enter a room, clear a room. How to immobilize someone with her bare hands. Then she went in and did some target shooting, which always calmed her down.

Her father had started bringing her there in middle school to learn to shoot. He was insistent that she learn to defend herself. Their family, like many with their means, were targets, he disclosed. They'd gotten threats. The thought of a kidnapping, in particular, kept him up at night. He also insisted on self-defense classes, which had come in very handy with the Sutton incident. She didn't want to think about how that might have gone if she'd had a different kind of dad.

And as she let her mind wander back to their

unusual father-daughter bonding sessions at Patriot Shooting Center, she knew it was time to find out the truth. She tried to think about what her mother had said: Would it really make a difference how she felt about him if her father wasn't actually the man who'd fathered her? Would she love him any less? Was his love any less real? Of course not. Many people were adopted or had sperm donors, so what did it really matter? She decided to look at it in purely clinical terms. She and Lila needed to know. When she was filling out medical forms for Lila, she was doing her daughter a disservice. How could they know what risks they carried or what to look for if she didn't even know her own genetics? Her father was her father, no matter what, but she was ready to know the truth about her biology.

Victoria made a stop at her mother's house on the way to see Wade. She and Jack had decided to spare her mother the details of Victoria's latest predicament. Her mother knew about Jenna's disappearance, and she was frantic about the possibility of Sutton coming after them. At Jack's insistence, she'd gotten round-the-clock security. They'd let the nanny go because her mother didn't trust anyone else to be with Lila right now, so they were all pitching in for now. It seemed unnecessary to burden her with the minor issue of Victoria's legal problem until it became a real issue, and they were both sure that Murray could make it go away.

Victoria was happy her mother had someone. Stark really looked out for her, and she was hoping that maybe he was staying with her at least some of the time, although she didn't see any evidence of him taking up residence at her mother's house. But since her mother was a private person, she didn't pry. She got the feeling they both wanted to take things slowly, which, under normal circumstances, would be fine with her. But these weren't normal circumstances. His car wasn't in the driveway when she pulled in and parked. She started in, a little disappointed for her mother's sake but happy for the chance it would give them to talk privately.

"Where's Lila?" her mother asked. She was dressed in her exercise clothes, no makeup on. Victoria didn't ask her about Jack.

"Home with Nick. Father-daughter time."

A faint smile graced her mother's face, and Victoria could tell it brought up mixed emotions—fond memories of Victoria's dad swinging her around by her hands as her feet flew up in the air, solemn memories of her uncle walking Victoria down the aisle in his place.

"So, what did you want to talk about?"

"I want to talk about Dad." Victoria took a deep breath. She was ready.

"Oh. Okay then. Let's sit. Anything in particular?" Her mother was playing coy, but Victoria was sure she knew what was up.

"I'm ready to find out the truth."

"Good. I think that's wise."

"How?"

"We'll do it with Dr. Mason. She'll send it to a private lab. No names." A concierge doctor was one perk of wealth that Victoria thoroughly enjoyed.

"Okay. But can I ask something else? About that time period that the two of you separated?" When her mother had initially dropped the bombshell on her, she'd been too upset, too confused, and too angry to ask much of anything. She'd just walked out, and it had taken a few weeks before Victoria could even talk to her again. They hadn't broached the subject since.

"Sure. What is it you want to know?"

"How was it afterward? With Dad? Like, once you got back together after the separation?"

"I guess it was a little awkward at first. And we both agreed, no questions. But once we found our rhythm again, the whole separation thing started to fade. It started to feel more like a movie or a dream. Not like something that actually happened to me."

"How long did it take?"

"Oh, I don't know. A month or so? And, of course, I found out I was pregnant soon after we reconciled, and that redirected our focus. We just carried on."

"But how did you feel, like...on the inside? Being back together?"

"I felt...content. I knew it was where I belonged, with your father, and the separation was a mistake." Her mother had a warm smile on her face, and it broke Victoria's heart because she knew that, whatever she had with Jack Stark, it wasn't the same.

"That must have been reassuring."

"It's strange, you know. It wasn't like I didn't enjoy my little fling with Sam. Because—"

"Mom! Stop!" Victoria covered her face with her hands, cringing at the thought of it.

"Let me put it another way. I don't regret the separation. Like I said, your father and I met when we were so young. If the separation hadn't happened, maybe we'd both always be wondering if we were missing something. This way, we knew we weren't. I knew where I belonged, and it was with your father. And he belonged with me."

"Whose idea was it? The separation?"

"It was pretty mutual, believe it or not. And so was the reconciliation. So don't you worry. We were very happy from that point on."

Victoria longed for that feeling. The feeling that she was where she belonged with Nick. Maybe it would come to them again. Maybe she just needed to give it more time.

"Victoria?"

"Yes?"

"Is there something else you want to talk about? About you and Nick, maybe?"

She did need someone to talk to, but she couldn't even sort out her own feelings right now. "Not right now, Mom. Some other time."

"I'm here if you need me." She and her mother were getting there, one step at a time.

They said their goodbyes and Victoria went on her way. She checked her phone before she started driving and noticed that there was a text message from Randy Ramirez. He was flying up and wanted to interview her and Nick. *Just what I need.* The thought of Randy and her husband in a room together made her uncomfortable. Very uncomfortable.

Victoria met Wade over at his place. It was a larger two-bedroom, two-bath. It didn't front the Hudson, that was out of his price range, but he had a nice view of the river and the new bridge that spanned it from his balcony. He'd made his spare bedroom into an office. It was quite a setup. Four large monitors, a mainframe, and a bunch of other hardware she'd be hard-pressed to identify.

"Great place, Wade."

"It suits me."

It was the first time she'd seen his apartment. It was a little awkward being out of her element, but she didn't want anyone to know she was meeting with him. Wade claimed that what he was doing for her was pretty standard. Nothing really that hard to do. She wanted him to teach her so she wouldn't leave any breadcrumbs on her quest to find Sutton or implicate him somehow and put him in jeopardy.

But before she could open her mouth and ask, he started right in on something else.

"Victoria, I know you don't believe in psychics, but—"

"I never said that."

"You didn't have to."

She let out a sigh. She didn't really have time for this. But then she didn't want to offend him either. She was sure he believed he had a gift, and she wasn't completely sure he didn't. She just didn't really care that much about it. It didn't seem relevant.

"Did something happen? Along those lines?"

"I had another feeling when I was researching Sutton." Wade said his gift was called clairsentience—the ability to feel other people's feelings.

"And? What did you feel?"

He sat with his head cocked to one side like he was struggling to find the right word. "Desperation," he said at last. Then he got a serious look on his face like he was calling up the memory. He sat for a moment, his brow furrowed, and then continued.

"There was anger there too. But more than that, I felt a strong sense of...well, desperation is the best way I can describe it."

"Desperation?"

Wade shrugged. "Do with it what you will, Victoria. I have no idea what it means. I just felt I should pass it on."

Victoria wasn't expecting that. She'd expected him to say *rage* or perhaps even *fear*. But then again, if

Sutton was on the run, he would feel desperate, wouldn't he? She didn't have the heart to point out to Wade that he was probably just making a perfectly logical inference.

"Thanks for letting me know. That's interesting. Desperation."

"Yeah."

"So, have you found anything? Any traces of him anywhere? Or of Jenna?"

"Not yet. I've been using facial recognition software, but so far I haven't gotten any hits on him or Jenna, aside from what the police saw near her house. It's pretty easy to avoid getting picked up on them. Hats. Masks. Glasses. They'll all mess with it. It doesn't help that the train station cameras are on the blink a lot."

"Right."

"I'm keeping tabs on social media. That sort of thing. But she hasn't posted anything so far. I've crowdsourced their photos to some of my networks."

"What else can we do?"

"There's only so far I'm willing to go, Victoria. I won't do anything that will land me in prison."

"I know, Wade. That's why I wanted to meet you here. Can you teach me some of what you do? Just start with the basics. Like if I give you the name of someone, show me how you would start digging. And then, if I want to find something out but it's too risky, could you tell me—hypothetically, of course—how to do it? That wouldn't be too much for you, right?"

"Hypothetically, no. What did you have in mind?"

"Let's start with Jenna. How would I find out if there was someone else in her life? Someone else who could have assaulted her?"

"That's not too hard. We can start with dating apps and social media and see where it leads us."

"And the facial recognition software. Show me that too."

"Okay. Let's get to work."

They continued on her little mission. It wasn't really that hard. It was just a question of how to do it and also cover her tracks, and Wade had tips about that too. It was a productive session.

Victoria walked in the door late that afternoon, a full load of groceries in her arms, to a napping daughter and a relaxed husband binge-watching some crime show on Netflix.

"Hey, Vic. Where've you been?"

"Out and about. Visiting with my mom. Nothing special."

"Need any help?"

"No, you stay put. You look engrossed." She went into the kitchen, set down the groceries, and started to put them away. Then she heard Lila on the baby monitor waking up from her nap and switched gears. She went over and looked at the screen. She looked fine, but Victoria was eager to go up and get her. As she was walking through the living room, Nick called over to her.

"It's that series I told you about."

"The one about the Russian spies?"

"Yeah. It's good. You'd like it."

"Looks like I have some catching up to do."

"Sorry, I should have waited for you."

"It's fine."

He went back to his show, and she went up to get Lila, vowing that they would have a nice evening. A nice, drama-free Sunday evening where all the action was confined to the television set. She brought Lila back and set her in front of the television with Nick.

With the two of them occupied, Victoria went into her home office and sat down to compose an email. She went back and forth about how to address it, how to start, and how much to disclose, knowing that she'd have to score a face-to-face appointment before she came clean about what she really wanted to know.

Did your ex-husband ever hurt you?
What was it like being married to a narcissist?
Oh, and, do you think he could kill somebody?

She settled on something short and vague: *I'd like to talk to you about your ex-husband. I'm a former student of his.*

Sutton's ex-wife was a smart woman, a professor of sociology. She'd catch her drift. The only issue was, what would she do with it? Did he still have a hold over her? Would she blame Victoria for ruining their lives? Even if she didn't blame her, had she moved on? Would she simply ignore her, not wanting to revisit that period of her life? Or would she welcome an opportunity to help bring him down?

EIGHTEEN

It was Monday morning, and Victoria had just returned home after dropping off Lila at her mother's house. Randy and Detective Sanchez were stopping by to have a chat with them about the case. She was more than a little nervous about having Randy and Nick in the same room, but she tried to convince herself she was just being paranoid. She hadn't done anything besides a little harmless flirting. But was flirtation ever really harmless?

She'd secured some evidence the day before that Jenna had engaged in a relationship prior to the incident with Sutton that seemed to have ended pretty abruptly, but Victoria was keeping that to herself for now. Her digging had led to a thirty-something bartender in Scottsdale, but that's as far as she got. He was a good-looking guy who, according to his social media feed, seemed to have moved on to a perky blonde.

"How long do you think this will take? I have to be in the city by one."

Nick was starting his new position in finance the following week, and he had some meetings in the city to prepare for it. This was a great opportunity for him. Before the Angie Hansen scandal, he'd been one of the top real estate brokers in the area and the owner of his own firm. But when it came out that he'd had an affair with a client—and was later accused of her murder—he decided to sell the firm. In a small, close-knit community, a scandal like that was the kiss of death, but in Manhattan it would be different. This was a fresh start for him, and she didn't want to ruin it.

"I have no idea. But I can't imagine it taking that long."

"What do they want, exactly?"

"Sanchez said they want to talk to us about Jenna Williams. But I'm guessing they also want to find out if we had anything to do with Sutton's disappearance."

She hadn't asked him again about where he went that day, and she still wanted an explanation. More importantly, she hoped he'd have something to tell the detectives if it came up today. The gate buzzer sounded, and she went to greet them, hoping to get it over with quickly.

Randy felt his pulse race a bit as he walked to the door of the Mancusio residence with Detective Sanchez at his side. Their home was a bit less impressive than he'd imagined it would be, given their reputation. It was a stunning home by most people's standards, but then, they weren't most people.

The door opened, and Nick Mancusio stood before him. He'd seen his photo splashed all over the media, but he presented a bit smaller than he'd imagined. He was a few inches shorter than Randy and not quite as muscular. He had that movie-star handsome look, though. Even Randy could see that much.

"Nick Mancusio," he said, holding out his hand and flashing a blinding smile. *Are they veneers, or does the guy use some kind of teeth whitener?*

"Detective Randy Ramirez," he said, enveloping Nick's outstretched hand with his larger one and gripping it firmly. Victoria was now by his side.

"You already know my wife, I take it." Mancusio rested his hand on the small of Victoria's back as he spoke.

"Yes. Hey, Victoria. Nice to see you again." Randy smiled at Victoria, and he saw Nick Mancusio's jaw tense up.

"Hello, Detective Ramirez," she replied, shooting him a curt look that told him to watch it.

Maybe Sanchez picked up on the tension because she stepped in. "Of course, I need no introduction. We've all been seeing a lot of each other over the past year or so. So, you know the drill, folks. Let's get started."

Sanchez marched over to the living room and sat on the larger side of their white leather sectional, and Randy sat next to the detective. Victoria and her husband sat close together on the smaller side, Mancusio's hand resting on top of hers, which sat on her thigh. Randy noticed that the house didn't look fully lived in. It was sparse. A few tasteful pieces of art. A few family photos. No books. No telling artifacts. Nothing too personal, as if they'd been stashed in a witness protection program with a new cover life, trying not to reveal too much. Maybe that was because they'd only recently moved in.

"So why are we here, Detectives?" Mancusio leaned back into the sofa cushions looking totally at ease. If he had something to worry about, he was very good at concealing it.

Sanchez started off. "We talked to Victoria about the day before and the day of Sutton's disappearance. She's been able to account for her whereabouts. But we haven't spoken with you. Can you tell us where you were the day before and the day of Sutton's disappearance?"

"I thought you wanted to talk to us about Jenna Williams' disappearance," Mancusio said, and his jaw stiffened again. Victoria tilted her body away from her husband and crossed her leg to the opposite side, displacing his hand.

"Would you indulge me? Please?" Sanchez said.

"I was in Brooklyn the day before he disappeared. With my parents. And later that day, I came back here."

"How much later?" Randy asked.

Mancusio looked over at his wife. "I guess it was probably after midnight?" He shrugged.

"That's pretty late to get home from a visit to your parents. What were you doing in Brooklyn?" Sanchez asked.

"I went to get some materials for our gallery opening. Our order's been held up in the supply chain bottleneck. My family has a construction business. They fronted us some supplies. That's not a crime, as far as I know."

"What kind of supplies?" Randy said.

"Drywall. Lumber. Mud. The usual stuff."

Sanchez narrowed her eyes on Mancusio. "So, can your parents corroborate your being there until...what time would you say? Eleven o'clock or so?"

"Sure."

"And Dr. Mancusio, can you confirm the time your husband got home?" Sanchez asked.

Victoria let out a sigh. "No, I'm sorry. I fell asleep before he got in. I didn't hear him come in." Then she looked over at her husband. "I'm sorry, Nick."

"You have nothing to be sorry about, Victoria. I have nothing to hide."

"So, what time was it when you saw your husband?" Sanchez asked, still looking relatively friendly.

"About seven in the morning. I woke up, and he was there, next to me in bed." Victoria replied.

"And what time did you fall asleep?"

"Around eleven, I think."

Sanchez turned to Mancusio and gave him a hard stare. "Even if we could verify that you arrived back home at midnight, which we might be able to do with GPS, it seems like a pretty long time to be at your parents' house getting supplies. So, is there anything else you want to tell us?"

"I have nothing more to say. And if you want my GPS, get a warrant." There was an uncomfortable silence after Mancusio spoke, and Randy was sure there was more to it.

"We had an argument," Victoria confessed.

"Victoria! You don't need to tell them that! It's none of their business."

"I do. Because it was all my fault." Victoria looked over at Sanchez. "It was my fault we had an argument, and I don't blame my husband for being upset with me. You see, I kept the real reason for my trip to Arizona from him. And I didn't tell him about the threatening text messages from Sutton until that morning, and I should have. So, when I finally told him what was going on, he was understandably upset. He went to his parents' house to cool off. His leaving had nothing to do with Sutton. And I'd like you to stop harassing my husband. We've all been through enough."

"I see," Sanchez said. "So, you didn't get supplies from your father?"

"Yes, I got supplies! And we're done here, Sanchez. I'm not under arrest again, am I?"

"No, Mr. Mancusio, you're not under arrest," Sanchez replied. "Maybe we could get your GPS and—"

"I've had it with this crap!" Mancusio's eyes widened as his finger shot up into the air, his cool exterior evaporating in the heat of the moment. "My family is being threatened. A woman is missing. And you two sit here and accuse me? And my wife? I'm asking you to leave my house now. And don't come back unless you have a warrant. And if you bother either of us again, I'll file a harassment suit." Mancusio stood, his hands balled up like he was ready to pounce, but Randy was sure he wouldn't. Still, he had a sharper temper than one might expect from a pretty boy.

Then Randy stood up, and Sanchez followed suit. Victoria, who up until that point had just been staring up at her husband with a blank look on her face, finally rose from the sofa. After a tense moment or two of Mancusio breathing through his nose, he walked away toward the kitchen, shaking his head, and leaving the three of them standing there in silence.

"I'll see you two out." Victoria walked them to the door with barely another word, opened it, and shut the door behind them.

Victoria turned back to Nick, who had made his way back into the living room.

"Idiots," he said.

"I didn't expect them to ambush you like that. I'm sorry."

"It's not your fault. That's just how they roll." He came closer and touched her cheek, and it was then that she noticed the look in his eye. At first, she thought it was anger, which would have been at odds with his soft touch, but then she realized it was something different. It was hunger. Hunger for her.

She was sure it was just jealousy, that he'd picked up on the subtle cues between her and Randy. But it didn't matter. He wanted her on some primal level, and she wanted him too because having a man look at her like that was intoxicating. It lit her up inside. He needed her. Only her. And that was enough for the moment.

"Thanks for defending me."

He pulled her into him and held her tight, like he wanted to possess her, his head in her hair, kissing her behind the ear, running his hands over her back, exploring her in a way he hadn't for so long. And then their mouths met and they melted into one with an urgency that been lacking lately. He lifted her up and carried her over the sofa where they frantically stripped off their clothes. Then Nick slowed it down a bit, making her wait. He traced his fingers lightly over her body, heightening her senses to a fever pitch, building her desire. He kissed her in all the right places, and by the time they gave in to their mutual lust, she was lost in it. It was glorious and different and confusing all at the same time.

Afterward, she was expecting his customary *I love you*. But that wasn't what came out of his flushed lips as he looked into her eyes, casually stroking her hair.

"So, why were you at Sutton's house?"

"Huh?"

"Why were you at his house that morning? You never really explained yourself to me."

"I told you, I just wanted to see him in person."

"I don't believe that, Victoria. That's not a reason."

She let out a sigh, knowing this wouldn't sit well.

Nick was a macho guy, and the thought of his wife stalking someone with a Glock in her hand wouldn't sit well. But she told him the truth anyway.

"I wanted to see if I could get to him. If I needed to for some reason."

"I see. Do you think you could do it?"

"Do what?"

"Murder someone, Victoria."

"If I had to. To protect Lila."

"I don't see it. I don't think you have it in you. And if you don't, you shouldn't put yourself in a situation like that."

"And what about you, Nick? Do you have it in you?"

"I'd kill Sutton with my bare hands if I could find him. But now I can't. You should have come to me, Victoria. You should have told me before you went off like that."

"I should have. I'm sorry." They stayed there for a while in each other's arms, and Victoria realized that many of their marital problems could likely be traced back to the same issue. Nick felt emasculated because she didn't need him. Angie Hansen had given him what she hadn't, the chance to feel like a strong, protective man.

"But since we're coming clean here, what time did you really get home that night?"

"Around three."

"Where were you?"

"I wasn't anywhere near Sutton."

"That's not what I asked."

"I'm not sure you want to know."

"I want to know, Nick. I need to know."

"I was at church, Victoria. I went to light a candle. And I just stayed a while longer than I expected. I needed some time. So you see why I can't give them my GPS. How would that look? And I didn't do anything to Sutton. Not because I didn't want to. Because I never got the chance."

Because of you, he might as well have added, but he didn't need to because she could fill in the blanks. He'd betrayed her by sleeping with Angie Hansen, a woman who was still haunting his conscience, and she'd betrayed him by putting them all in mortal danger. Could any couple get past a mess like this? Should any couple be fool enough to even try?

NINETEEN

After a morning of tension followed by a mind-blowing release, Victoria had been content to spend the rest of the morning in her office, shutting out all the factors of her life she couldn't control and focusing instead on the ones she could. Work had always been like that for her, and perhaps that's why she enjoyed it so much. She was starting to pack it in for her afternoon trip to Connecticut when her phone buzzed. It was Randy calling, so she took the call. She hadn't talked to him since she'd escorted him out their front door earlier that morning.

"Hi, Randy. What can I do for you?"

"I'm sorry about the way things went this morning, but I've got some good news for you."

"You got Sutton?" But then it dawned on Victoria that even if they picked him up, with Jenna gone, they'd have nobody to press charges against him. What then?

"Not that good but close. Looks like Sutton may have left the country. Three days after he disappeared."

"How do you know?"

"We caught some security cam footage at the Miami airport. He was in the international terminal.

There's one of him walking from a distance and another close-up of his face, but it's at an odd angle."

"And they didn't intercept him?"

"He must've gotten fake papers, or they would have caught it. He grew a beard. He looked different, so my team didn't catch it until earlier today. We're pretty sure it's him, but we're trying to get a few more eyes on it. I can forward it. Maybe you can weigh in. And I'll send all of it to Detective Sanchez. She can compare it to the security cam footage from your house."

"Sure, send it over." She clicked on the image, and there he was, looking up at the camera, a faint smile on his face.

Then she watched the video footage. The walk. The mannerisms. It was him. And she was sure he wanted them to see this. He wasn't stupid. Why else wouldn't he try harder to disguise himself? But she had to play this carefully. No detective wanted to be outclassed by a smarty-pants art dealer.

"What do you think?" Randy asked.

"It's him."

"Well, I guess that lets you and Nick off the hook for his disappearance."

"Sure, but don't you think this is all a little too...convenient?" Victoria replied.

"You mean the fact that he's looking at the camera?"

"Yes."

"I thought that too. It could be that he wanted us to see him. It's not that hard to fake out the security algorithms with a hat or some glasses, and I'm sure he knows that. So I agree that he probably did it intentionally. To let us know he outsmarted us. Once he cleared security, he'd feel pretty safe. He's got a big ego, and he's smug. And once he's out of the country, he can go anywhere. He's got enough money to live comfortably for a long time."

"What if it's a diversion? What if he's just trying to make us think that's what he was doing? Letting us see him at the international terminal?" Victoria asked.

"And what then? He has a chance to get out of the country and doesn't take it? He stays here and risks being arrested? Why on earth would he do that?"

"I don't know. To kill me, maybe? To kill my family?"

"Look, he's not going to come after you today, Victoria, so why don't you relax a bit and try not to think about it for a bit for a change?"

"I'll try."

"And I'm sorry if I ruffled some feathers at your house earlier."

"It's okay. We're both just sick of it. It's been a rough year." She knew that wasn't really what he meant. He shouldn't have been so informal with her. He knew better, and she figured on some level he absolutely did mean to ruffle Nick's feathers.

"I know. I would be too. Well, I'm headed back to Scottsdale. If you need anything before I leave, let me know."

She knew he was floating her an opportunity to see him in person, but that's the last thing she needed right now. A harmless flirtation in Arizona was one thing. It wasn't part of her real life. But having him in her home was all too real, and she didn't need that kind of complication now—or maybe ever.

"Have a safe trip back, Randy."

Catherine Sutton was now a full professor of sociology at a small liberal arts college in eastern Connecticut, not too far from Tarrytown. She looked older than Victoria but not as old as Sutton, a petite woman whose shoulder-length dark hair had a few strands of gray peeking through. She was attractive in a hip scholar sort of way, with her wire-rim aviator glasses, pale skin, and serious countenance. Victoria thought it odd that she'd kept his name after the divorce. She was also surprised that it was her husband who had filed for divorce, not Catherine. But she was willing to meet with Victoria right away, and that could only mean one of two things. Either she was out to get revenge, or he still had a hold over her and she wanted information. So far, it wasn't going as expected.

"So, what were you doing in my apartment that night?" Her voice was a bit deep for a smaller woman.

"He asked me to come up and get some articles he'd flagged for me," Victoria replied.

"This was after you'd gone out for drinks?"

"Well, yes. He asked me to go for drinks. Rather, he insisted that I go with him."

"And you didn't find that odd?"

"I found it uncomfortable," Victoria replied.

"Then why did you go?"

"I didn't feel like I had much of a choice."

Sutton gave her a hard stare. "And then?"

"When we got to the apartment, I asked about you. If you were home. And he said you were out of town. Then I got really nervous."

"Maybe he took that the wrong way."

"What do you mean?"

"Maybe he thought you wanted to make sure the coast was clear. Make sure I wasn't home."

"I didn't mean it that way. I told him I wanted to meet you. I said I was looking forward to meeting you."

"I'm not saying you meant it that way. I'm saying

maybe that's how he took it." They were both silent for a few moments. "And then?"

"He wanted me to have another drink with him. I said no and just asked him for the articles. But then he got upset. He told me to sit. He *ordered* me to sit and have a drink with him. But when he walked into the kitchen, I rushed for the door. To try to leave. At that point, I was willing to risk my grade. My degree, even."

This was always the hardest part for her to recount because it was truly terrifying. The way he ran to the door and overpowered her. Bolted the door shut. Spun her around. Called her a tease. Started to force himself on her, his hands everywhere. But she got through that part while Catherine Sutton looked down toward her desk, avoiding eye contact.

"He was so strong. He was all over me. I couldn't free myself. My only move was to play along. So I pushed him away a bit and asked him to stop. I said I wanted to slow things down. I told him I was just nervous. That it was a big step for us. I acted coy. I asked him to get me a drink. And it worked. It pleased him to hear me say that. He started to calm down. And then he backed up and asked me what I wanted. Then I had a clear shot, so I karate-kicked him in the groin. As hard as I could. And he went down."

Catherine's eyes widened, and Victoria shrugged. "I've had some training."

"I guess."

"He was lying there in a ball on the floor, and I bolted. He called out to me as I left. Said if I told anyone about it, he'd kill me. So I didn't. I just left college the next day and never looked back."

"And you never knew until recently that your family was behind the investigation that got him fired?"

"No. I never knew."

"You're a smart woman, Victoria. I find it hard to believe that you didn't know what would happen if you went up to my apartment that night. And you really didn't know who was behind his demise? You expect me to believe that?"

"I guess I'm just a trusting kind of gal, Catherine." Victoria gave her a hard stare. Was she actually defending Sutton's actions? That would mean she was still on his side—and coming here was a big mistake. "I mean, how did he explain it all to you? When it all came out about his other students? Did he blame it on us?"

"You look like you're judging me for questioning your story. But you, of all people, should know how it feels. To want to believe your husband. This disrupted not only his life, but mine too. What did your husband tell you about Angie Hansen?"

"I don't think that's relevant here."

"He told you that it was her, right? That she'd come on to him?"

"Again, I'm not here to talk about me."

"We're not so different," Sutton said. "You know how that feels. To want to believe your husband."

Victoria hardly thought it a proper comparison. Angie Hansen was a willing and eager participant. "You don't believe me?"

"It's not a question of whether I believe you. With someone like him, he actually believes his side of the story. I mean, let's get back to why you're really here. To find out how dangerous he is, right? To try to predict what he might do next?"

"Yes."

"Well, to do that, you have to get into his head. People with his kind of narcissism, they see the world differently. Grandiosity. What does that mean? It means an inflated sense of self. How could you *not* want him? And if the self is under attack, they react with a vengeance. They're highly competitive. How do you think I survived?"

"I'm sorry. What are you getting at?"

"How do you think I managed to get free of him, Victoria? It's not that easy to get away from someone like that in one piece."

"I don't know."

"I had to figure out his game. And beat him at it. But without him even knowing I was playing."

"I'm not sure what you mean."

"I had to act like I believed him. I'm pretty good at it, no? You just had a little taste of it. I had to act the faithful wife. Blame the flirty college girls. Stand by him. Act like I was hurt. Jealous, even. I had to make him see me as pathetic so he'd stop wanting me and file for divorce himself. And it worked. If I'd divorced him, if I'd gotten angry, he'd have taken it all out on me. Blamed me for my inadequacies that drove him to the other girls. So that's how I survived. Like you, I played along. Although, I'm sorry to say, I never got the chance to kick him in the balls."

Victoria's head was spinning. She didn't know what to believe anymore. Which part of this was the act? The woman seemed a little off. But she pressed on. "What was it like, if you don't mind my asking? Being married to him? Did he ever hurt you?"

"His tactics were mostly emotional, not physical. The silent treatment, using sarcasm, gaslighting. If I fought back, he would grab my wrists sometimes. Punch a wall. But he never actually hit me. It was just there in the background, the threat of it. His physical power over me. But then, when he started moving on to coeds, he got bored with me. He didn't interact with me that much. It was liberating in a way. But I was still trapped. If I'd asked for a divorce, he'd have retaliated. So I had to make him think it was his idea."

"Is that why you kept his name?"

"It's not the only reason. By that time, many of my publications were under my married name. We married when I was very young. He'd swept me off my feet. So smart. So charming. They can be like that. But yes, it did help with the narrative a bit. The jilted wife, pining away. She couldn't even let go of his name."

"Has he ever bothered you again?"

"No, and I don't expect that he will."

"Do you think he has the potential to get violent?"

"Of course, Victoria. You've read the literature. They all have the potential to get violent. Especially if they're provoked. But he's not stupid. And if he inherited that much money, my best guess is he would just go somewhere else and start over. It's like a compulsion. He has a need to find the next victim to manipulate. Try Costa Rica. He always talked about going to Costa Rica."

They wrapped things up, and Victoria was left with more questions than answers. Which was the real Catherine Sutton? The jilted, pining wife? The shrewd survivor? Or was she some twisted, desperate combination of the two?

When Victoria pulled up to her mother's house, Stark was there. Usually, she'd be happy, but today she would have liked some alone time with her mother. Their relationship was moving to a better place. She was starting to view her mother in a new light, as a real person with flaws and strengths and rich life experience. Victoria didn't have many female friends; she'd always had trouble relating to other women. The closeness she was starting to feel with her mother was comforting, but it also alerted her to the fact that she'd missed out on something, keeping other women at arm's length.

"Hello, Victoria."

"Hi, Jack. Where're my mom and Lila?"

"She took Lila upstairs to change her. I wanted to touch base with you anyway."

"Likewise."

"Any news on your end?"

"As a matter of fact, there is. Ramirez just called. They claim they have footage of Sutton at the Miami airport, leaving the country."

"I heard that."

"Of course, that was after he and Sanchez came to our house and grilled Nick."

"I heard about that too. She's just doing her job."

"Right. And they were wrong. Again. So, do we get an apology this time?"

"I doubt it."

"So, what happens now?"

"I don't know. I assume they'll keep looking for Jenna Williams, but with Sutton possibly out of the country, it's a lot less likely there was foul play involved."

"Where does that leave my family?"

"Yes, Jack, where *does* that leave our family?" Her mother had heard the tail end of the conversation as she entered the living room with Lila in her arms.

Lila smiled and let out a squeal when she saw her mother. Victoria reached out and took her, hugging her tight.

"Hello, my little angel. I missed you!" Lila continued to babble away. On a few recent occasions, Victoria thought she'd heard her say *mama*, but it was never directed at her. Lila was moving on to consonants, so it was probably just part of her new repertoire. Still, it should be soon, maybe in another month or two, and Victoria could hardly wait to hear her say it and make it official. She still couldn't quite believe it herself.

"Well, of course, it means neither of you is under suspicion anymore. Which is a positive development. But it does leave you in limbo as far as Sutton. But the longer he stays away, the more likely it is he won't come back. I say we just keep the security and see."

"I don't buy it for a minute. He wanted us to know it was him. That's why he's looking at the camera. He's not stupid," Victoria said. "And we have no way of knowing if he actually left."

"Maybe it's his way of thumbing his nose at all of us," Jack replied.

Victoria knew it was futile to protest that theory.

"Have you gotten anywhere on Jenna Williams?" Victoria asked.

"There's another guy from her recent past I'm checking out. He seems to go through a lot of women. That could be nothing, or maybe not. Are you still wanting to pursue this investigation into her, given the new information?"

Victoria did, but since she seemed to be equally good at finding information, she decided it was better to keep it to herself for now and take Jack off of the case for the time being. It was really up to the detectives in Arizona to pursue Jenna. She was their witness. Their responsibility. She didn't feel Jenna posed a threat to her. Mostly she just wanted to know if Jenna had been telling the truth about Sutton for her own peace of mind, to see if she could trust her own judgment.

"I think you can hold off on her for now. But could you keep looking into Sutton? Keep an eye out? Keep digging around, see if anything turns up?"

"Of course, Victoria. Anything you need."

"Victoria, can you join me in the kitchen, please?" Her mother turned and walked away, not waiting for a reply, and Victoria followed. Her mother had the DNA kit her concierge doctor had dropped off.

"Oh. Right." Victoria refused to attach any significance to this event. *Purely a clinical matter.* She followed the directions in silence and handed the kit back to her mother without comment.

"Do you want to stay for—"

"I need to get going now." She turned from her mother, and they made their way out to the living room and said their goodbyes. It wasn't until Victoria had strapped Lila into the car seat and seated herself behind the steering wheel that it hit her. *What if my father isn't my father?* A wave of emotion came over her, and she started to sob for all the times she'd shared with him and for all the times she'd missed. And for sweet little Lila, who would never even get the chance to meet him.

After Sandra closed the door, she turned to Jack with a curious look on her face. "So, what do you think she's really up to?"

"I think she's taking matters into her own hands. Victoria won't give up until she finds him." *Or he finds her.*

Jack wasn't convinced that Sutton had left the country, but he didn't see the sense in stressing them out even more. He planned to get with Lexi about it tomorrow and keep digging on his own. When he had something of value—comforting or alarming—then he'd share it with them. Ruminating over the what-ifs wasn't a productive use of anyone's time.

"I want you to track her, Jack. Keep tabs on her. Don't let her do anything that would put her in danger."

"Do you really think that's a good idea? It's a pretty big breach of trust. What if she finds out?"

"She's my only child, and she's my responsibility. And if I'd encouraged her to report Sutton to the police in the first place, maybe things would be different. This is my fault as much as anyone's."

"Your fault?"

"I thought I was doing the right thing back then. Protecting her by just making it go away. But we let him get away with it. If he'd gotten some kind of criminal record back then, maybe..." Sandra started to tear up. If there was one thing that pushed Jack's buttons, it was a crying woman—and not in a good way.

"Sandra, none of this is your fault. And he didn't really get away with it, not totally." Jack walked over and hugged her, and she pulled herself together pretty fast.

Jack had his share of regrets—the biggest one being his failed marriage—but he and his daughter had moved past it. There was enough guilt in this family to fill purgatory. They seemed to be stuck wallowing in it. Maybe if they could rid themselves of this guy for good, they could finally move on.

"Just keep track of her for me, Jack. Keep abreast of what she's doing. I know Victoria, and she's not going to let this rest."

"What about Nick?"

"What about him?"

"Will he let it rest?"

"I'm not sure how much he can do with Sutton on the run."

"What's your sense of his family? What kind of reach do they have?"

"I'd assume it's pretty regional." Sandra started to clean up Lila's things, walking around and working off her nervous energy.

"Do you think his family was behind the prison hit on Malone?"

"I've never cared enough to think about it. But his family isn't the only one with connections, Jack. We're just much more circumspect in our approach." She smirked at him.

"Duly noted! I'll try to stay on your good side." He thought about telling her he'd once considered the possibility she'd hired someone to get rid of Angie Hansen on behalf of her daughter. But with those steel blue eyes staring into his soul, he reconsidered. She might take it as a compliment, but he didn't want to chance it. He was more into her than he let on.

She stopped what she was doing and strode slowly over toward him. He loved to watch her walk, her petite body with its charm school posture tempered by a slight feminine wiggle. Was she conscious of the effect it had on him?

"Wise decision," she whispered, placing her index finger on his lips. He towered over her wispy frame, but she was the one exuding all the power.

"I have to say, it's kinda hot, this tough girl thing you've got going on." He pulled her in for a kiss.

"I figured a guy like you could take a little heat," she replied.

"Oh, I can take a lot of heat; don't you worry about it."

And the remainder of Lila's toys were left scattered on the floor for the time being.

TWENTY

Another week had passed, and nothing more had happened. Everyone else seemed to be moving on, banking on the fact that Sutton had left the country and assuming the threat was pretty much gone. Since they weren't home most of the day, Victoria and Nick had reduced the security team to evening hours and overnight.

Victoria continued to keep up on her tactical training and her behind-the-scenes research. She was trying hard to believe that her life could go back to normal, but she didn't really believe it. Still, she tried to think about what Stark said. The longer they went with nothing happening, the less likely it was that something would happen, so she was happy about the one-week milestone. Perhaps weeks would turn to months, months would turn to years, and it would all just fade away.

She'd just dropped Lila off at her mother's house and was now back home. She was planning to work from home that day. Nick was at his new job in the city, which was working out fine. He seemed to love it. He was making great money already, and it had unlimited potential. And she really enjoyed the time alone in her home.

She'd just finished tidying up in Lila's room and was walking out the door when she heard a voice.

"Hello, Victoria." It was very low. Very faint. So faint she thought she could be imagining it. "You've done something different with your hair." It sounded like Sutton.

She took a few steps back toward Lila's room as her heart raced. *Where's my weapon?* Her bedroom. A few doors down. Then she heard a crackle and turned around.

"I like it."

She realized the voice had come from the baby monitor. She could hear someone breathing. Then it just cut off. She'd heard stories about this happening, but the installers had assured her their router was secure. She grabbed her phone and waited to see if he would speak again, thinking she could record it. But nothing more happened, and she was left in a state of confusion with no proof that it had ever even happened. She called the police and went to get her weapon, planning to keep it handy until they arrived.

She tried not to panic. She needed to think clearly. When had she gotten her hair cut? Maybe three days ago? It was quite a bit shorter and a shade lighter. Could he notice that through the baby monitor camera? Or had he seen her somewhere else in the house? Had he maybe hacked their whole security system? Could he see and hear everything? Or was he around, somewhere close by? Was this how he seemed to know so much about them? Had he been listening in on their conversations? Her mind raced, thinking about what information she might have disclosed.

When the officers arrived, they checked the entire house. As she expected, there was nobody there and no signs that anyone had been there. The officers told her to follow up with Detective Sanchez and went on their way. She called Sanchez and filled her in. Then she called Nick and left a message. Then she called the security company that had installed their upgrade and asked them to send someone over. Finally, she called Wade and asked him to come over and to be there when the tech team came, thinking he'd have a better read on if their so-called hack-proof measures were truly so.

About an hour later, she and Wade were at her house, mulling over the events of the morning and the case in general while they waited for the security tech people to arrive.

"How close would he need to be to hack the baby monitor?"

"With the kind you have, he could be anywhere in the world. With the older, walkie-talkie ones, a hacker would need to be close, not much farther than your yard. The kind you have, it's web based. They could be anywhere. But you don't have it connected directly to the internet, so he'd have to have hacked your router somehow. All your devices could be vulnerable, so don't use anything until they come and check it out."

"I guess that's good and bad. It means he may not be a direct threat, but then it'll be harder to convince the police to keep up the search if they think he's just toying with me."

"Maybe he *is* just toying with you."

"Maybe, but do you know how hard it is to live like that? To never know? I have to find him, Wade! I have to know for sure where he is. Have you had any luck with facial recognition?"

"Not yet. I'm trying. If he wants to beat the algorithm, it's not that hard. A mask. A hat. Glasses."

"So I've heard. That's exactly why I know he meant for us to see him at the airport. He's too smart to let that happen. Anything else in his background? Can you take me through it again? Everything you've uncovered?"

"Like what?"

"Any other violent offenses? Any patterns in his past? Anything to lead to where the money might be?"

"I can't hack bank accounts. Well, I can, but I won't. I'm...unwilling." Wade gave his head a firm nod, seeming pleased with himself for finding just the right word as if they had all day, which they certainly did not.

"I'm not asking you to hack bank accounts. Just take me through everything one more time."

He started looking through his file, rattling off various facts.

"He has a clean police record, as you know. Job history was pretty steady after he was let go from the college. He inherited money from his father a few years ago. Almost a million. He doesn't do social media, so there's not much there. He's got a Netflix membership. He used to belong to a gym, but he let it lapse a few months ago. Oh, and this is interesting. I didn't notice this before. I wonder if this means something."

"What?"

"I was looking at his Strava feed from a few months ago to see if I could find any patterns as to where he went. To maybe see how he made his escape, because the paths behind the house have spotty GPS coverage. I was thinking he might have walked there and just continued into a dead zone."

"And?" Victoria looked at him, her eyes wide and her patience wearing thin.

"Anyway, I just realized that he slowed down quite

a bit over the last month or so, from a jog to a walking pace. And look at the distances over time. He wasn't going as far anymore."

All at once, something clicked. A bunch of disparate pieces in the back of Victoria's mind suddenly snapped together, front and center. "Wade! Oh my God. Something just hit me."

"What?"

"I don't know if there's any connection, but when Jenna told me about the assault, she said she thought Sutton stopped because he had to, not because he wanted to."

"What does that mean?"

"I have no idea, and neither did she. She just told me it was a gut feeling. The way he looked at her. That it wasn't regret. And that he had to stop, for some reason."

"Had to stop?"

"Do you think maybe his strength was getting sapped? That's why he backed down with Jenna? She said when she shoved him, he fell back hard. She was surprised by her own strength. Chalked it up to her adrenaline pumping. But what if she wasn't stronger? What if Sutton was weaker?"

"That's an interesting theory."

"There's something else. I might be grasping at straws here, but bear with me."

"I always do, Victoria." He smirked at her.

She shot him a look and continued. "The woman he assaulted. The call girl. She died a few years back of some sort of medical condition, Randy told me."

"And?"

"What if he caught something from her? What if Sutton is sick?"

"Sick? Hmm."

"And when I saw him outside his house, he was

thinner than I remembered. Oh my God. What if I'm right? How can I find out?"

"I draw the line at hacking people's medical records, Victoria. Why don't you take your theory to the police and see if they can get the information with a warrant or something?"

"I have to think about it. What if they don't believe me? Plus, I'm not sure how that works. He hasn't been convicted of anything. Isn't there some kind of doctor-patient confidentiality? Would a doctor even tell the police? Do they even have to?"

"You're asking me?"

"I'm thinking out loud, Wade."

"I'm sure the police can get a warrant for the medical records of a fugitive. At least give them a chance. It'll help them with the profile too."

"You're right."

"I know."

"So, Victoria, if you're right, if Sutton's sick, how might that make him feel?" Wade had a smug smile on his face, which confused her.

"Huh?"

"Remember? I told you I had one of my feelings about him? And I told you he was feeling..."

"Desperate. You did say that, Wade."

Victoria had to admit it was a pretty weird coincidence. But what good was this gift if he couldn't use it to find Sutton?

"Maybe I'll make a believer out of you after all. But come to think of it, if he's really that sick, he'd need medical care. Wouldn't he be reluctant to run?"

"No, Wade. Not if it's too late. If he's terminal, he's got nothing to lose. And that, I'm afraid, would explain everything."

"Yeah, I guess it would."

"Let's step up our facial recognition software efforts

around the area. Airports, Penn Station, Grand Central, rental car companies. Start looking in the archives for anything from after he was spotted at the airport to around the time of Jenna's disappearance. Could you put some photos up of him with a hat or glasses or something? Just to see if maybe we could trip him up?"

"I can try to create something. That's not a bad idea. I'll also crowdsource his photo to my network again."

The gate buzzer sounded; it was the tech representative for the security company that had installed their router along with their whole supposedly airtight system. They went around the house, checking everything. Wade and the technician rambled on about demilitarized zones and default optimization, and then the technician asked her if she had, by chance, disabled remote access. She told him she had no idea what they were talking about and suggested they do their jobs and figure out how to give them the tightest security money could buy, or she'd fire them and find someone who could.

"Sorry. I'll dial down the tech babble." The technician looked a little sheepish, and she felt bad for snapping at him. "Do you use the camera remotely? Like when you're away from home to check on her?"

"Yes. Sometimes. But not often."

"Can you live without that feature?"

"If it means we'll be more secure, of course."

Wade went on to explain that if they had been using the monitor to check up on Lila remotely when they were away from home, that would create more vulnerabilities in the system. She confirmed that she could live without that feature, so they tightened things up. There were also some software updates that hadn't gone through on the router, so they did those and then went up to check the baby monitor and camera and performed updates on those. Then they changed all the passwords, and the technician informed her, yet again, that their security system was indeed the best that money could buy.

After the technician left, she turned to Wade. "So, what do you think? Are we secure?"

"Nobody's ever really secure from hackers, Victoria. They're always one step ahead of everyone. I'd keep the security detail outside for the time being and switch to an old-school baby monitor if I were you. At least that way, if they hack it again, you'll know they're close."

"Good idea," Victoria said.

"And keep your devices off when you're not using them, especially if you're having sensitive conversations. I'll go pick up a few more goodies and come over and modify it a bit more tomorrow. For now, disconnect everything from the internet that you don't really need. When I come back, I'll double-check for any attacks or intrusions." Wade reached into his bag.

"And here's a mobile hotspot. Use this to connect to the internet when you need it. But if you're doing anything sensitive, I'd do it at the office until we're sure you're good."

It was all very disturbing, but the chances of Sutton targeting her at her house were slim, even if he did have a death wish. If he wanted to kill her, he needed to be sure it would succeed, and this would be the hardest place of all to pull it off. Of course, anywhere else, she was in his crosshairs.

She called Randy, and he didn't pick up, so she left a message: "Call me. It's urgent." She needed help with her theory about Sutton's health. If she could find out for sure that Sutton had a fatal illness, they could maybe just disappear for a while and let nature take its course. But she needed to know. Soon. Maybe he couldn't get her at home, but now she needed to watch her back everywhere, even online. *How long can I live like this without losing my mind?*

To get her mind off of home, Victoria had gone into the office to work for a few hours. Then she'd stopped to pick up Lila on the way home and filled her mother in on what had happened. Stark offered to stay at the house with her mother for the time being, and they had overnight security posted outside. There wasn't much more any of them could do to feel more secure.

Now she was home, still feeling a bit uncomfortable and not very secure. It was close to six, and Nick hadn't come home yet. He'd been curt on the phone earlier when she told him about the monitor. She didn't know if that was just work stress or his attitude toward her in general, but she was getting sick of his mood swings. She cozied up with Lila for a bit and got her fed, then she started to fix herself some dinner while her jams played softly in the background. Lila liked to bounce around to the music while Victoria cooked.

She heard a call coming in on her phone. *Randy. I hope he has some good news.*

"Hi, Randy."

"Hey, Victoria. Detective Sanchez filled me in on what happened. That must have been terrible for you. I can't even imagine. How're you holding up?"

"I'm okay. Really. But I wanted to run a theory past you." She went on to explain it to him. The canceled gym membership. The shorter runs. The fact that Sutton hadn't fought back much with Jenna. The dead victim from the cold case. He agreed it was worth looking into and said he'd talk to Barrett about a warrant. He also said he'd see if Sutton's former boss could shed some light on his whereabouts. Where he might go. People he might reach out to. He asked if Victoria could remember anything about his family, but nothing came to mind except that he was from a suburb of Philly.

"Do you know anything about his medical history?" Randy asked.

"No, not really. I know he was a pretty regular exerciser, but he was also a heavy drinker. Hard liquor. He was always asking students to go out and party. He could hold his liquor too. I've seen him drink a lot, but I never saw him drunk or even tipsy."

"That's good information. Sounds like a candidate for liver trouble. If he's got that high a tolerance, he's likely done some damage."

There was a lull in the conversation, and she was about to sign off, but then he continued, and part of her was happy he did. It was nice to just talk to someone for a change, not argue. She'd been pretty cold to him when he was in town, and he didn't deserve it.

"So, how's everything else? How's the gallery?"

"Oh, it's going okay. We're on schedule to open soon."

"And how's your little girl?"

"Lila? She's fine, thanks. She's babbling away. I can't wait to hear her first word."

"It's even more wonderful than you're imagining."

"You have kids?"

She turned and saw Nick standing in the doorway. She hadn't heard him come in with the music in the background. *How long has he been standing there?*

"Yes, a son. Six years old. I share custody with my

ex."

"Oh, well, I really need to go now. So just keep me updated, okay?"

"Uh, sure, Victoria. Will do. Have a good night." They hung up, and she turned to Nick, who looked deadly curious.

"Who was that?" Nick asked.

"Huh?"

"Who *was* that, Victoria? It's a simple question."

"Uh, it was Detective Ramirez. Checking in on us. And I wanted him to check on something for me. I have a theory-"

"You wanted to check on how many kids he has?"

"It's not like that, Nick!"

"What's it like then, Victoria? You don't see me on the phone after hours chatting with Sanchez about her personal life."

"He was just making conversation."

"Again, Victoria, detectives don't just 'make conversation,' especially after hours. Don't bullshit me. What's going on? Did something happen between the two of you in Arizona?"

"No! Of course not! We were just talking, Nick. I'd never cross that line."

"Maybe you didn't cross the line, Victoria. But you walked right up to it."

"What's that supposed to mean?"

"I'm going for a run." He turned from her.

"*Wait!* I have to tell you something. It's important."

"Later, Victoria. I need to clear my head." He kept walking.

"It's dark, Nick. Please be careful," she called out to him. But she knew better than to protest further. And he was off.

He was like that. He'd come back. He always did. And the run would calm him down.

LITTLE LOOSE ENDS

Victoria busied herself with Lila and the comfortable routine of her mundane household chores while conflicting thoughts bounced around in her head. *I haven't done anything wrong. Have I?*

It was well past eight o'clock, and Nick still wasn't back. More than two hours had passed since he'd gone out for his jog. He'd taken his cell with him. She went to see if he'd come back for his car and left again, but it was still there. She fired off a text but got no reply. She wasn't really concerned. It was probably just his way of making her stew in her own guilt for chatting it up with Randy Ramirez.

She was heading back up the stairs when there was a knock at the door. *Did Nick forget his key?* She looked out the viewer. It wasn't Nick, and it wasn't the security team. It was the police, and she felt a wave of nausea wash over her. She hesitated, knowing that whatever was on the other side of the door was going to be bad. She opened it and faced them, trying to steel herself for what was to come.

"Ma'am, I'm afraid I have some bad news. Your husband's been in an accident. A hit-and-run." Her knees buckled, and she crouched to the floor with her head in her hands. *So much for my woman's intuition.*

TWENTY-ONE

Jack and Sandra were snuggled up on the sofa in her family room, watching *The Mentalist* reruns. Sandra loved crime shows with a touch of humor, the very kind of shows that Jack tended to avoid, given his background. But he put up with them for her. Besides, the fact that she had a thing for wisecracking detectives seemed to be working out pretty well for him.

He didn't really watch the shows with her; he read instead. Parallel play. He preferred thrillers with fate-of-the-nation-at-stake plots. Everyone needed their fantasy escapes, and since he'd never lived in that world, it was a good one for him to inhabit for an hour or two a day.

They were interrupted by a sound that neither of them had heard in so long that it took a second for him to realize exactly what he was hearing. It was Sandra's landline ringing. Until then, he hadn't really tuned into the fact that she still had a landline.

"Who could that be?" Jack asked.

"Probably a telemarketer," Sandra replied.

But then Jack flipped over his cell and saw a series of texts. He glanced over them and felt his stomach sink. "Sandra, check your cell."

"What is it?" Her face went pale as she read the somber expression on his face. "*Jack?*" Her voice shot up a few octaves.

He thought she might just have a heart attack, so he spit it out quickly to let her know that, although it was bad, it wasn't her worst-case scenario. "It's your son-in-law. He's had an accident. Victoria's trying to contact you."

A momentary look of relief washed over her face. "I thought—"

"I know what you thought." He hugged her tight and then let her go, his hands resting firmly on her shoulders. "Now take a deep breath and call her. She needs you."

Jack watched as she called her daughter and then sprang into action. Nick had been hit by a car while he was jogging—a hit-and-run. His injuries were not likely to be fatal, but they had to get him into surgery right away. They needed to go over and stay with Lila while Victoria went to the hospital. So out the door they went, barely stopping to grab their phones off the sofa.

"Need your purse?" Jack asked as they got in the car, noticing its absence.

"No. Let's just go." He started the car and peeled out, not even bothering to tell the security team where they were headed.

A hit-and-run. That seemed a little too much of a coincidence. *Maybe Victoria wasn't so paranoid after all.* Jack needed to step up his efforts to find Sutton before something even worse happened. It was starting to get personal for Jack now. Very personal.

Victoria stood back and watched helplessly as the medical personnel at Northern Westchester Hospital prepped her husband for surgery. They told her it could have been a lot worse. From what they could piece together, either the car had only grazed him, or he had somehow leapt to the side just in time to avoid a direct hit from behind. The car hit him on his left hip and thigh and sent him flying up in the air. He landed on his right side and also hit his head, and they were awaiting the results of a catscan. A fellow jogger a mile or so behind had stumbled upon him unconscious and called it in, and that, they claimed, was another lucky break. He had some broken bones. Right now, they needed to get him into surgery to set his leg.

"We're taking him back now, Mrs. Mancusio. We'll keep you posted."

Nick's parents were on their way to the hospital along with his older brother, Mark. And now she needed to talk to the police, see what they knew about who did this to her husband. She was sure it was Sutton. And she knew now that all of them were in constant danger. Would they finally believe her now? And if they did, then what?

"Have you found any evidence yet?"

"We're just getting started, ma'am. It was a pretty deserted stretch of road."

"Are there any cameras? Maybe near that complex of stores?" Nick had been jogging in a residential area that was very wooded, the homes lined with tall trees, colorful leaves still clinging to their branches—his normal route. It would be hard to see anything on the road even if the homes hidden behind the trees had cameras. But the road where he was hit butted up against a complex of stores, and she was hoping maybe one of them might have a clearer view of the road.

"We'll try everything to find this person. I promise you."

"I have a feeling it might not be random. He may have been targeted." She went on to explain the situation and was pretty surprised that the officer hadn't heard much, if anything, about it.

"You can follow up with Detective Sanchez about that in the morning."

She was frustrated that nobody seemed to be taking this case seriously. Last year, she couldn't go anywhere without being swarmed by reporters. Now, nobody, including the police, seemed to care that a sociopath was out to get her family—a sociopath with nothing to lose.

Just as they were finishing up, Nick's family showed up.

"Victoria, sweetheart, how are you holding up?" Nick's mother hugged Victoria tight against her chest. She was a zaftig woman who might have been referred to as "stacked" in another era, matronly but with a hint of sensuality that flowed from her long, dark hair and ruby red lips. She was never without her makeup, even tonight. They'd hit it off right away the first time they met, even though they were from different worlds.

"Hi, Anna." She was the quintessential Italian mother: warm, funny, demonstrative, the opposite of Victoria's mother with her stoic sense of emotional restraint. She'd always made sure her daughter-in-law felt comfortable in their Brooklyn Italian family, a culture that was so delightfully different from her own. She loved the way they all talked over each other, how food was the central feature of all occasions, how so much emotion was jam-packed into every interaction, even the quieter ones. Then she turned to his father.

"Hi, Joe." Nick's father was a different story. He'd always been kind to her, and she knew he would do anything for them. But to say he was a man of few words was putting it mildly, especially when it came to women. He was a man's man, and Victoria could see her father-in-law in Nick when he was in his serious mode. But her husband's macho core was wrapped in a sterling sense of humor and an uncanny ability to charm even the most difficult of people, attributes his father lacked. Still, he was a proud and commanding patriarch, and she knew he would do anything to protect them.

"Hi, Victoria. How's my son?" Joe's thick head of hair had grayed a bit over the past decade, but he was in no danger of losing it anytime soon. His dark eyes were the same shade as Nick's, but their shape was different. Nick had his mother's smiling eyes. Joe's eyes never smiled; they just stared straight into the soul. Maybe it was because he didn't blink much and seemed to hold a gaze a bit longer than normal, but she always felt like he could read her mind.

"They just took him into surgery. The prognosis is good. Where's Mark?"

"He's parking the car," Anna replied.

"I'm gonna walk out and meet him." Joe turned and left, leaving Victoria alone with her mother-in-law, which was fine with her.

They passed the time with stories of Lila and her milestones. Anna vowed to come up and see her granddaughter more often. Westchester was like another planet to them, and Victoria knew that they wished they lived closer, even though it wasn't really that far. She thought that might have caused some resentment on Joe's part. That and the fact that after he'd met Victoria, Nick had abandoned the family construction business and gone into real estate up near her family.

"So, how are you two doing these days, dear?"

Had Nick told them about their recent issues? He'd gone up there after their argument, so maybe he had. *Ugh.* She didn't like that thought. Or maybe his mother was assuming that his affair was a hard thing to get over? She had been almost as upset with Nick as Victoria had for his transgression, which was surprising. He'd always been her golden boy.

"We're good, Anna."

She absolutely did not want to get into anything right now, and thankfully Anna didn't press the issue. Then Nick's father and brother came back, and they passed the time talking about the Giants game while she and Anna read on their phones. Finally, after about another two hours, which seemed like an eternity, the doctor came out.

Joe stood first and then Victoria. The doctor did his best to address them both, but Joe's eyes were like magnets, pulling him in. He had a commanding air about him, and the surgeon seemed to have an instinctive feeling that this wasn't the kind of guy you wanted to piss off. He informed them that the surgery had gone very well, but they needed to keep Nick under observation for a few days to make sure there wasn't any swelling in his head from the concussion. He assured them it was all routine and that he'd make a full recovery, including the broken arm and leg, the latter of the two perhaps requiring some physical therapy.

"Thank you, Doctor." Joe gave him a nod, and the surgeon was off, seeming eager for the escape.

Then Anna started to sob, and she fell into her son's arms. Mark was a slightly taller and decidedly less handsome version of Nick and a carbon copy of his father in terms of personality.

"It's fine, Ma. It's all good. Your boy's gonna be just fine." Mark held her while she let out her pent-up emotions. Everyone knew that Nick was her favorite, the youngest of her four boys, and none of them seemed to care.

Victoria didn't know quite what to do with herself, a bit uncomfortable during this public display of emotion, so she did nothing. She just stood there, silent, taking it all in. Then she thought about their drive home. It was so late.

"Do you all want to come and stay over at our place for the night?"

Anna looked at her husband, and he answered for all of them. "I think we'll go home and come back in the morning, Victoria. It'll take less than an hour at this time of night. But thanks for your offer."

She was actually relieved. Her mother? Stark? All of them together? Not good. They said their goodbyes, and they all went on their way. Everyone except Nick, who had a few days ahead of him as they watched for the swelling, and she felt bad that she didn't even have the brain space to ask the doctors about the implications. But then, neither had anyone else. For now, he was okay, and tomorrow was another day.

TWENTY-TWO

Randy had to hand it to Victoria. She had figured out what all of them had failed to deduce: Sutton was a sick man indeed. And he had to agree; it was possible Sutton would stop at nothing to get back at her—if he was well enough to do anything at all. They needed to step up the efforts to find him before it was too late.

After Victoria presented him with her theory, Randy was able to obtain a warrant for Sutton's medical records. It took some persuading—on top of Barrett calling in a few favors—since their case was so thin. But he used that very fact to convince the judge that it otherwise made no sense for Sutton to skip out on the charges. In all probability, they would not stick. So why else would he risk it? And even the judge could see that if they were correct about his fatal illness, he could make for a very dangerous fugitive.

Sutton had stage four liver cancer, likely brought on by a case of Hep B he'd gotten a while back coupled with a lifetime of heavy drinking. It was amazing he'd looked as good as he did when he was arrested, but some people were like that. They got away with it until the last possible moment when the veneer fell away and the hard living caught up with them all at once. He might look completely different by now, which might account for why they weren't getting many hits on his whereabouts.

According to the records, he'd received the diagnosis about eight months prior, and they'd given him between six and eighteen months to live. That explained his decision to run. On the plus side, it was just a matter of time before the Mancusios would no longer need to worry about him, but it was anyone's guess how fast he would decline. The specialist said Sutton could last a lot longer, or he could be dead already. Some people deteriorated gradually, but some took a steep dive.

The news of Randy's discovery was starting to spread around the office, and since he hadn't had a chance to tell anyone it was actually Victoria who'd figured it all out, he was being billed as somewhat of a hero.

He heard Barrett's heels clicking as she approached his door. "Good work, Ramirez." And she was on her way.

Did Ginny Barrett just give me a compliment? Was the brevity of the visit her way of letting him know he was off her unofficial probation list? Or was she just busy? She didn't even stick around long enough for him to ask her if he could go back up to New York to help Sanchez with the investigation, but he was sure she would approve. He needed to see this through. And now that he knew Sutton had nothing to lose, he was more concerned about Jenna Williams' disappearance. She was his witness. His victim. His responsibility.

His phone rang.

"Ramirez here."

It was Detective Sanchez, letting him know that Nick Mancusio had been the victim of a hit-and-run the night before. He got up to speed, feeling a bit guilty for giving the guy such a hard time, and then went to find Barrett. He needed to get up there and do something to help out. And he needed to do it soon, before something even worse happened, maybe next time to Victoria or Lila.

It was just before nine in the morning, and Victoria was on her way up to see Nick. She was feeling a bit numb about everything. She hadn't talked to Sanchez yet, and she was still troubled by the fact that last night she hadn't been able to convince the police this wasn't some random accident, even though it seemed obvious to her that her husband was targeted.

She walked into Nick's room. He was awake but still groggy from the pain meds, facing away from her. She went over to his bed and sat in the chair next to him. She reached over and rested her hand on his arm, but when he tensed up, she removed it, hoping she hadn't hurt him.

"How're you feeling?"

He turned to her, and she tried not to wince when she saw the bruises on his face. It occurred to her that he hadn't seen himself, and she didn't want to let on how bad he looked.

"I've been better." He seemed a little distant, but then maybe it was the pain medication.

"Do you need anything? Are you in any pain?"

"I'm fine." He looked off to the side again rather than up at her, and then she knew it wasn't just the pain meds. He was still upset with her. Was it still about the phone call last night? Or was it the fact that he blamed her for his near-death experience?

"So, they say you're lucky. It could have been worse."

"I don't feel very lucky."

"I'm sure." There was an awkward silence. "Do you remember anything?"

"I remember my wife chatting up some detective on the phone in my kitchen before I left."

"I'm sorry, Nick."

"So you admit it?"

"Admit what?"

"Never mind."

"Do you remember anything about the accident? I'm on my way to see Detective Sanchez."

"She was here already. I told her what I know. Which isn't much. She can fill you in. If this screws up my new job, I'll—"

"It won't. They'll understand." Victoria gave his water pitcher a shake. It was still half full.

"That's not how the world works, Victoria. I need to get better and get out of here."

"They said it'll just be a couple of days."

"We'll see." At least he was looking at her now.

"They're not going to fire you, Nick. And even if they do, we don't need the money. You'll find something else."

"No, *you* don't need the money!" What was he talking about? It was true that the trust was in her name, but all of their other assets were joint, and it was a pretty substantial amount.

"I'm sorry, Nick. Is there anything I can do?" She knew that nothing she could say would make any difference with the mood he was in. She'd be better off leaving and waiting until it passed.

"No. Thank you. I think you've done enough."

"Come on, Nick. I said I was sorry. What more can I do?"

"And I said I was sorry too. Over and over and over. But you couldn't move on. Every day, the little digs.

The guilt trips." It was true, and she could see that now.

"I'm trying, Nick. I really am."

"I guess sometimes trying isn't enough."

"What more can I do?"

"I want you and Lila to stay over at your mother's house for the time being."

"I don't think it's really necess—"

"Stop it! She's my daughter too, Victoria! I don't care if you want to be reckless with your own safety, but you're not going to do it with my daughter. I don't want you two staying there alone right now."

"She's *our* daughter, Nick."

"You asked if you could do anything for me. That's what you can do."

"Okay, I'll stay over at my mother's until you get out. I need to get going. I'll stop by later." She touched his hand again and went to kiss him, but he pulled away. *Okay, if that's the way you want to play it.*

She started toward the door.

"Victoria?"

She turned around, expecting some sort of lame attempt at an apology.

"Yes?"

"I can't do this anymore. I want a divorce." And then he turned away from her.

She could think of no appropriate retort, so she turned, walked out the door, and kept on going.

When Victoria pulled up to her mother's house Stark's car wasn't there. She was glad because, at the moment, all she wanted was to be alone with her mother and Lila. She'd had it with men in general. Her mother opened the door and instantly knew something was up. Victoria opened her mouth to speak, and she felt a gut-wrenching wave of emotion strike her.

"I want to t-talk. I'm ready...t-to..." And then the deluge broke. She started to sob right there on the stoop. Her mother pulled her into the house and into her arms, shutting the door behind them. She ushered Victoria to the sofa, rubbing her back as they walked, and sat her daughter down. Then she left her to cry it out while she went to get some tissues. Victoria's sobs woke Lila up from a nap. She started wailing, but Victoria was powerless to help her. After a few minutes, the tears slowed to a trickle.

"He could have been dead. Lila's father could have been dead."

"But he's not, Victoria. Has he taken a turn for the worse?"

"No."

"So what's the trouble?"

She sucked it all in and looked up to see Lila in her mother's arms, smiling at her. She couldn't help but smile back. Then Lila started to belly laugh, and Victoria couldn't help but laugh too, with tears and snot running down her face. Her mother handed her a tissue, and she made a halfhearted effort to clean herself up. Then she balled up the tissue, threw it to the side, and reached for her daughter.

"Come here, you! Do you think Mommy's funny? Is your mommy a funny bunny?" She held her cheek to cheek and then sat her on her lap.

Her mother seated herself in an armchair kitty-corner to them and handed Lila her learning cube to keep her occupied.

"Nick asked me for a divorce."

"Oh, he's on drugs, Victoria. He doesn't know his own mind. He'll come around."

"I don't know about that, Mom. Things have been pretty tense lately."

"Well, you two have been through a lot. It's understandable."

"We've tried marriage counseling, but it hasn't really helped."

"Telling your problems to a complete stranger? I'm so surprised that hasn't cleared things right up." Her mother's eyes widened.

"People say it helps."

"People say a lot of things. It's pretty simple, Victoria. If you want the marriage to work, you both figure out how to make it work. If you don't want it to work, it won't, and there's nothing anyone can do for you."

They sat there quietly for a while, watching Lila try to fit a square piece into a triangular space in her cube. When she started making a fuss, Victoria went to guide her to the right slot, but her mother intervened. "Let her figure it out."

She didn't feel like arguing, but she knew this was what it would be like if they moved in, and none of them could take much of that for very long.

"So, Victoria, do you want it to work? And are you willing to do whatever it takes?"

"I don't know, Mom." What exactly did her mother have in mind? A lobotomy? Infidelity was a hard thing to get past. But was infidelity their problem or just a symptom of something deeper? Was it ever really about one thing?

"Well, that's what you need to find out."

"How?"

"I don't know, Victoria. For your father and me, it was a trial separation. But we didn't have a child yet."

"He said he wanted a divorce, Mom."

"I expect he'll change his mind. But do you want a

divorce? Maybe you do."

"No. I don't want that for Lila."

"I'm not talking about Lila. I'm talking about you. Do *you* want a divorce, Victoria? Do you still want to be with Nick or not?"

"I don't know."

"Well, he's probably picked up on that, so it seems like you've got some soul-searching to do."

"Nick wants me to stay here with Lila while he's in the hospital."

"I think that's a good idea. Now, do you want some coffee? Breakfast?"

"I'm actually pretty hungry." Her mother got up to go to the kitchen.

"Mom?"

"Yes?"

"I want to see the DNA results. Today."

"Right now?"

"Maybe after I eat?"

"Good plan."

Lila was getting restless, so Victoria put her on the ground, letting her blow off some steam with her power crawls. She was getting faster, and it was more and more work to run after her. She could pull herself up now and get into all kinds of mischief, and Victoria expected her to be an early walker. Things would only get worse then. She would need to bring a nanny back into the picture soon, especially with her gallery opening next week and Nick being in the city all the time with his new job. *And possibly his new home.*

Her previous nanny was long gone, snatched up by one of the many equally busy but not quite as wealthy families in the area, so she was starting from scratch. She could probably steal the woman back with the right incentive, but that seemed a bit cutthroat, especially if she was going to try harder to have some female friends in the future.

Her mother came in, and Victoria put Lila in the playpen. Then they chatted about nothing in particular, sipping coffee and nibbling their scrambled eggs, toast, and fruit. It felt almost like a normal day, but when she felt satiated, she reminded herself that it wasn't.

"Okay, let me see it." Victoria held out her hand, and her mother gave the envelope to her. She turned it over to open the flap, carefully at first, trying to gently nudge it, but it was sticking. Then an urgent need to know came over her, and she just ripped the side off, pulled the paper out and unfolded it.

"And?" Her mother's wide eyes reminded Victoria that this was a big moment for her too. All these years she'd never known who was the father of her child.

"It says the results of the paternity test are negative."

"Oh my God!"

"Wait, that means—"

"Sam Coleman isn't your father, Victoria. Your father was your father! Oh my God, Victoria. I can't believe it. I'm so relieved!" Her mother's hand went to her stomach to steady herself as tears of joy started flowing from her eyes.

"Wait. Sam Coleman's *not* my father?"

"I have to see it for myself. Let me see it!" Her mother snatched the sheet of paper from Victoria's fingers. She looked down at it and then held it up to the heavens. "See? She's yours, Hugh. All yours!"

"Wait, Mom."

"Yes, Victoria?"

"Now, you're sure it's only the two of them? There's no other secret rendezvous you want to tell me about? 'Cause now would be the time." Victoria flashed her a sly smile.

Her mother bonked her over the head with the DNA results, but she was still smiling. "Such a smarty-pants! But I guess I had that coming. Yes, Victoria. I'm sure! Your father's your father, in all ways possible."

They reached over and hugged each other, both of them laughing and crying at the same time. Then Lila joined them. Victoria turned to see her standing up, holding the rail of her playpen, bouncing up and down, laughing her head off, eager to get in on the fun. She picked her daughter up and brought her over with them. Although she wasn't a religious person, Victoria said a tiny prayer that somehow, her father was here with them, sharing in their joy.

TWENTY-THREE

A third week had passed since Sutton's disappearance, and there was nothing new on any front. Nick's hit-and-run case was going nowhere, and her marriage was in limbo. She and Nick had decided on a trial separation, which was fine with her. Victoria was staying at her mother's house with Lila, and he was at their place. He was planning to get a temporary rental in the city near work starting that weekend, so she was in the process of moving back home. They all agreed that with a round-the-clock security detail they'd be safe there. She and her mother were doing well enough, but she didn't want to push it.

It was early morning, and Victoria was at the office, but she needed to get over to the gallery. The grand opening was this weekend. Her big return to center stage. And it needed to go well. Nick would have Lila the entire two days—they were alternating weekends—so she could focus on work. There were some upsides to the joint custody arrangement. And she reminded herself that he wasn't dead. Lila could have no father at all, and then where would she be? Things could always be worse, and she tried to remind herself of that every day. They'd had no further incidents or hacks on any of their electronics, and they all felt pretty confident that the house was secure. She had opted for old-school baby monitors, though. Two sets. One for her and one for Nick. *Is that how Lila's life will be from now on? Two sets of everything?*

At least Nick's recovery was going faster than expected. He was still on crutches for the broken leg, so he'd hired a nanny to watch Lila a few days a week and tend to the house for him. It made her uneasy thinking of another woman in her home. She had no idea who the person was, and that made her even more uncomfortable, but she needed to get used to it. If they got divorced, that's how it would be. And, plus, it wasn't like the woman was alone with Lila. Nick was still home, recovering. At least until the weekend, when he was moving to the city.

It was hard to sort out how she felt about her marriage because the separation didn't feel quite real. It felt more as if he'd gone away for a while, and she was visiting with her mother. She expected it to hit her more when she moved back home. And if it didn't, that would be good to know. Maybe she was ready to move on after all.

"Hey, how's my favorite supermom?" Charles popped his head into her office.

"Not feeling very super today."

"Fake it till you make it, babe." Charles didn't seem overly concerned about her separation from Nick, and she guessed that made sense. He'd never been a big fan of her husband's.

"Don't worry, I will. I'm just having doubts about the gallery. The exhibit. All of it."

"It'll be fine. You worry too much."

"I think I worry just the right amount."

"How's the hot detective?"

"I'm assuming he's cooler now. It's November. Even Arizona's pretty temperate this time of year."

"Very funny. Okay, you don't want to play. My only chance to live vicariously, old married guy that I am. But fine."

"I know for a fact that your marriage is still sizzling hot, and you're not even forty, so don't blame it on Roger. You're just trying to get me to move on because you never liked Nick."

"That's not true."

"Isn't it?"

"I'm not falling for this. I'll wait until you're divorced. I don't want this coming back to bite me in the ass. You get back with him, and it's like, *You hate my husband. Blah blah blah.*"

"Oh, come on. It's always been obvious there's tension between the two of you. You act so awkward around each other. I can't stand to be there when you're in the same room together. Why is it like that?"

"I don't know. I think he just feels so uncomfortable around me. I know the type. I've dealt with it my whole life."

"What type is that?" Charles gave her a wide-eyed look that said *Duh*. "Wait. Are you saying he's homophobic?"

"Not overtly."

"Not at all! I swear. You're misreading him. He's uncomfortable around you because you're from money, like me. He's always felt out of place in our circles. He's from Brooklyn, Charles. He's out of his element here."

"I mean, maybe at first. But still?"

"I don't know. He's pretty happy to be working in the city again. Our whole marriage has revolved around my world."

"Are you excusing his affair now? Because he's from Brooklyn? Like Angie? And she was from *his world*?"

"No! Not at all. That's not even what I meant. Let's just drop it, okay?" There was no sense in going down this road with Charles. It wasn't at all productive. She'd gone to work to forget about her personal problems, not analyze them. Maybe there were some drawbacks to being in business with a close friend, but she couldn't imagine it any other way.

"Consider it dropped."

"So let's review the plan for the opening."

And they went about their business, and Victoria was able to block out, just for a few hours, all the insanity of her life and focus on pleasant details like what time to bring out the first round of passed hors d'oeuvres and whether to go with a moscato or a sauvignon blanc for their white wine option.

Charles had left for the day, and Victoria was alone, working late in her office. She was about to call it a day. She'd done all she could at the gallery and was feeling better about it. Lila was with Nick, and she wasn't too eager to get to her mother's house. She saw a call from Wade coming in and picked up.

"I got a hit on facial recognition! At a convenience store in Peekskill."

"Oh my God. Can you text it to me? I'm going down to the station. Can you meet me there?"

"Not right now. I have a job to finish up."

"Okay. Send me everything you have." Victoria called down to the station, but Sanchez was gone for the day. She called Stark, and he said he'd meet her there. A strange combination of fear and excitement coursed through her veins. Might they actually be able to track him down after all?

But then what? That thought kept nagging at her.

What had he done that they could actually prove? Jenna wasn't around to press charges for the assault. They were unlikely to be able to tie him to Nick's hit-and-run. He had skipped out on a court appearance; that much was true. But Jeff Malone only got fifteen years on his plea deal for murder two. What would Sutton get for his minor transgression? Probation? But she couldn't worry about that now.

As she walked into the station, she heard her phone ping. It was a text from an unknown number.

It's a shame about Nick.

She charged into the station, eager to get their tech people on it, although she was sure most everyone had left for the day. She left a message for Wade asking him to come to the police station when he finished up, thinking that maybe he could fill in some of the blanks if their top people were gone. As she sat and waited, her mind drifted to Sutton and how much he'd screwed up her life.

Even though she had an ulterior motive for the therapy sessions, she had to admit that her therapist had a point. What happened to her was a violation of trust. Nick had mentioned it many times, that he felt she held back. That she was closed off. She had always attributed it to their cultural differences. But maybe there was more to it. She was so young when the incident happened, not quite fully formed. Perhaps if it had happened later, when she was more confident, she would have handled it differently. But then that's what made Sutton a predator. He wouldn't go after a strong, confident woman, would he?

Victoria's car was in the parking lot when Jack arrived. He hurried in to meet her and found her waiting in the lobby, which didn't surprise him. This wasn't exactly a high-priority case, and it was late in the day.

"I called Detective Sanchez; she'll be here in twenty." He turned to the officer at the front desk. "Is there anyone on the tech team we can talk to while we wait for Detective Sanchez?" The officer was young. Apparently new. Jack didn't recognize him, and it seemed to be mutual, which didn't sit well with him. He'd only been gone a few months.

"I'll call back to them. What did you say your name was?"

"Jack Stark."

The officer's eyes widened, and he snapped into action and picked up the phone. "Yes, I've got Jack Stark here to see you." He turned to Stark. "He said he'll be right out. Sorry for the delay."

Jack held his hand up and gave it a quick wave as they walked farther into the precinct. Soon they were sitting in an interview room with a technician. Victoria showed the photo and the text to him. The photo wasn't very clear, but you could see him in profile. It was hard for Jack to think that anyone could make a positive ID from it, but it was possible.

"It's him. I'm sure of it. Can you trace the phone?" she asked.

"Maybe. It's a burner but thankfully not a dumb one. I can try an IMSI catcher, but it might be out of range."

"And?" Victoria looked over at Jack.

"It means he can try to ping it and get a location. The old-school phones were harder to trace, but they're in short supply these days. The ones they sell now, we have more tools to track them. It's harder to keep them off the grid."

"Do you need a warrant?" Victoria asked.

"Nope."

Victoria and Jack waited while the technician did his thing. Then someone called out to Jack that someone was here to see Victoria. Jack went out to find Wade Higgins in the lobby, and that was the last thing he needed right now.

"Hello, Detective Stark."

"Hello, Wade. I'm retired now. Just call me Jack."

"Hi, Jack."

"Come. Let's see if we can put our heads together." Jack winced a little when those words left his lips. He'd probably rather get a root canal than collaborate with Wade Higgins on anything. But Lexi and Victoria seemed to be fans, for some reason he couldn't fathom, and he didn't want to make an issue of it. Just as they were walking in, Lexi showed up. She and Wade shared a mutual interest in otherworldliness. Apparently, her aunt also had "the gift," and he was quite happy to let Lexi and Higgins chat it up while they all walked back to the interview room.

"So, where are we on everything?" Sanchez asked the technician upon arrival.

"I got the IMEI."

Jack turned to Victoria. "That's the actual identity of the phone."

"And it was purchased at that store in Peekskill," the tech guy said.

"He's using a smart burner?" Higgins asked.

"Yeah."

"That's odd," Higgins replied. "The texts Victoria got before. They were from old-school phones."

"The older ones are harder to hack, right? So why's he using a smart burner now?" Victoria asked. But nobody had a chance to answer.

"I've got him!" The technician stood up and clapped his hands together. Then he sat back down. "Well, I have a location on the phone, at least."

All eyes turned to Lexi. She sprang into action and ordered a team of uniforms to the address—no sirens, she instructed. Peekskill was at least a thirty-minute drive, so they'd never get there in time. All they could do was sit tight and try to monitor any further movement on the phone. In the meantime, she called Randy Ramirez to let him know they had a hit on his fugitive.

Victoria's unanswered question lingered in the air. Why would Sutton suddenly opt for a more traceable smart burner?

About ten minutes later, the officers reported back that they'd found the phone, but not Sutton, sitting on the stoop of a small home in a working-class area of Peekskill inhabited by a now quite confused and mildly agitated elderly couple. The husband had called their attorney son, who informed the officers that they would have a lawsuit on their hands if they didn't explain themselves. It had ended fairly amiably as far as the elderly couple was concerned. But it left them with proverbial egg on the face, and Jack knew it was only a matter of time before the department would tire of this, lose interest, and move on.

Victoria was fuming as she drove away from the police station. But then, she should have known better. She shouldn't have taken the bait. Of course Sutton knew they could track him with a smart burner. He was way too clever to get tripped up by something like that. Now what? It seemed she couldn't win. If she hadn't told the police, they'd never have found the phone. She could only assume he wanted her to tell the police. But why? And how much longer would she be able to keep them engaged in this wild goose chase of hers? Not very long, in all likelihood. Maybe that was why he'd done it. He knew that they'd all look ridiculous, and then maybe a higher-up would get tired of it and pull the resources to track him. She should have kept it to herself a bit longer, until she knew for sure that she had him.

But how? Wade wouldn't have been able to do that trick with the phone. They'd told her it was proprietary NSA-level software. Maybe it was and maybe it wasn't. But even if they could get it, in all probability Sutton wouldn't come at her the same way again. She needed to go on the offensive. Get one step ahead of him. Just stay calm and think logically.

There was something gnawing at the edge of her consciousness. Something about Sutton and his past. Peekskill? Did he have a relative in Peekskill? Or somewhere on the Hudson? She let her mind wander on the drive back to her mother's house, thinking back to the brief conversations they'd had back when she was an undergrad.

Then it hit her. He had an aunt who lived across the river in a town called Danburg. She remembered it now. He'd mentioned it one time. And he used to go to some camp on Storm King Mountain. *Yes!* They had talked about the river and how different the view was depending on what side you were on. That had to mean something. And it would make sense that he would go somewhere familiar. An aunt in Danburg. It was better than nothing.

And it really was the perfect place to hide out. At first glance, Danburg didn't look like a dangerous place. A little run-down, maybe. Some parts more so than others. But not the kind of place you'd fear walking around at night or even during the day. But the crime rate was shockingly high, especially for a small town, and it would be an easy place for a fugitive to blend in, or at least easier than the more exclusive towns on this side of the river. So she decided she'd focus on Danburg and go from there. Step up the facial recognition there. It wasn't much, but it gave her some hope. And she really needed hope right now. Very badly.

TWENTY-FOUR

Victoria still had a business to run. This gallery was her dream, and she wasn't going to let Sutton get in the way of it. Her idea for the opening was to use the gallery space to connect the Hudson River school's rich history and its contribution to American art with more contemporary American artists who held the same reverence for American landscape and nature. She did this by combining an educational exhibit highlighted with a few high-end pieces combined with a selection of more contemporary artists from different regions of the country, showing off the various landscapes. She hoped to funnel leads from the retail gallery to her private art dealership while also giving emerging artists a chance to develop a following. And she could also educate people about the Hudson Valley region and its importance.

Right now, she was having a moment of self-doubt, hoping it wasn't too much for people to take in. This evening was the VIP opening, invitation only, and she was single-mindedly focused on it. It signified not only her return to the art world after her brief maternity leave but her return to the limelight after a year of turmoil and humiliation. She had skipped her educational foundation's annual fall gala benefit, instead opting to donate a percentage of the gallery proceeds, so it had been over a year since she'd been in the public eye. She needed the evening to go well.

The guest list included a veritable who's who of Manhattan's elite, most of them rich and unknown but a few who might garner some media attention. The timing was good. They were headed into late November and peak tourist season had already passed, so the town was still lively but not packed to the brim. Christmas was just around the corner, and they were headed into prime shopping season. Hopefully, sales would go well and perhaps spill over to the other shops and restaurants in town eager to capitalize on their traditional October momentum.

Victoria had arrived at the crack of dawn to get things ready and had gone back to change into her evening attire, and there was nothing much to do but wait. She was putting the finishing touches on the displays just as Charles walked through the door.

"What do you think?"

"It looks amazing, Victoria."

"Are you sure? I know we went back and forth about what to put in this central spot, but I decided on the Thomas Cole."

"It's perfect."

"What about the background information? It's not too pedantic?"

"What? No, you worry too much. It's not like you're giving a lecture. If people want to read it, they can read it. If they don't, they can move on."

"Okay. Give it a spin. See how it feels."

Charles walked around the gallery while Victoria checked again on the refreshments and fussed with the placement of the reception table.

"It looks great. I'm glad you mixed the regions together. I like the way the brighter pieces from

Hawaii and the Southwest offset the more muted tones of the Northeast and Pacific Northwest. And this one. It's spectacular. Those cliffs. Where is it?" Charles asked.

"North shore of Kauai. Marionette Taboniar is the artist. I'm due for a trip back there. Haven't been since high school."

"And I like the Nicole Miller on you too. But careful you don't break your neck in those shoes."

Victoria rarely wore heels, but today she was sporting a pair of red-and-white Manolo Blahnik pumps to complement her royal blue dress in line with her very American art theme.

"My feet are going to hate me tomorrow."

"If you live that long."

"Very funny."

She looked around the gallery. She'd made her dream a reality, and that counted for something. It was time to get back in the game, and she was ready.

"I have to run out for a bit. I'd say break a leg, but in your case..."

She whacked him with a program. "Stop! You're making me paranoid!"

"I'll see you around six." Charles left her alone with her creation, and she had to admit, even to her critical eye, that it all looked amazing. Then she felt a pang of sadness that she and Nick weren't sharing this moment together. He'd done an amazing job on the renovation. But this was her dream, not his, and he was off pursuing his own now.

In a moment of weakness, she took a few photos and texted them to him. After a few minutes, he texted back with a smiley emoji and a photo of Lila with a face full of strained carrots. That reminded her that however spectacular this gallery was, it was only her second-greatest creation.

Randy had gotten into town that afternoon. He'd heard about Victoria and Nick Mancusio's separation from Sanchez in the context of the case. Mancusio apparently had secured a place in the city near his new job, and Victoria had just moved back to her house from her mother's. Although he had to admit the thought of seeing Victoria again gave him a rush, he felt a hint of sadness for their baby daughter. Victoria hadn't been in contact with him since that last phone call the night her husband was hit by a car. He always suspected there was a story there, but he hadn't felt comfortable enough to call and ask her. He decided that stopping by her gallery opening might be a good way to run into her.

He walked in, and was greeted by a young man at a reception table.

"May I have your name, please?"

"Oh, I didn't realize you needed to have..." He glanced at the name tags and recognized one of the names—the former mayor of New York City. He felt like an idiot for just dropping by.

"Yes, tonight is invitation only. Tomorrow we'll be open to the general public." He looked himself up and down. Jeans. Sweater. Leather jacket. *Yup, that's me. The general public.*

He was about to walk out the door, when he saw Victoria. She caught his eye and held up a finger to say *one minute*. He waited, and she headed over. She'd always been dressed casually when he'd seen her before. Jeans, maybe a nice blouse, so he wasn't prepared for what he saw coming at him. She wore a royal blue dress that hugged her trim figure. The hem sat above the knee and showed off her long, lean legs, which extended gracefully into a pair of four-inch-heel designer pumps. He'd never seen her legs before, and it was worth the trip just to get a glimpse of them.

"Randy! Nice to see you."

"I'm sorry, I'll come back tomorrow. I didn't know that—"

"Don't be silly. It's fine. Nate, can you make Detective Ramirez a name tag, please?"

"Of course. How would you like it to read, sir?"

"Randy Ramirez is fine."

"So, do you want to come and take a look?"

"Yes, of course."

Then someone called out to Victoria, and he could tell she was conflicted about leaving him, fish out of water that he was.

"Victoria, it's your big night. Go. We can catch up later."

"Are you sure?"

"Absolutely."

"Maybe tomorrow? Do you have plans?"

"Plans? No, I'm kinda new in town."

"Right." She flashed him a polite smile. "Well, please stay and enjoy the opening, and let's shoot for tomorrow. We can put our heads together and make some progress on the case."

"Absolutely." *Of course. She wants to work on the case.*

"Great."

"I'll let you get back to your guests."

An attractive man around Victoria's age called over to her and started to walk over to them. Was this her date? Had he totally misread her?

"And who's your mystery guest?" The man didn't seem jealous. It sounded like he was teasing her.

"Charles, this is Randy Ramirez. The detective from Arizona I told you about? Randy, this is my business partner."

"I've heard a lot about you," Charles said, his hands full with his drink and some flyers.

That surprised Randy. Why had her partner heard so much about him? Maybe this wasn't hopeless after all.

"Glad you could make it. But I'm afraid I need to borrow Victoria for a while."

"Of course. I'll be fine."

Charles put his hand on Victoria's shoulder and guided her over to a cluster of VIP-looking people in the corner.

Randy went to have a look around the gallery, and he had to say, even though he wasn't an art aficionado, he thoroughly enjoyed the exhibit. The paintings captured the essence of the different regions of the country, and as a visitor to the region he found the educational part about the Hudson River school painters surprisingly engaging. Overall, it seemed to be a brilliant idea for marketing both the region and its artwork.

He remembered the first time he saw her, walking into the precinct with a baby strapped to her front, a frightened new mother in need of his assistance, and thought how it might be different if that's who she really was. But here in her element, he could see she was Victoria Vander Hofen—and she was totally out of his league.

———

Jack arrived with Sandra to a jam-packed scene filled with important people, and he couldn't think of a worse way to spend an evening. But Sandra looked lovely, even more elegant than she had at Victoria's charity function over a year ago when they'd first met.

LITTLE LOOSE ENDS

And she was in her element, making the rounds. Jack stopped to chat with the mayor, who was quite surprised to learn that he and Sandra Vander Hofen were a couple. It was their first time in public together, and it was sure to raise some eyebrows. Then he noticed Randy Ramirez standing around with a dazed look on his face. *What's he doing here?* Jack excused himself and went to find out.

"Randy! I didn't know you were coming."

"I wasn't. I sort of crashed the party. With Victoria's blessing, of course. I was actually on my way out."

"I'll walk out with you. Any news on the case?"

"We're working on all of it. Trying to get a hit on Jenna Williams or Sutton."

"What's your best guess? Do you think Sutton had anything to do with Jenna's disappearance, or do you think she just ran?"

"Jenna's pretty street-smart. My guess would be that she just cut her losses and bolted. We're not ruling it out, that he may have done something to her, but they're not going to let me stay on this case forever. It's just not that important in the overall scheme of things."

"I know. I get it. Lexi Sanchez said the same thing. Especially after he sent us on that wild goose chase."

"What's your plan?"

"I've got some irons in the fire trying to track him. Old sources of mine. I'll let you know if any of them pan out. I suppose he could even be back in your area. He could be anywhere."

"I know. We're keeping tabs."

"Let's keep in touch."

"Sounds good. I'll be going now, Jack."

"Throwing me back to the wolves, eh?"

"You better get used to it with that family."

"I guess."

Randy left, and Jack went back into the reception.

Sandra called out to him as he made his way past the reception table. "Jack! I was looking all over for you. Come meet my friend."

She grabbed his arm and off they went. Even though he'd rather have been home reading a book, it made him happy to see Sandra so excited, and he knew that part of it was because of him. She'd been alone for a long time, and so had he. Too long, so he didn't complain. He charged around the room with her, making the rounds, snatching the occasional canapé off a passing tray and popping it into his mouth to stop his stomach from grumbling.

TWENTY-FIVE

The opening had gone even better than she'd expected. An article in the Sunday *New York Times* called her exhibit a "brilliant call to action" on the importance of preserving America's natural beauty in the face of climate change, and the local media praised her for helping to spotlight the region's importance in the overall history of the country and development of its art. There were a few reviews critical of the fact that the exhibit focused on landscapes instead of on some of America's more pressing social issues, and one noted that it lacked edginess by failing to include some more abstract interpretations of landscape. But she'd expected that, and it didn't bother her at all.

With her opening out of the way, she had time to focus again on her mission of finding Sutton, and she planned to spend the morning on it before going over to check on the gallery. Now that she was back home, she'd set up the facial recognition software program on her home office computer and had it scanning the area around Danburg. Narrowing the focus might help get a hit. She'd also done some digging and found that Sutton's aunt had died about five years back. Her house had been sold, but Victoria figured she'd hone in on that neighborhood, thinking he might go somewhere familiar. She was interrupted by the sound of her phone and thought it might be Randy. But it was not.

She and Nick had been texting, but they hadn't talked on the phone recently. She picked up immediately, her mind flashing to Lila and her safety.

"Is something wrong?"

"No. Nothing's wrong. I just saw the Sunday *Times*. Congratulations."

"It's your victory too, Nick."

"Not really."

"How's Lila?"

"She seems to be a real city girl. Loves Central Park. The carousel was a hit, but not as much as the ducks."

"At the pond?"

"Yeah."

There was a prolonged silence as she pictured Lila's face, full of joy, laughing at the ducks. And she'd missed it. "Was there anything else?"

"Um, no. Not really. I know it was a big night. I just wanted to say congratulations."

"Thanks, Nick. But I need to go now."

He sounded a bit disappointed that she'd cut it off, but then what did he expect? He was the one who'd asked for the divorce. Or separation. Or whatever the hell this was. And she didn't appreciate the mixed messages, even though she had sent him that text yesterday. It was all so muddled and confusing, and it made her very uncomfortable. One way or another, she needed to get her life back on a definitive track. Either cut her losses and move on or get back together and try to make it work. She wasn't planning to live in limbo forever.

She thought about Randy and his visit to the gallery the night before. And her powerful attraction to him the first time they'd met. He was the first guy she'd had any attraction to since the day she met Nick, and she wondered about that. What would have happened if she'd met Randy prior to Nick's affair, back when she was happily married? Was it just a coincidence that it had taken that long to meet another man she was attracted to, or was it because the affair had fundamentally changed things forever?

She knew Randy was interested in her, and she had every right to pursue him. So what was stopping her? Was it the fact that she hadn't been with another man in over a decade? Or the idea that there would be no turning back if she went down that road? Maybe some time with Randy was just what she needed. A chance to find out if she was ready to move on. She called him and left a message suggesting they meet up for an early dinner, and then she got back to her mission.

Since Sutton was likely a very sick man, she was checking footage from hospitals and clinics in the area. He would probably need palliative care at some point, so she started to research home infusion IV services. There were two main companies in the region, both on the Westchester side of the Hudson. She called both, but only one serviced the town of Danburg. Then she found a way to hack into their delivery calendar and found two clients with Danburg addresses—the first information with the potential to lead somewhere.

She was trying not to get her hopes up. The whole Danburg thing could be totally wrong. Maybe he wasn't even there. And Sutton could still be doing just fine as far as his health. But she needed to keep trying. Keep moving forward, even if the chances were slim.

But then she got a hit on facial recognition at a gas station in Danburg. Sutton was in the driver's seat of a car, his head tilted out the window like he was asking the attendant a question. It was hard to make out the make or model. His face was clean-shaven, and he didn't appear to be aware of the camera like that time at the airport.

I've got you, Sutton. And I'm coming for you.

She planned to go on a reconnaissance mission the next day to the two residences on the other side of the Hudson to see if there were any signs of him at either of them. That was enough progress for one day, so she closed up shop and headed to town to check on things at the gallery.

It was almost six, and Randy had texted that he was on his way over for dinner. He had eagerly accepted her invitation and asked her to go out, but Victoria decided that eating in public was too risky, so she offered to host him. She and Nick were still married, and most people didn't have a clue they were even separated. She didn't want to fan the flames of gossip and speculation. She'd thought about cooking, but she didn't have time. And on some level, she knew her mother was right; she wasn't that great a cook. She didn't have much interest in improving, either, but she did appreciate a good meal, so she picked up some takeout from Mint, one of her favorite spots in Tarrytown.

The sound of the gate buzzer alerted her to Randy's arrival, and she let him in, preparing to face her first date—if this was a real date—in over a decade.

"Hey, Victoria." He wore khakis and a navy polo shirt, and he smelled great. Whatever he was wearing for an aftershave, it certainly had an effect on her.

"Hi, Randy. Come in."

He handed her a bottle of pinot noir and started to

lean over like he was going to give her a peck on the cheek, but then he pulled back and rested a hand on her arm instead. She felt comforted that she wasn't the only one confused about the meaning of tonight's rendezvous.

"Thanks for having me over."

They made some small talk as they made their way to the living room. She asked him to have a seat while she grabbed some wineglasses from the kitchen. *So far, so good.* Of course, as far as the case was concerned, this was going to be a one-way street. She wasn't giving up anything about Sutton until she knew for sure that her information was good.

They continued with their chitchat, and after a bit, they made their way over to the dining room table. She'd set the table so they would be kitty-corner. It felt intimate, but not too much so. She'd thought about candles but decided against them.

"You shouldn't have gone to so much trouble," he said.

"Don't worry. All I did was set the table. The food's from Mint. I'm not the greatest in the kitchen."

"I would have taken you—"

"Not a great idea. Everyone knows me around here."

"Right. Good thinking."

So far, the case hadn't come up, and although that wasn't the primary purpose for the invitation, she did want to know his thoughts. She learned that he was divorced and shared custody of his son, and he was educating her a bit about the challenges of the two-household situation. *If nothing else, maybe he could be a good friend.*

"So, have you made any progress on the case? Any idea where he is?"

"Not yet. But we're working on it."

"How hard?" She offered him a hesitant smile.

Randy shrugged. "There's a limit to how many resources my department will put toward a case that seems to have moved out of our jurisdiction. But I'll do what I can. How about you? Anything from Stark?"

"Nothing useful." She let out a sigh and her shoulders sank. "I don't know how much more I can take of this." Then Randy put his hand on top of hers. It felt good, so she tried to let herself be vulnerable for a change. "I'm just so tired of living like this, Randy. Wondering if today is the day he finally gets me. First, the affair. Then the murder case. Now this? Living in fear all the time? For me? For Lila?"

"It doesn't show. And your opening was spectacular, by the way."

They paused, and Randy took a sip of his wine.

"Thanks." The reminder of her gallery and her career snapped Victoria out of a rare moment of weakness. "And I'm sorry. I'm fine. Most of the time I'm fine. I shouldn't burden you with this."

"Don't be sorry, Victoria."

"Let's just forget it and enjoy our dinner." She noticed that he looked a little disappointed that she'd pulled back, but she was a private person, and she'd shared enough for one night.

They talked more about their backgrounds. He had a degree in criminology with a minor in psychology from the University of Arizona, and he'd gotten extensive training in criminal profiling. She talked a bit about her graduate work at Columbia. She left out the part about meeting her husband there, that fateful day on the Columbia quad with her hair blowing in the wind while he watched her try in vain to produce a decent sketch for her drawing class. She told him about the nonprofit she'd started that provided college scholarships to students pursuing degrees in fine arts and art history. And she realized that getting to know someone was a lot of work. What to leave out, what to include.

As they got to the end of the meal, she offered him coffee, but he declined. Then she suggested they take their wine to the living room. She was walking in front of him, but he was very close behind, so close that she could feel his breath on the back of her neck and take in the intoxicating mix of the musky aftershave and his rugged masculine scent. It lit her up inside. It was new and exciting and different. She thought it would feel weird or awkward, but it didn't.

As they got to the sofa, he bent down to put his wineglass on the coffee table and his head grazed the side of her neck, heightening her senses. As he stood back up, she placed her glass down and turned to him. Their lips met in a frenzy of abandon as they grabbed each other and gave in to their mutual attraction. He was so tall, it strained her neck to kiss him, but she didn't care. After a while, he lifted her up and placed her on the sofa, and they made out for what felt like an eternity.

Then they started to take their encounter to the next level. It felt good, his hands on her. She let him explore her body a bit, and she followed suit, raw energy overriding her inhibitions. His hands were large and powerful, yet he stroked her leg gently. She ran her hands over his muscular back, and the kissing grew more intimate. But then something hit her, and it stopped her dead in her tracks.

Birth control!

She'd been trying to get pregnant for so many years that the issue of birth control was completely off her radar. She placed her hand on his, hitting the emergency brake. Randy's reaction was immediate. He pulled back, sat up, and brushed himself off.

"I'm sorry, Victoria. We should take it slow."

"Don't be sorry, Randy. You didn't do anything wrong." She remembered how it felt when her mother had come clean about her paternal predicament. The last thing she wanted was to be on the other side of that conversation, with her child staring back at her in disbelief. *Ah, well, you see, I'm not really sure which one's your father.*

"You're not ready. It's fine. We got carried away, is all."

"It's just not great timing." How could she be so stupid? Her mother had been ten years younger. Practically a kid. Victoria wasn't a kid. She needed to do better. For all she knew, she could be pregnant right now. As much as she wanted a sibling for Lila, this wasn't the way to go about it.

"It's all about timing, isn't it?"

And from that point on, things were painfully awkward between them. After a bit, he went on his way. They talked about next time, but she felt like they both knew it wasn't going to happen. What were the chances of ending a marriage and then meeting the love of your life on your very first date in over a decade? Next to zero, she imagined.

Randy was a great guy, and she was for sure attracted to him, and it was good to know that she could be attracted to someone besides Nick. But he was too good of a guy to use while she was still on the rebound. And right now, she didn't need that kind of complication in her life anyway. She had to focus on finding Sutton and eliminating that threat from her life once and for all. Only then would anything else even matter.

Randy wasn't that surprised by the way things had turned out. He realized it was unprofessional in the first place to even let things go as far as they had, and it was totally unrealistic to think that things could ever work with her. Her life was here, and his was in Arizona. He'd realized that the minute he'd walked into the gallery, and he was disappointed in himself for even taking her up on the dinner offer. She was in a vulnerable state, and he should have known better.

Plus, he still had a job to do. Tomorrow he would meet with Detective Sanchez and try to make the most of his time here since he was pretty sure they wouldn't send him up again. He thought back on that night on the phone, when she'd hung up very abruptly. He had the feeling that her husband had overheard them. It didn't matter to him in terms of Victoria and their relationship, but it held some significance for the case. Was Sutton escalating? Had he taken out Jenna Williams and then tried for Nick Mancusio? Or had Mancusio been distracted by his emotional state when he was out on his run?

He reminded himself that Nick and Victoria Mancusio weren't his responsibility, so he decided tomorrow he would focus on Jenna Williams. She was his witness. He'd go over to the apartment again, check video in the area, ATMs, and see if he could find some evidence as to what happened to his witness. And, of course, there was his fugitive. He for sure needed to focus on finding him.

But as he got in his car and drove away, a feeling of sadness washed over him in spite of himself because he knew it would be the last he'd ever see of Victoria Mancusio.

Victoria picked up the wineglasses to head in and clean up from dinner when she caught a glimpse of her photo on the fireplace mantel. It was taken in Central Park, the upper part near Columbia, a few weeks after she met Nick.

She set the wineglasses back down, walked over, and picked it up. That smile on her face. It could light up the whole room. She remembered the feeling, looking into Nick's eyes as he snapped away on the camera and joked with her at the same time. He was taking a photography class, and she was playing the model. When was the last time she'd smiled like that? When was the last time she'd felt like that? Her hair was really long then, and Nick had captured it perfectly, with the sun glistening above and stray hairs blowing around in the wind like sparkling strands of spun gold.

She remembered that day because right after he took the photos she'd told him about what had happened with Sutton. They hadn't slept together yet, but things were headed in that direction. In fact, she hadn't slept with anyone since the incident—and it had been over a year—not so much because of Sutton, but she'd lived at home during her senior year of undergrad and there hadn't been much opportunity to date. Then she'd met Nick the beginning of her first year in grad school. Nick was in his second year of an MBA program, and she was studying art history. It was a fairytale courtship.

After the photo session, they made out for a bit, standing in the woods, and then they started walking, hand in hand, slowly back out. Their passion for each other was at a fever pitch, and she was thinking that could be the night they consummated it. She couldn't even remember how the topic of Sutton had come up. Something about her wanting a female advisor for her master's, if she was remembering it correctly. She hadn't wanted to talk about it, but he'd pressed her.

They sat on a bench for a bit as she recounted the incident. After she got through the story, he leaned over and touched her cheek, ever so softly.

"Babe," he said. Then he pulled her in close to him.

She didn't make any noise, but silent tears rolled down her face, dampening his shirt. She could feel the warmth of his skin on her cheek. It felt nice. He caressed her hair and gently rubbed her back as they sat in comfortable silence while a symphony of Central Park's signature birds chirped around them. They were still far enough in that they didn't hear much street noise. It was magical. A perfect early fall day with the warm breath of summer still lingering in the air, and it filled her with a sense of security and happiness.

After a bit, she looked up at him. "It's fine. Really. I'm okay. It wasn't that big of a deal. I don't know why I even mentioned it."

"Not a big deal? Of course it's a big deal. And really, we can take it slow, Victoria. I'm not in a rush. I want to get to know you. All of you." He brushed the hair from her face, leaned over, and gave her a gentle kiss. It was then that she noticed a different kind of look in his eyes. It was somewhere between sympathy and reverence. But his desire seemed to have faded.

"I'm fine, Nick. Really. I am." Although she'd been appreciative of his tenderness at the time, she remembered feeling a bit concerned that the passion seemed to have left his eyes. She thought that he might hold back, and she didn't want to be treated with kid gloves. She wanted all of him. His passion. His desire. How could she have that if he felt sorry for her? As she looked back on it, could she fault him for going after Sutton and roughing him up? He'd meant it as a gesture of chivalry, even if it had backfired.

And it was all starting to hit her, the magnitude of how royally and completely Sutton had screwed up her entire life. He'd robbed her of the chance to discover the depths of her own passion, to explore her budding sexuality on her own terms. She couldn't help but wonder if things would have been different if she'd never told Nick. Or, better yet, if it had never happened at all.

She thought about what her therapist said. Had the incident closed her off emotionally? Made her less able to be vulnerable? Hardened her in some way? It had certainly damaged her relationship with her mother. For over a decade, she'd misjudged her. Blamed her for sweeping it all under the rug. She could see now that it had affected her more than she'd known. It might even have ruined her marriage. Yes, it was clear to her how much damage this one man had caused. And now he had the audacity to threaten her. Her family. Her daughter.

He was going to pay for all of it.

TWENTY-SIX

It was Monday morning, and Victoria decided to wait for the rush hour traffic to clear before heading out on her drive to Danburg. Lila was staying with Nick for the next three days, so this was her chance. The two houses were on opposite sides of town. She decided to check on the one closer to the bridge first. Maybe she'd get lucky.

She did a quick burst of cardio on the Peloton and then some Pilates, which seemed to be getting her abs back in top form. Then she practiced her martial arts for a bit before deciding it was time to go. She'd just gotten her weapon serviced. She loaded it up and then went over her vehicle with an antitracking device to make sure it was clean. She left her cell phone behind, opting instead for the old-school burner she'd picked up the other day. And then she was off.

She drove past the first house and crossed it off the list. There were kids' bikes in the yard. Toys. It didn't look like a place Sutton would be. The second house had potential. It was in a more run-down section of town—buckled sidewalks, some homes with broken windows. The house itself looked pretty deserted, and it butted up against a vacant lot. It was worth a closer look, but she'd have to come back at night to check it out thoroughly. She'd tell nobody about this. Not until she knew for sure she had him.

And maybe not even then.

Jack was sitting in his car, waiting. He had followed Victoria over the bridge to Danburg and then lost her. He didn't want to make it obvious he was following her, so he'd stayed a few cars back. She was a pretty nimble driver, and when she cut in front of a garbage truck, he followed just in time to see her veer off to the right, but not in time to catch her.

He knew one thing for sure. Victoria had no business in Danburg if it wasn't related to Timothy Sutton or Jenna Williams. Rather than driving around aimlessly, he decided to park by the bridge and watch for her to drive back over, scanning his police radio for any emergencies so he could spring into action if needed. Of course, she could go home another way, so he wasn't going to wait all day. If she didn't drive over in an hour or so, he'd find a reason to call her. So far, it had been about twenty minutes.

About ten more minutes passed before Jack saw Victoria's sporty Mercedes coming his way, headed for the bridge. He watched as she drove onto it, relieved that she was still in one piece, but knowing full well that something was up. There was nothing on the police radio, though, so he started up his car and went on his way, very conflicted about what to do next.

Under cover of nightfall, Victoria returned. She parked a few blocks over from the target home. This time, she'd driven an older car she'd rented through an app using a fake name, knowing her car would stand out in that neighborhood. Besides, she didn't want anyone to be able to track her car's GPS if she actually went through with what she was contemplating. She approached the home through the vacant lot next door. She was dressed in black, her hair tucked inside a hoodie.

She made her way to the front of the house and saw that the window curtain was open, offering a peek into the living room. She could see in, but nobody would be able to see out. And there he was, sitting in an old recliner, watching television. She knew she should pull out her burner and call the police. But she didn't. Something deep inside her compelled her to see this through herself. She had a need to face him after all this time. And what if she called the police and they couldn't do anything? There was no witness. What if he turned it around on her? Accused her of being a stalker? What if he got arrested and hired someone to kill her? Or Lila?

She went around the back of the house to see if she could find a way in. There was an open casement window, but it was only slightly ajar. She nudged it up ever so gently, hoping the TV set would drown out any noise. Then she crawled through it.

Victoria made her way through the house in silence, clearing each room as she went. But as she approached the living room she had to fight an urge to abort the plan—she'd come this far, and she needed to see it through. But suddenly, it somehow seemed a bit too easy. *Did he draw me here intentionally for some reason? And why is this just dawning on me now?*

No, she was probably just being paranoid. Having second thoughts was normal. Around the next corner, she'd have him in her sights. *Easy does it.* She took a deep breath and entered the living room, gun drawn, prepared to end it once and for all but totally unprepared for the image before her.

Aside from that dark morning in Arizona, Victoria hadn't seen Sutton in over a decade—but it might as well have been a century. Their theory was correct. Timothy Sutton was a dying man. A dying man with nothing to lose. She took in the sight of him, propped up in an olive green recliner that was so threadbare she could see through the fabric at its corners. His thin arm dangled off the side along with the IV line that ran from above the chair down into his vein. He looked like a hundred-year-old man. Her gun was pointed straight at him. She wondered what he'd done with the money that was missing. He certainly wasn't spending it on this dump.

"Victoria Vander Hofen. What took you so long? You look well."

"I guess I can't say the same for you, Tim."

"Dark humor doesn't suit you, Victoria. Surely you can do better than that."

"I'm just getting started."

"Oh, come on now. We both know you're not going to shoot me, or you would have done it already. So why don't you put the gun down? I'm no threat to you now."

"Shut up, Tim. Just shut up!" She'd shot Malone—in self-defense—but this wasn't self-defense; it was murder. He was right. She couldn't murder him. Is that what he'd been counting on? She kept the gun trained on him anyway.

"You're a tease, Victoria, but you're not a murderer."

"Keep talking like that, psycho. You're making it easier."

"I really liked you, Victoria. You hurt my feelings. I thought we clicked. What changed your mind? Was it my substandard faculty housing?"

"You're delusional."

"Maybe, with all these meds. But I still think you can do better than Nick. He's the only reason we're both here."

"You're the only reason we're both here."

"Just call it in to the police already. Or put me out of my misery. Either way, it makes no difference to me."

She held the gun on him with her right hand and pulled out her phone with her left, fumbling a little while she kept an eye on him. He was half dead anyway. What was the point of having his murder on her conscience?

"Not so fast, Victoria. Drop the gun."

Victoria froze. She recognized the voice behind her and cursed herself for not anticipating this. Of course Sutton had a backup plan. She wasn't about to turn around to find out if the threat was genuine, but Victoria kept her gun drawn.

"I said drop it, Victoria." Jenna came closer and tapped the butt of a gun between Victoria's shoulder blades. She could feel the other woman's breath on her neck before Jenna took a step back.

"I'll put it down, Jenna." She didn't dare move a muscle. "Can I bend down and put it on the ground?"

"Sure. I'm not going to shoot you. Not yet. Tim and I have a little business to settle."

Victoria placed the gun on the floor to her right then stood back up. She was able to get a glimpse of Jenna and gauge how far away she was. She could probably disarm her from that distance, but she'd only have one chance. She wasn't going down without a fight. Then she heard Jenna take another step back. *Damn.*

"Make the transfer, Tim."

Sutton pulled a laptop computer out from under the blanket that was draped over his lap and started tapping the keys, his hands struggling to do even that simple task. Victoria didn't move. Jenna was behind her, gun pointed. It took longer than it should have. He had to start over a few times, and Victoria worried that Jenna would get impatient. It felt like an eternity, but it also gave Victoria time to think. She'd have to time it just right if she was going to disarm Jenna after she got the money because it was pretty clear to her what was supposed to happen next.

"It's done. Half a million. All yours, Jenna."

"Let me see the screen."

Sutton turned the computer around to her.

"Read me the numbers." Sutton turned the computer back around and read the numbers, slowly, to what Victoria assumed was the offshore account that Jenna had memorized.

"I've held up my end of the bargain. Now it's your turn, Jenna. Finish her off," Sutton said.

"A deal's a deal." Jenna took a step forward, and Victoria sprang into action. She spun around and kicked the gun from Jenna's hand with a hard blow from her leg, the force of it sending Jenna to the ground along with her weapon, which slid across the floor. Victoria tried to go for the gun, but Jenna grabbed her leg and pulled her to the floor so forcefully that she felt her leg almost leave the socket.

Then Victoria saw Sutton struggling to get out of his chair. He was going for Victoria's gun. Jenna was the bigger threat, but Victoria's gun was closer. In a split-second calculation, Victoria made her choice. She lunged toward Sutton and her gun. He managed to grab it, but she was sure he wouldn't have the strength to fire it; he had trouble even picking it up. She still had a chance.

She knew she'd miscalculated when the look on his face changed as he fumbled with her gun, because from his vantage point, he could see what Victoria failed to realize until it was too late. Jenna had already recovered her gun. A strange calm came over Victoria as she prepared to die. She thought about her daughter. Would she even remember her? Then she heard a muffled shot. Sutton slammed back against the recliner, his eyes wide and his mouth agape, and the gun fell from his hand. Jenna came closer, pointed the gun at Sutton, and fired it a second time, putting him out of his misery once and for all. Victoria watched in stunned silence as the blood seeped into the light blue cotton fabric of his t-shirt.

All Jack could do now was wait. He had arrived just in time to see Jenna pull a gun on Victoria through the front window. All along, he'd felt in his gut that Victoria wouldn't be able to go through with it and murder Sutton in cold blood, and he was relieved that he'd been right about her. He'd thought about rushing in, breaking down the door, but then Jenna might take Victoria hostage or shoot her, so he snuck around the back and went in through the open window, arriving just in time to see Sutton with a gun on Victoria. Then Jenna fired two shots into Sutton's chest and lowered her weapon. He tucked himself back behind the doorway, not wanting to cause a panic, waiting in silence, ready to jump in.

Jenna stood there seemingly in shock while Victoria struggled to process what had happened. Jenna's gun was still in her hand, pointed down. Victoria's gun had dropped from Sutton's hand to the floor by his chair. She thought about going for it, but Jenna must have sensed it.

"Don't move, Victoria. I don't want to shoot you."

"What *do* you want, Jenna?"

"I want to leave here and never look back."

"Me too. We both want the same thing. And we both got what we wanted. So, can you put the gun down?"

"How do I know you won't call the cops?" Jenna asked.

"Why would I call the cops?" It was then that Victoria noticed the silencer on Jenna's gun. And it dawned on her that they could actually get away with this.

"But we have to get out of here. The shot wasn't as loud as it could have been, but it was loud enough."

Jenna just stood there.

"And another one would surely make it worse, Jenna. So can you *please* put the gun *down?*"

"I want you to go get your gun first. And take out the clip."

"Okay, I can do that. But then you have to do it too."

"Okay." Jenna kept her gun on Victoria while she retrieved her Glock and took out the ammo.

"Now you."

Jenna followed suit, keeping her word.

"So, was that your plan all along? To kill him after he wired the money?" Victoria asked.

"Pretty much. Until you went all *Charlie's Angels* on me."

"I had to do something, Jenna. You had a gun pointed at my back."

"I wouldn't have used it on you," Jenna said.

"How was I supposed to know that?"

"He got what was coming to him. I've got no beef with you."

There was a long, tense pause.

"So now what?" Victoria asked.

"We go. They'll find him sooner or later."

"Sure. But don't you think you should wipe the place first? I'm wearing gloves. Your prints are everywhere," Victoria said.

"Probably a good idea. You go. I'll finish up and head out."

"And don't forget to destroy the computer."

"You're kind of a control freak, Victoria. Has anyone ever told you that?"

"Nope. Just you, Jenna."

They both wore wary smiles, the tension still palpable.

"I'll be going now." Victoria turned to head out the back of the house. She had so many questions, but with Jenna and her mercurial disposition, she thought it best not to push her luck.

"Probably a good idea. Good luck, Victoria," Jenna called out to her.

"Good luck to you too, Jenna."

Victoria didn't turn around again. She just kept walking. She was pretty sure Jenna wouldn't shoot her in the back. Pretty sure, but not certain.

Jack stayed a few paces behind Victoria and watched as she got in her car and drove away. He walked back to his car and got in, relieved that a predator was off the streets, for good. He started up his car and headed back over to the other side of the river, secure in the belief that this whole ordeal would soon be behind them and they could finally get on with their lives.

TWENTY-SEVEN

A few days later, Victoria got a call from Detective Sanchez. The police had found Timothy Sutton dead in a home in Danburg. A driver from a medical supply company had called it in. Sutton was using a fake name, but the authorities found his real driver's license in with his belongings. Sanchez said it looked like a robbery gone bad. They didn't find any of the missing money, and the place had been ransacked. Maybe Sutton had flashed some cash around the wrong people. They were all waiting for the ME's report.

From what Victoria was able to piece together, Sutton had rented the place in Danburg about a month prior. He must have caught up with Jenna around that time and offered her a deal, knowing that he was getting too weak to do much damage on his own. Victoria's theory was corroborated when she caught some security footage of Jenna in Peekskill the day they found the cell phone, but so far, there was no evidence that she'd run Nick down that night. Now Jenna seemed to have vanished again, which was fine with Victoria.

One question still haunted her: Did Sutton ever actually assault Jenna, or had she made that all up so

Victoria would relocate her? Someone had hurt her; that much was for sure. But if Sutton hadn't done anything, why did she kill him? And if she could kill someone like that in cold blood, for money, what else was she capable of? But she couldn't worry about that now. If Jenna wanted to kill her, she'd had her chance. And Jenna had Sutton's half a million plus the money she'd given her, so chances were it would all simply fade away. The worst the woman might do is hit her up for more money if she blew through the rest too quickly. Victoria had learned her lesson, and she wasn't going digging for answers this time. She called Nick, left him a message about Sutton, and then went about her business.

Today was Thanksgiving, and she was headed over to her mother's house to help her cook and then join in the festivities. She was making mashed potatoes in advance to bring over. *Hard to screw up mashed potatoes.* Jack's daughter and her fiancé were stopping by, so it was sort of a big day for the family. She and Nick were splitting Thanksgiving Day. Lila was with Nick now. They would spend part of the day in Brooklyn, and then he'd bring her over for dessert. They'd reverse that for Christmas. It wasn't ideal, but neither of them wanted to completely miss Lila's first holiday season, and half a day was better than nothing.

Victoria walked into her mother's house with her casserole dish of mashed potatoes. She was supposed to help her mother with the cooking, but she got distracted.

"Hey, Victoria. This is my daughter, Lisa, and her fiancé, Steve." Jack certainly seemed eager for them to meet.

"Nice to meet both of you. And congratulations on your engagement." She was surprised to see them there so early.

"Thanks!" Lisa said. "We can't stay too long, but we wanted to drop in and at least meet you. We still have to drive to Connecticut to see my mother, and then it's over to Steve's parents in Rye for dessert."

"Sounds like a whirlwind of a day."

"You get used to it."

Jack's daughter was in her late twenties, quite a few years younger than Victoria. She was a math teacher at a local public middle school, but she looked more like a perky kindergarten teacher, the kind all parents wanted for their child, with just the right mix of warmth and authority. Lisa's hair was dark and about the same length as her own, and she gave off a kind, friendly vibe that Victoria found comforting. If she was at all intimidated by the Vander Hofen wealth, it wasn't showing.

"Let me bring this to my mother, and I'll be right back."

"I've got it, Victoria. Have a seat." Jack held out his hands, and she passed him the dish, leaving her no choice but to sit.

"Steve, would you like to join me for a tour out back?" It wasn't so much an offer as a directive. Steve followed him out of the living room, leaving the two daughters to talk.

Victoria figured their mutual interest in education was good common ground, so she told Lisa about her foundation, which provided college scholarships for students in the arts. Lisa went on to point out that the arts programs had been severely cut back in most middle school programs, and it gave Victoria the idea that maybe she could expand to fund extracurricular programs for students in the younger grades. They were interrupted by Victoria's mother.

"Can I get you ladies anything? Coffee, maybe?"

"None for me," Lisa said.

"I'll take a cup," Victoria said.

Just then, Jack and Steve came back and joined them. It was nice, all of them sitting there, but her own family's absence was conspicuous. She found herself grateful for the fact that Lila was coming over later. And for the fact that she existed at all. As bad as it was to think about starting over, it would be even worse if she were childless. She would never really be alone, and that gave her some comfort. After a bit, they said their goodbyes to the happy couple, and Lisa and Steve went on their way.

———

Jack closed the door and turned back to the living room. Sandra had gone to check on dinner. It smelled great, and he was starved, as usual. It was only going to be the three of them for the actual meal. He was pretty used to this joint custody holiday thing, but he sensed Victoria was feeling a bit blue about it.

"Missing Lila?"

"Yeah."

"It's the worst part of divorce. The kids."

"But the best part of a failed marriage?"

They both smiled, but he knew she was putting on a brave face. His thoughts turned to Lisa and Steve, who seemed so solid, so happy. But didn't everyone in the beginning? Maybe Nick and Victoria had looked like that too. Of course, he shouldn't be filling himself with worry about a marriage that hadn't even happened yet, but what kind of father would he be if he didn't?

"That too."

"I enjoyed meeting Lisa. And I'm not just saying it."

"I know, Victoria. You're a terrible liar, so I'd know if you were."

She looked briefly at him, a curious look on her face.

Jack wasn't planning on telling anyone what he'd seen the other day. Morally, he could live with it, and he wasn't a police officer anymore. As a PI, he had a duty to his client. And Victoria was more to him now than a client. They were on their way to becoming family.

"Well, it seems like you two have a lot in common, more than I would have thought."

"She's very easy to talk to," Victoria said.

"Yes, I guess she is." Jack noticed that Victoria was avoiding eye contact.

"Nick's coming by later to drop off Lila," she eventually said, "so at least I'll get to spend time with her."

"I'm glad. How did he take the news?"

"What news?"

"About Sutton."

"He was relieved, of course. Very much so. Like all of us."

"You think he had anything to do with it?"

"Nick? With Sutton? *No!* I mean, they said it was a robbery, didn't they?"

"Yes. But then, you never know."

Victoria narrowed her eyes at him. "It wasn't Nick. I'm sure of that."

"I'm glad."

"So, what's your best guess about what happened?" Victoria asked.

"I don't care enough about Sutton to give it much thought. And from what Sanchez told me, I doubt this case will be a high priority." He saw her breathe a small sigh of relief, her shoulders sinking a bit.

"But what's your best guess? You knew him better than I did."

"A robbery. It's not a great neighborhood." She started to walk away but then turned back and looked him straight in the eye. "Unless Jenna Williams was able to track him down. I wouldn't want to get on her bad side. She's a real piece of work."

"I got that impression." Jack held her gaze for a bit, and then Sandra called them in for dinner. "But then it's not our problem anymore, is it?" Jack said.

"Nope, it's certainly not," Victoria agreed.

Jack flashed her a knowing smile. "So then...let's eat." Jack put his hand on Victoria's back and guided her into the dining room, eager to dive into a good home-cooked meal, his stomach grumbling even more than usual as the savory smells filled the room.

Her mother's gate buzzer sounded; it was Nick. Victoria didn't quite know how to play this. Should she ask him to stay for dessert? Would he even want to? It was all such unfamiliar territory. She decided she'd ask him to stay. Even if he brushed her off, it was good to be the bigger person. For Lila's sake.

She opened the door, and he was standing there with Lila in his arms. He leaned over and gave her a peck on the cheek.

"Come in," she said. He handed Lila to her, and then she noticed he had a shopping bag hanging from his forearm. He held it up and then placed it on the floor and took off his coat.

"Goodies from my mother."

"Eggplant parmesan?"

"Of course. And some of your other favorites."

"Tell her thanks."

"Tell her yourself. Sorry, that came out wrong. I mean, you're still allowed to call her, Victoria. She'd love to hear from you."

"Right. I should do that." Nick looked good. Happy.

Her mother and Jack walked over and said their hellos, and her mother invited him to stay for coffee and dessert. He accepted. She expected it to be awkward, but it wasn't. It was pleasant and comfortable and easy, and she almost forgot for a bit that they were separated.

None of them wanted to talk about the case, but she knew they were all beside themselves with relief that the threat to their family was gone, and that relief was reflected in the convivial mood of the evening.

Then Nick announced he had to leave, and it brought her back to reality. But it was an everyday reality that she could live with. Marital issues. Considering the insanity of the last year or so, it was nothing she couldn't handle.

"I need to work tomorrow, and I've got a long drive back to the city."

"Right. I'll walk you out." Nick said his goodbyes to her mother and Jack and kissed Lila. They continued to the door.

"I'm glad that's going so well. You like it?"

"I love it."

"That's great, Nick."

"And the gallery. It's going better than you even expected."

"It is. It's been a good few weeks for both of us, I guess." *Yet it happened while we were apart. What does that say?*

"I guess it has." They both seemed reluctant to end the conversation, and their unspoken words lingered in the air.

"Drive safe," she said.

They hugged and Nick went on his way. Victoria decided she was ready for some alone time. Since it was Thanksgiving, she was trying not to feel sorry for herself. Instead, she took inventory of all the positives, the most important one being that they were safe now. Jenna Williams was a minor loose end, but she wasn't afraid of her. As long as Victoria didn't go on the offensive, the worst thing she might do in the future is ask for money. Overall, she couldn't complain. Her career was moving on to a new level, her mother was happy, and whatever that little interlude was with Jack, she was sure he was trying to tell her that, whatever his suspicions, he had her back. He wasn't a substitute for her own father, but it was more than she'd had in a long time, and it was nice.

Victoria was in bed drinking an herbal tea and reading a few more reviews of her gallery opening when she heard someone calling. She'd forgotten to turn off the ringer. She was going to let it go to voicemail, but then she saw it was Nick and picked up.

"Hi. Is everything okay?"

"Yeah. Everything's okay."

They were both quiet for a few moments.

"What's up?"

"I wanted to hear your voice."

"And how does it sound?"

"Truthfully, a little nasal. You coming down with something?"

"You're hilarious, Nick."

"I know. Actually, your voice sounds...great." Nick's voice sounded steamy, sexy. Like she remembered from their early days when they'd talked on the phone

for hours on end.
"Yours isn't so bad either."
"Oh yeah?"
"Yeah. I've always liked your voice."
"What do you like about it?"
"The accent, I think."
"What accent?" Nick asked.
"Your Brooklyn accent."
"You talkin' to me?"
"That sounds more Jersey Shore."
"Oh, so you're an expert now?"
"Not an expert, per se. I just have a good ear."
"That's a real claim to fame, Victoria. You should put that on your dating profile."
"I'll take that under advisement."
"So, Victoria. Are you?"
"Am I what?"
"Dating?"
"We're separated, Nick."
"Yeah, I know. I'm not meaning to pry. I just thought we might want to come up with some kind of agreement. You know, I take Tinder. You take Bumble. So it doesn't get awkward. I mean, what if we match?"

Victoria smiled in spite of herself. *Classic Nick Mancusio.* This was Nick's go-to move if he ever got her upset. If he could make her laugh, it all went away. When had they stopped laughing?

"You don't just 'match,' Nick. You have to swipe first."

"You sound like a real expert."
"Not really."
"Well, you're pretty swipe-worthy, Vic. In a moment of weakness, I might just do it."
"I'm not on any apps, Nick."
"Neither am I. I prefer to go old-school."

"And how's that working out for you?"
"I don't know yet. Would you like to have dinner with me?"
"You're asking me out on a date?"
"Yes."
"Well, it's not really fair. It's hard to say no because I already know what a great date you are."
"Maybe I've changed."
"So you're appealing to my innate sense of curiosity?"
"If that's what it takes."
They both paused, and she thought it didn't sound like a bad idea. "Okay. One date. What do we have to lose?"
"Only everything."
Neither of them was ready to end it. That much was clear. But she wasn't ready to go back to business as usual. Even if he said he was sorry and asked to come back home, she wasn't ready yet. They'd rushed things once, and it had all exploded. This time, they'd take it slow.
"Okay," she said. "We'll take it one date at a time."
"One date at a time."
"Yeah. See what I did there?"
"I did. Very clever. How about Saturday night?"
"That works. Good night, Nick."
"Good night, Vic."

EPILOGUE

One month later

"What are you doing?" Victoria called out to Nick, who was relaxing on the lanai, looking out at the spectacular view. Well, not quite relaxing. He was sitting up straight, taking it all in, like a kid at Disneyland who couldn't decide which ride to try first.

"Wondering why we don't do this more often."

"The eleven-hour flight? The five-hour time difference?"

"You're a hopeless romantic, Victoria."

She walked up behind him and gave his shoulders a rub. It had been pouring sheets of water all morning, but now the rain had slowed to a trickle, and the verdant and jagged Makana Mountain—or Bali Hai, as it was more commonly known—was bathed in rays of sunlight that streamed down from the clouds. A rainbow straddled the turquoise and cobalt bay that fronted their suite. It was one of those sights you had to see to believe.

"I hope my secret's safe with you." She leaned over and gave him a kiss, and then he placed his hand on hers. They stayed like that for a while.

They'd decided to simplify the whole awkward

Christmas family situation by spending it on the island of Kauai. They knew it was the rainy season, but it didn't bother them too much. They were spending a few days on the rugged North Shore and then would maybe catch some sun on the south side. They had actually been lucky. The first two days were pretty nice, and she didn't mind a little rain.

As far as their relationship, they were inching along, taking things slow, and that was fine with her. They'd sold the house and bought a property on the Hudson in Briarcliff Manor, a few houses down from where they lived when all the insanity started. It had a spectacular view, maybe not quite as spectacular as this, but close enough. Nick's job was going better than either of them had expected, and he was already making a small fortune. He purchased a condo in the city with a great view of Central Park. She was spending some of her time there, and for once in her life, she was going with the flow. Sometimes they were all together, sometimes not. At some point, they'd probably have to make some kind of decision about where things were headed, get on some kind of set schedule, but Lila was still a baby. They had time. Years, maybe. And it was nice to finally be out of crisis mode. They were living their lives, one day at a time, and it felt great.

She still had so many questions, but this time she wasn't going digging for answers. When they found out that it was a very scared and remorseful teenager who'd clipped Nick that night when he was out on his run, she felt a bit better about Jenna. She'd watched the young woman shoot Timothy Sutton in cold blood, so she knew she had it in her. But it made her feel a little better to know that Jenna hadn't run down her husband, and she didn't expect Jenna to bother her again.

She and Nick never talked about any of it. Nobody in her family did. Sutton was gone. They were safe, and the rest of it didn't seem to matter much anymore. Little loose ends she could live with. She saw no point in telling Nick what had happened that night. And he never asked. If it came out somehow, she'd deal with it then.

It was all starting to blend into the background, and she expected that would only increase over time, especially with the news she was planning to spring on him tomorrow. For today, she was content to sit and enjoy a magical Christmas Eve, just the three of them, with raindrops and sunrays dancing in harmony on the white sandy beach below.

Three months later

Was it really him, you're probably wondering. Or did I pull a fast one on everyone? I've kept you in suspense long enough. Yes, it was Sutton—sort of. He did most of what I said he did, but not all of it. Let's just say he did enough of it. And I have to say, he got what was coming to him. The world's a better place without him. Don't you think?

And the other guy? The one who left me gasping for air? I don't have to worry about him anymore, either. I heard he died in a hiking accident a few months back. Tough break, but then he was a stubborn one. I always told him it was dangerous to go hiking alone, but then you know how guys can be.

Victoria heard Nick coming down the stairs. She lifted herself up slightly and stuffed the letter under her butt, along with the envelope postmarked Mexico City.

"Hey! What'cha up to?" he said.

"Nothing, really. Just watching the fire dance around. It relaxes me."

"Looks cozy. I'll join you."

"Wait, can you get me some tea first? Please? My stomach's a little queasy."

"It's a little late for morning sickness, isn't it?"

"Go figure."

"You're drinking for two. You want a double?"

"One will do, thanks."

Once he went on his way, she pulled out the crinkled letter, smoothed it out a bit, and continued reading, knowing the herbal tea wasn't going to be enough to soothe the knot forming in her stomach.

So, I'll be coming back to the States soon. I bet you're thinking I'm going to ask for more money, but you're wrong. Know why?

I got a book deal! Can you believe it? It's a thriller. Two frenemies team up to get back at a common enemy. Think Mean Girls meets Thelma and Louise. You'll love it. And don't worry, Victoria, they both live happily ever after. - J

Victoria crushed the last loose end into a ball and tossed it into the crackling fire. She watched as it began to unfurl, the flames licking the edges of the paper, slowly at first, and then devouring it as it crumbled into ash.

Nick returned with her tea, and they sat there for hours, watching the fire burn itself out until barely an ember survived, the last chapter of their harrowing ordeal behind them and the rest of their lives ahead.

ACKNOWLEDGMENTS

To my readers, thank you so much for taking the time to read my second novel, *Little Loose Ends*. I also want to thank everyone who read my debut novel, *Killer Motives*. I'm beyond grateful for the positive feedback I've received from readers and reviewers. I'm also very appreciative of the support I've gotten not only from my close friends and family, but also from my wider circle of associates and acquaintances. I'm honored that so many of you took a chance on me. A special thanks to my friends Robin and Carl, who went above and beyond to get the word out about me.

My thanks goes out to the many people who helped me with this new project. It was a challenge writing a stand-alone sequel with the right combination of new information and backstory, so I'm very thankful to my beta readers who provided critical feedback to try and help me get the right balance. Thanks to my husband Rick who read countless drafts, offering many suggestions, large and small, which helped refine and improve this novel, and to Susan, Donna, and Alan who offered constructive criticism and feedback. A big thanks to my daughter, Erica, who inspires me every day with her resilience and her big heart. Mama's always got your back.

A special thanks goes out to my editor, Julie MacKenzie, for her expert editing, her dedication, and her sense of humor. She literally worked through a hurricane to meet my deadline and get the edited manuscript back to me in time. Thanks to Ivan Zanchetta for his outstanding covers, and to Sharon Kizziah-Holmes at Paperback Press for her excellent formatting services. Thanks to Laurence O'Bryan and his team at BooksGoSocial for their marketing support and advice, and thanks to Dr. Jennifer Roost for her consultation on legal and ethical issues in medicine. A special thanks to author and historian Dr. Pamela Sakamoto for her encouragement, support, and expert advice, and to author and historian Dr. Carl Ackerman for his publishing advice. And thanks to all my favorite mystery and thriller writers out there who have inspired me over the years and continue to do so. Please keep writing!

I would very much value a rating or review on Amazon, Goodreads, or Barnes and Noble. I read all of my reviews and gain valuable feedback and inspiration from them. Thanks to everyone who has taken the time to rate or review one of my novels. I know how busy everyone is, and I really appreciate it. I'm hard at work on my next novel, a psychological thriller set in Silicon Valley. Look for that around summer, 2023.

If you'd like updates, please sign up for my mailing list at www.bonnietraymore.com.

ABOUT THE AUTHOR

Bonnie L. Traymore is an author, historian and educator with a doctorate in United States History. She is the author of the page-turner novel *Killer Motives: A Hudson Valley Mystery*, and an award-winning non-fiction writer with a love of mystery and thriller novels. Originally from the New York City area, she and her husband have two children and reside in Honolulu, Hawaii. *Little Loose Ends* is her second novel.